GOD OF LIES

SOULLESS EMPIRE BOOK 3

JADE ROWE
SASHA LEONE

1

KIRA

The vodka fumes from the grizzled old Russian are enough to ignite fires. Or make a girl drunk if she sits long enough with him.

If someone naïve were to walk in, they'd find

this place oozing the wrong sort of danger—unglamorous, bloody, the kind to get you dead.

Even the most daring keep away from places like this.

Except, of course, for me.

I'm here for a story. If I can get it.

I need to get it.

"Mr. Lenin," I start again. "You said you could tell me something about life behind the Iron Curtain, for my paper."

Only self-control prevents my eyes from tearing up as he veers in again, his hand snaking out to graze my breast. I shift to avoid the contact, doing so in a way that won't insult him.

"You are too pretty to be here alone," he says, downing his vodka and slamming the shot glass on the bar. "But let me taste you, and you won't be."

He veers in for another kiss and grope, and I move just enough to escape the brunt of the unwanted advance.

"Let me try you," he says, "and I'll tell you whatever you want."

Another two drinks appear on the bar, even though my first is still untouched. This time, his hand lands in a firm grip on my thigh. I count to ten before I put my hand on his.

"If you can't share the information here, Mr. Lenin, I'll go elsewhere."

I apply pressure and bend his finger, just enough to capture his real attention. Then I peel his hand away.

Lenin nods, rubbing the scar on his face.

I don't know his real name, not that I'm sure he does either. Men of his age didn't bring much with them from Mother Russia. A name was probably seen as a frivolity. He's had plenty gifted to him since then, though, and he's a font of knowledge, if I can get to it.

If he doesn't try and rape me or kill me first.

He might come off as a drunk old Russian, but he used to be powerful in his day, and that kind of power lingers, no matter where he might sit on the ladder now. All I know for sure is that he's somewhere on the ladder.

Everything about him screams Bratva—from the tattoos to the scars to the bar he gets shitfaced in. We're deep in the Russian enclave of Chicago; its dank low lights don't come from a need to create atmosphere, but rather from the need to do business in the dark and have private drinks.

It's soaked in the blood of organized crime.

I'm looking to get my boots dirty.

That's why I'm here, after all.

If I want to get ahead, make a name for myself, find a way into the biggest, most powerful organized crime ring this city has ever seen, I need to start at the bottom.

I need to start at a bar like this, no matter how much I hate the place and the Bratva.

There is no other way in.

"Drink, Karenina. What is it you want to know?"

Lenin takes a big chug of his drink, and I hold back a look of disgust.

My heart beats fast.

There's no asking him about what I want directly, but if I can win the confidence of a man like this, I know he'll start talking—even if it's for a price.

"It's Kira. I—"

"Kira. It's short for something. Russian, eh?" He laughs, but it doesn't touch his eyes. They remain hard and cold. A warning.

"No. Grew up right here in Chicago," I say, deftly shifting from his wandering hand.

But now he sways in even closer, and in the low light, I can see the savageness of the slashing knife that disfigured his face. "I ask again. What do you want to know? Mother Russia or Bratva?"

"Both." I hold still, because I know being here's beyond dangerous, but I also know chances like this don't come around often.

Lenin could be my key.

"Come home with me, Karenina, and I'll tell you."

The blood heads right down to my toes, leaving my skin cold and clammy. "I'm good here."

He pulls back, turns away, and orders another drink.

Shit.

Every lead and rumor from all the sources I've scraped up, paid off, and flirted with have led me here.

None of them dared cross the line into the Bratva territory I'm interested in. Of course they wouldn't.

Rumor has it that the shadow king they worship is a butcher like the underworld's never seen.

Andrei Zherdov.

He's rumored to rule with an iron fist.

It's a miracle I even have a name.

"I can see you're a great man," I tell Lenin, buttering him up once again. "One who's more than familiar with how the families work here and in Russia. You came to Chicago for a better life, did you not?"

Maybe if I go in sideways, slide under his ego, I can find an entrance.

But the old Russian just scoffs. I'm losing him.

Not again...

My focus fades, and I become keenly aware of the chatter swirling around us. The voices speak in English and Russian. Even if I can't translate all the words, I can understand their implications.

I'm being watched.

Not by one person, but by many.

Some with a predatory air, others with mild curiosity. But they don't make a move. I must be right; Lenin still has sway, at least in here.

That's a good sign. Sort of.

"I like you, Karenina." He nods to my drink, and I finally pick it up, only taking a baby sip as he downs the rest of his.

It's so sharp and bitter I have to physically hide my grimace.

"Don't like vodka?" Lenin laughs.

"Not my favorite." I lean in, aware of the invitation this man will take from it, but I'm desperate for information. "Did you ever work for Zherdov?"

The air seems to stiffen around us. He gives me a long look and runs a finger down my arm.

It takes everything I have not to smack him away.

"Perhaps."

This time Lenin switches seats so he has me boxed in. A greedy hand arrives on my inner thigh, and he starts to massage me, moving up. I close my hand on his thick wrist.

"Perhaps not."

"You used to be one of the Bratva's most feared enforcers, didn't you?"

His eyes narrow, and he moves closer, hand shaking my hold like there's a bug on him. I'm helpless to do a thing as he wraps his fingers around my throat.

He doesn't squeeze, just lets me feel the power he holds. "Be careful."

"I'm just asking questions," I gulp.

"Questions can get you killed."

"Is this how you show your strength? Assaulting women?" I say, so low he might miss it.

But Lenin's paying attention. He smiles, baring his sharp, uneven teeth. "I've killed for lesser insults."

"You have your hand around my throat." I force myself to meet his eye. "And I can already tell you're a very powerful man."

He waits a slow count to ten before he lets me go. "You like power?"

"I love power." I'm on dangerous ground. I know how to manipulate my way out of most situations with a handsy man. I know how to do it without insulting him—or insulting him just enough to stroke his ego—but this man's different. More dangerous.

Still, I'm so close. I just need to keep my cool for a little bit longer.

I shift and cross my legs, pulling my bag onto my lap. "Tell me all about Zherdov, your work."

"And you'll make it worth my while?"

"Yes." I nod, my little barriers in place.

I need this.

The story that no one else can get. But if I do it, my career can finally start, my dreams will become real, my revenge—

"Very well. Come to my place, then," Lenin calls my bluff. "And I'll give you everything you need."

Alarm bells start ringing at his sinister tone. That's when it really starts to sink in. No one here's going to help me if he tries anything. No one at all.

"No. No." I shake my head. "Here is good, I..."

Lenin grabs my wrist. "I have information, little reporter, but not here. Too many eyes and ears."

Every instinct tells me to cut things short, to stop here. But beneath the ambition and desperation that usually tug me through dangerous situations, something even more powerful urges me on.

Hate.

"You'll have to behave," I say ignoring the ominous malice in his grin. "And maybe..."

Suddenly, my bag starts to vibrate.

It's like the bar goes quiet.

What, are we not allowed phones here?

"Now who could be calling you at a time like this?" Lenin taunts.

He must enjoy seeing me squirm, because he finally lets me go so I can awkwardly pull out my phone and look down at my screen.

A bolt that's half dread and half relief shoots through me. It's my editor-in-chief.

Get back to the office. NOW.

"Problem?" Lenin chuckles, reading my expression like a book.

I glance around, planning my escape.

If there was one person who could pull me off a story, it's Mitt Calhoun. Editor and all-round exploitative bastard. He knows none of the seasoned reporters will touch this story.

He uses it like a carrot on a stick for me and other ambitious junior journalists at the paper. And I play right into his hands. Every time.

If only he knew the truth.

"Fucking hell," I mumble. I stand up and start to text my response.

Then, Lenin's greasy hand grabs my wrist. "Where are you going?"

"I have to—"

"You agreed to come with me."

"I-I have to go to the bathroom."

His eyes narrow, then he points to the back of the bar. "Hurry up, then." To my surprise, his fingers fall from my wrist.

I don't wait around to let him second guess his decision. Hooking my bag on my shoulder, I scurry toward the backroom, ignoring the open leers as I do.

I just need to make it out of here.

The bathroom is disgusting: Broken seats, stained bowls, and graffiti everywhere. Worst of all, though, there's not even a window to escape through. Heart beating fast, phone buzzing, I take a breath and poke my head out of the door.

That's when I see it.

In the narrow hall between the Men and Women bathrooms is one more door, almost completely hidden behind peeling graffiti. The sign above it flickers dully. Exit.

"Please work."

Holding my breath, I press on the bar. It creaks open.

I don't wait around to thank my luck. The second I'm in the dirty alleyway out back, I start running, somehow finding my way through the trash and dumpsters to where I parked my beat-up, rust-bucket of a car.

With my pulse still on fire, I slide in, praying the engine will catch. It finally does on the fourth try.

Just like that, I'm off, heading for the offices of the Chicago Daily.

"Thank the fucking lord," I sigh, a satisfying wave of adrenaline crashing through me.

But before I can settle into the excitement of another daring escape, my phone starts ringing again.

I can't catch a break. All I can do is pop in my earpiece and answer.

Mr. Calhoun's roar is immediately on me.

"When I say now, I mean now."

I bite back a retort. I need this internship, both as a stepping stone for my career and for my own personal reasons. If I didn't, I'd have bitten back at the fucker long ago.

"On my way, Mr. Calhoun," I assure him, swallowing what little is left of my pride. "I was just out chasing a lead for the story."

He clearly isn't impressed. "A better one than that fashion girl, I hope."

I wince. That one still hurts.

"I think so." I take a sharp turn on a forgiving corner, taking a little bit of my anger out on the road. "Hey, is this Bratva related? Because I think I was really onto—"

"Of course it's Bratva related," he interrupts, then pauses. "Do I ever call you or Tate for any other reason?"

Tate.

The other junior reporter on this case.

I tighten my grip on the wheel.

"I'll be there in a few minutes," I sneer.

By some miracle, I manage to avoid getting pulled over as I weave through the streets. There isn't a second to waste.

I park and rush into the building, taking the elevator to meet Mitt... and probably Tate too.

Sure enough,

outside Mitt's office leans the smug figure of my journalistic nemesis, Tate Parker. "Out fucking guttersnipes for a story?"

"Oh, is that where you were?" I snip back.

Tate's struck a nerve. Too many of these leads are like Lenin. But it's not like I have a lot of options.

"Just you wait and see what I was out doing," he responds, his smug grin growing even bigger.

I narrow my eyes, my heart lurching.

Fuck. What does he have?

"There you are. Finally." Mr. Calhoun pokes his balding head out from the small conference room adjacent to his office. "Come in." His glasses are sliding down the bridge of his nose and sweat stains are visible under his arms.

He looks like he slept here.

Hell, it wouldn't be the first time.

"As you know," he starts, turning his back on us as we follow him inside, "there have been rumblings that a brutal Russian crime syndicate has started to overtake this city's entire underworld. Some of that influence even seems to be seeping into legitimate areas of Chicago. From politics, to big business, to fashion... apparently."

He's looking at me while he says it, and it takes all I have not to wince away. He will never let me live down what happened with my last lead—Yelena. "You want to be the first to break it, like me. Isn't that right?"

"I—"

"Well, too bad." Now it's Tate's turn to interrupt me. "Because I've cracked the case wide fucking open. And it doesn't have anything to do with fashion shows or clothing lines. Figures, you put a girl on a man's case and—"

"Shut the fuck up," Mr. Calhoun barks, clicking on his key remote. A projector groans down from the ceiling, pointing toward an empty whiteboard. "We're not here to gloat. We're here to get to the bottom of this fucking story. Now, listen. Tate's not completely full of hot air. He did get something for us. Something big."

Tate can't help but gloat. "Real big," he says. "I've uncovered our first high-ranking Bratva official. At the Russian consulate, no less."

I nearly sink through the floor. "No way."

Mr. Calhoun clicks another button, and a collection of screenshots appears on the board.

"Security footage of a recent break-in at the consulate," he starts to explain. That's all I hear before everything goes silent.

The other two start talking, but I don't hear a thing.

Because I recognize the man in the images.

Ilya Rykov.

"No fucking way."

Fear and dread roll through me.

... Along with something else.

Something darker and more thrilling. Something I immediately hate with all my being.

The man in the photo is gorgeous—even more so now than I remember him being when we were younger.

His dark beauty shines through the shitty quality of the captured security footage.

Dark and devilish, and with that blade's edge of evil.

What the hell is he doing back in America?

"You know, Kira," Tate's grating voice pierces through my shock. "I've always been the better—"

"What the fuck did I say about gloating?" Mr. Calhoun scolds. He looks at me, and I shake my head, trying to come back to here and now. "I'll give credit where credit is due. You've finally broken the seal. We have our first real look behind the iron curtain. But I'm not sending you onto the stage, kid."

"What? Why not?"

"Because we have access to someone better for the job."

No. Please.

"Who?" Tate demands to know.

Mr. Calhoun's hard eyes stay glued on me. "Kira, do you think you have what it takes to get close to this monster?"

Ice slides down my spine. *Does he know?*

"M-Me?"

"If you want this job," Mr. Calhoun says, turning to study the photo before whipping back around to me, "along with a promotion, you'll need to get us inside this fucker's inner circle. Do you think you can do that?"

My head is spinning so fast I could pass out.

"How would I even..."

"Mr. Calhoun," Tate sputters. "I found him. I should be the one who breaks this. Plus, how is little miss Daisy here going to—"

Mitt raises his hand, and Tate immediately shuts up.

"The Bratva would never let a man into their inner circle. Hell, not a woman either. But a friend... an old friend..."

My heart drops through the fucking floor.

That seals it.

He knows.

But how?

"I'm not that monster's friend," I crackle.

Calhoun shrugs and reaches into his pocket, pulling out a folded print of an old Polaroid. "Maybe not anymore. But you did grow up together. Did you not?"

I'm too shocked to answer.

That doesn't bother Mr. Calhoun one bit. He starts unfolding the wrinkled Polaroid.

"When Tate came to me yesterday with this story, I got to researching the man in the security footage. I was even going to fire you and give the promotion to Tate... until I found a very interesting connection."

I try not to wobble as my legs go weak. I know where this is fucking going. But I still don't understand how he does.

He hands me the Polaroid print, and I take it, willing my fingers not to shake.

When I look down, my world shatters.

It's the first time I've had the courage to look at a childhood photo of my dead brother in years. And my eyes prick as I take him in.

"Mikhail..." I feel myself whisper, sadness seeping from my lips.

Then the anger sets in, tinged with fear.

Next to Mikhail, standing even taller and much broader, is a younger version of the man in the security stills.

Ilya.

"An insider," Mr. Calhoun says in a softer tone, "tells me they know where this man will be tomorrow night. You should 'bump' into him."

He continues, but I can barely hear him again. Hate roars loud in my ears. I remember when that bastard first came to Chicago, back when I was a kid and my brother and him were just teenagers.

It's his fault my brother's dead. I blame my father's death on him too.

I fucking hate him.

But what I hate even more is the school-girl's crush I had on him. How even now, looking at grainy photos of him all grown up, I can feel that rosy warmth.

I want to burn it to ashes.

"Well?"

I glare at Mr. Calhoun.

"No."

"Kira." He sidles in closer. "We can bring the Bratva down. Put this criminal in prison where he belongs, along with all the other scum he works with. And you'll be the reporter who did it. It will be your name under the headlines. Winning all the awards..."

He's barking up the wrong tree with all the adulation bull-shit. Sure, I want to be successful, but it's not worth getting close to that man.

There is something that might make it worth it, though.

Revenge.

Desire snakes through me, tangling with the hate. I could honor my father and brother by bringing down the Bratva, by destroying Ilya.

That would be better than all the renown in the world.

But to do that, I'd need to put aside my hate and treat Ilya like a long-lost friend.

I don't know if I can do that.

Breathing out, I shake my head. "I can't." I'm no actress.

There's got to be another way—

"I was afraid you'd said that," Mitt murmurs. "I hate to resort to blackmail."

That snaps me back to attention.

"Blackmail?"

He shakes his head. "I know your papers are fraudulent."

If I thought my heart couldn't drop any further, I was wrong.

"They're not—"

"Please do not lie to me, Ms. Arendelle... or should I say, Ms. Zhirkov."

The last name sends a hammer of black bile through my chest.

"You know, applying for jobs under a fake last name could lose you a lot of trust. And in this industry, trust is everything. How do we know you aren't hiding some awful secrets? A criminal record? Heck, we know you grew up with criminals. Why else would you hide your very Russian last name?"

"None of that is true," I croak.

"It doesn't have to be."

Tate mutters something I don't catch. All I can focus on is the powerful editor threatening me and my livelihood.

"I can make it seem bad," Mr. Calhoun continues. "People don't want trouble, and you seem like a whole lot of trouble, Kira Zhirkov."

I flinch at the sound of my real name.

There's no denying what's happening here.

Mitt Calhoun has me by the ballsack. If I struggle anymore, he could rip it right off.

So, I try to focus on the positive.

Taking a deep breath, I look back down at the Polaroid. Fear and sadness billow through me. But a deep, fiery hate rises through it all.

Ilya.

I could take him down.

No. I'm not being given a choice. I *have* to take him down.

"Fine. I'll do it," I say, grinding my teeth. "I'll take him and the Bratva down."

Mitt just nods. "That's what I thought."

I barely hear him. I'm already laser-focused on my task, desperately trying to find a way to make this work.

The solution creeps into me like a sickness.

Ilya always had a thing for pretty girls. I was just too young for him back then.

Well, I'm not too young anymore.

I know how men look at me.

I'll use that.

Maybe this time, it will actually work.

It has to.

I'll get close to that monster, and when I can reach his throat, I'll slash it open. Take him down.

For my father. My brother. For my family.

For revenge.

Anything. For. Revenge.

2

ILYA

1 day later...

"You could leave your cozy castle," I say into my phone, observing the activity around me as I walk the Chicago streets, heading to my destination. "Do this yourself."

Valentin laughs. "What? And let you get fat and soft in your big, padded computer chair?"

There's a strange vibration in the air, almost like I'm being followed, which is ridiculous. Only someone with a death wish would do that.

"Maybe I'll do some window shopping in Chinatown," I say, "see what they have in chairs. You can join me if you like."

"Only if you need me. Do you?"

The smart thing to do here is to stick together in numbers. But numbers can lead to wars, and too many of our people are looking for that. There's discipline, and then there's avenging the blood of a comrade.

The latter wins.

Always.

"Better for me to shop alone."

"Ilya." The jovial tone falls away, and I can almost see my friend flex his fist, eye his gun. "Whoever this fucking prick is, they're going around torturing then killing members of our Bratva."

I'm more than aware of this, and the lead I got points to a lot of things but also seems to reinforce other threads.

Chinatown. It's why I'm heading there. "I know."

"I put you on this," Valentin says, because he likes to repeat himself to drive home a point. Not with others. He drives those points home in other ways. But he knows me and feels this is worth repeating.

It probably is, but it won't make a difference if my lead pans out. Still, I let him get his words in.

"I put you on this to figure out who's doing this and why. It's very important."

"I agree, I like that chair." I half-smile. The chair as code isn't the best, but Valentin is a dog with a bone, and since he made fun of my chair, it's an easy bone to play with. And I know he appreciates it.

"I don't like this chair spending time in Chinatown."

"There are good deals to be had," I say.

He mutters something not nice in Russian. Chinatown isn't a safe area for Bratva, so English is best. I'm not scared. That was beaten from me as a boy. But I'm cautious. Smart. English opens more doors than Russian in this part of Chicago.

"If Lev Arshavin lives," he says, "after being supposedly tortured and questioned..."

"It's one of a kind."

"Yes," he says. "And maybe the fucker's a rat."

"Hazarding a guess and saying take that 'maybe' to 'definitely.'" Question is, who the fuck has he ratted to, and why?

Saving your own skin isn't worth much when a man turns on the Bratva, especially one run by us.

"Find out what he said and why he said it."

"If I can find him."

"You will," says Valentin.

He's right, I will. I'm fucking smart and resourceful. And I don't have a death wish. I'll flirt with it, but that's not the same thing.

I cross the road and head into Chinatown.

"If he knows who the mystery troublemaker is," I mutter, "I'll find out."

Along with what he's up to and why.

"Do it."

"I'd like to do more."

"Like kill?" My silence is Valentin's answer. I want the fucker dead, but I need that possible information. It's why I'm here. Alone.

"Are you about to lecture me like a pleb?"

"I'm about to lecture you like a smart man who doesn't like betrayal," he says. "And issue a warning."

I sigh and turn down the desired road. For obvious reasons I don't come into enemy territory often. My goal now is to scope out potential traps and escape routes.

"I know he was demoted."

Valentin utters a nasty laugh. "He's a fucking former Russian enforcer, one who was demoted—"

"Humiliated."

"—after his ties to the Triad were uncovered."

"But why? They don't let in outsiders more than we do."

I don't question Valentin's use of the word demoted. There's no out other than death from the Bratva. But he's been shut out almost completely.

There's sense to that. Watch them scurry and follow the shit.

"There's a nice little bar down here," I say. "Popular with some Westerners and locals."

"Be careful," Valentin says cheerfully. "I hear there's a lot of Triad members down there."

"Fuck you. Or I'll take your lady to the White Lotus for drinks and dancing and I'll win her over."

That earns a growl. Talk of Valentin's wife in such a way, even in jest, and you find out exactly where his sense of humor ends.

I continue my loop, glancing at the alley that leads from the back of the White Lotus—an elegant name for a seedy bar. Then, I casually stroll, giving the appearance like I'm trying to find a place to spend my hard-earned cash.

"I'll buy you some John Belushi for your birthday."

"Who?" the philistine asks.

Then again, old school Americana has never been his thing. I always loved it and found it handy from time to time.

"Going in."

"Be careful, Ilya."

Anyone else would take that as concern for my well-being, but we both know I can take care of myself. He means don't get fucking caught.

That's hard when you're six foot four plus, tattooed, and Russian. Even speaking English and most of my Bratva ink covered, I look exactly like I am.

I settle at the end of the bar, in the shadows, and order a beer and bourbon, a safe bet here.

"It's a mix," I say into the phone. There's a mix of nationalities in here, which solidifies my suspicion this is a meeting place beneath its dive bar surface. "And he's here."

I watch from the corner of my eye as Lev talks with a couple of Italians. No one I know.

"He smokes," says mama bear Valentin, who'll kill me if I call him that to his face. "So keep an eye out for him taking a break. Just remember, Chinatown's dangerous for a Russian. Especially a lone Russian."

"Not my first fucking rodeo."

I don't say it to Valentin, but he's got a point. I take a swallow of my beer and listen to him talk about what to do if I corner Lev. Like I haven't done this before. Many might dismiss him. I don't. He's letting me know how serious this is. And no one knows why.

Which, again, is why I came alone.

"Discreet is the name of the game," I say, taking another mouthful of the beer.

Lev moves from the Italians to some others, but no one who I can pick out as Triad. Obviously, I don't know them all, but I know the tells.

They don't give me a fucking thing.

"If the one who's torturing and killing our men finds out you're there..." Valentin pauses. "Your reputation precedes you."

"I didn't know you cared."

Lev's drunk. He's stumbling about, pulling his pack of cigarettes from his pocket. Drunk or drugged. Fuck. Or on drugs. Still...

"I don't. You getting made could complicate things."

"So it's true love, you and me?" I pull a cigarette pack from my pocket and put it on the bar.

Lev heads out to the alley. "Need a cigarette."

I hang up and place one between my lips, heading out too.

The moment I step out, I get the lighter ready. My gun's within easy reach, but for now, I'm taking a different route.

I flick the lighter, hold it out, and when Lev goes to ignite the tip of the cigarette, I grab him by the collar and move him behind the dumpsters to slam him against the wall.

"Lev, my old friend. I've been looking for you. Time for us to chat, don't you think?" I say in Russian.

He swallows, but instead of him shaking over seeing me, he's darting his gaze about.

"I-Ilya, please!" he answers in fast Russian. "Let me go."

I'm used to men being so afraid of me they almost lose their minds, and definitely willing to spill anything, so that if they can't be saved, at least I'll end them quickly. But this is new.

He's scared shitless of me, but something else scares him even more. And that snags my interest.

Who could possibly terrify this man more than facing me and the wrath of my Bratva?

"You've fucking crossed paths with the most brutal Bratva this city has ever seen," I say, coming in close, his shirt clenched in my grip. "Who did you sell secrets to? Hmm?"

Lev shuts his eyes tightly, trembling, and whispers to me. "I can't."

"The Triad?"

The man doesn't speak.

I pull a knife I've had hidden. I don't tend to slice and dice or carve people like pumpkins, but a knife has a way of instilling a deeper fear than a gun. But instead of focusing on the weapon, Lev's gaze darts around frantically. I follow his gaze to the alley entrance and the door to the bar, but there's no one.

"The Italians?"

"Ilya, please." He swallows. "I can't."

Can't. Won't. Refuses.

He knows.

And he's way too fucking scared of whoever it is to tell me.

That's a first.

"You were tortured?" I ask.

"Yes."

"And still you won't speak?"

The man's practically crying. I hold the knife to his throat, slice lightly, then move it down, right below his balls. One upward motion and he'll be singing castrato.

"Do your worst."

"Why the fuck are you so scared?"

Lev's eyes dart and he says, "You and—"

"Not scared of fucking me. The one who tortured you. You're clearly of use or you wouldn't be here, so why are so fucking frightened?"

"I can't," he repeats, his voice filled with genuine terror. "I'm sorry."

This is fucking new. I watch him. "I could kill you. Hand you to my men..."

"Whatever you want, do it."

I almost step back at that, and I ease the knife away. He's vastly more terrified of some stranger than the real threat in front of him right now. That's never happened before. My crew and I are usually feared above all else.

So what the fuck has this man—a man who got to walk away from his torturer when the rest of his crew ended up dead —so afraid?

He's made a deal, so—

Oh, fuck.

There are fates worse than death, and if Lev's been pushed into a corner by a monster worse than me, then... Those are some real and horrifying complications.

Suddenly, everything comes undone. I'm so distracted by the implications that I let up. For a scared man, Lev moves fast, going for the gun under his shirt. I slash his stomach with my knife, but he doesn't let go of the gun as he takes the element of surprise and body slams me.

I crash into the dumpster as he bolts for the door, screaming as he gets it open.

Lev's advantage is short-lived as I launch myself at him, dragging him from the door.

The fear gives Lev more strength, and he tries to fight me, grabbing at my shirt, his gun lost in the scrabbling.

But strength from fear's no match against a man of my size and with my skill. I knife him deep in the guts, pulling up.

Lev howls and grabs at my shirt, trying to use it to climb. I rip it off and wrap it tight around the fucker's throat.

I've got no fucking idea if the Triad inside heard him over the music, or how many of them might come racing out looking for a fight. This is dangerous. I need to fucking scram.

Pulling the knife from the struggling man as I hold him by my shirt, I slice his throat below the fabric, and then slam the blade into his temple.

Lev stops moving, and I pull out the blade and wipe it clean before grabbing his gun. I switch it for mine just as I hear the muffled music inside the bar stop. Shouts fill the air. Metal slides against metal, and the telltale sounds of weapons being readied fill the air.

"This fucking situation's really gone to shit, Lev," I say to the dead man. "Thanks a lot."

I got nothing of use. Nothing but the ignominy of being taken by surprise, and a dead man who can't fucking talk.

Fuck it all. I'm usually better than this.

Oh well, better luck next time.

I check Lev for other weapons or anything else that might be useful, but all he has is his cigarettes and cash.

Leaving those, I turn and start to leave. No matter how much I love a good fight, it's the smart thing to do right now. I'll be vastly outnumbered. And sure, I know my friends, Valentin and Andrei, would probably stay to fight and kill the lot, but I prefer to choose the smart thing over the fun and reckless thing—at least, I do most of the time.

Before I can take a step in the right direction, though, something catches my eye.

There's something silver glimmering in the low light of the alley next to Lev's body. I bend down to see what it is. Fuck. Another gun. Must have been in his sock. I go to take that. I'm not planning on fighting, but I'm ready for one, and part of being ready is not leaving weapons behind for your enemy to use on you.

My fingers wrap around the gun just as a nearby sound catches my attention. I whip around, gun aimed and ready to fire.

But instead of catching my second kill of the night, I do something I never do.

I freeze.

To my shock, a young woman stands in the alley ahead, surrounded by grime and trash.

Even through the dim, flickering light, I can tell she's gorgeous—long dark hair, electric blue eyes, and a mouth that immediately draws my attention.

The young woman's the antithesis of this whole area.

What the fuck is she doing here?

I'm about to ask when something stops me—a recognition that grows from somewhere deep inside me until it's as massive as a goddamn mountain.

I frown.

She looks familiar.

Very familiar.

I stand slowly.

It takes a moment, but... I know who she is. There's no mistaking it.

My god, after all these years...

"No. Fucking. Way."

Kira Zhirkov.

3

KIRA

I'm frozen in place.

Everything in me is locked on the man ahead. He's staring me down with a look I remember all too well.

Dark, deadly, dangerous. Delicious. In all the wrong ways.

Ilya.

Our eyes lock.

A part of me notes that he's shirtless, his tattooed perfection bloody after killing a man.

And he seems to almost instantly recognize me.

It sizzles hot along my veins, melting the freeze.

His mouth turns slightly at the corners. "Kira Zhirkov... it's been a while. Don't you look amazing."

That dark deep, velvety voice is burned deep in my psyche.

But he's no longer a boy. He's a man. Hot and—and I hate him.

"I-I can't say the same about you," I sputter back.

Ilya smiles, low and dirty, and he saunters up to me. "Just wait until you clean me up."

I open my mouth to return a barb when a burst of sound comes from behind him, and a door bangs open.

Ilya grabs my wrist and hauls me with him at speed. "It's not safe here. Come with me."

Without waiting for my answer, he throws me over his shoulder and then plunges me into a nearby car. We speed away as bullets ricochet off what's clearly bulletproof glass.

"You know, Kira, if you wanted to see me shirtless, all you had to do is pick up the phone."

"I don't have your number."

"Smart girl like you could have found it," he says, almost purring as I grip the seat. "I have faith."

The bullets have stopped, but the fear remains. This was a bad idea. He's not even bothered by the hail of bullets we just barely escaped from.

"If I was smart, I wouldn't be here..." I mumble, more to myself than to him.

He must have heard it, though.

"So what brings you to Chinatown's back alleys, Kira?" he taunts, a serious line undercutting his tone.

He's already suspicious. As he should be.

I need an answer.

Thing is, Mr. Calhoun's plans for me tonight changed last minute. He sent me here to sweet-talk some disgraced Russian and hopefully find a way in to meet Ilya. Who knows what happened to the more upscale place I'm dressed for. White Lotus isn't exactly sequins and silk.

"Too many people were around the front, so I..."

Shit.

"You're shy?" he says. "Couldn't wait to see me again after all these years?"

I came around the back and walked right into the lion's den.

"Hardly," I huff, trying to control my frantic breath. "I didn't know you were there. I wanted to see if I could get in another way."

"Maybe be quiet until you come up with something better."

With that, he switches on the radio.

I stay silent, trying to get my thoughts in order until we get to wherever we're going. Shit. Where are we going? This is what Mr. Calhoun wanted. Mostly. I've got a horrible feeling the person Ilya killed was the man I went there to meet. An informant, someone who knew Ilya.

A two-for-one. Get the dirt, get an introduction.

But there isn't a need for an invitation anymore.

Ilya parks in the basement of a fancy building. To my shock, he gets out and wordlessly drags me over to the elevators where he punches in a line of code. The doors open, and he hits the top button.

"What if someone sees us?"

"Embarrassed by me, Kira?"

"I mean you," I hiss. "You're covered in blood. I don't know if you've noticed, but others will. What then?"

He shrugs. "I'll kill them."

The elevator opens to a beautiful, expansive, modern penthouse. Ilya kicks off his shoes and socks, then puts his weapons on the kitchen counter as he walks by.

I could take a gun, but he'd just overpower me, and I wouldn't put it past a man like him not to kill me.

"What are you doing?" I hiss as he takes off his trousers.

I trail him into the bathroom as he turns on the shower. What else can I do? I still haven't quite registered what's happening.

"What does it look like?"

"Like you're showering."

"Give the girl a prize."

"Most people take off watches," I say, "not guns."

He grins. The black tattoos covering him move with his expression. I'm not a girl given to ink, but on him…

I shiver.

Christ, I hate him.

"I'm more interesting than most people." He leans in. "Look at you, practically drooling."

His Russian tongue slithers through the warm air between us.

"I see you still haven't gotten rid of that stupid accent."

He laughs. "I see you still haven't gotten rid of that shitty attitude."

"It's not going anywhere." I glare.

He sneers.

"And neither are you."

With that, Ilya trails a finger down over my bare skin at the top of my dress, down between my breasts. His touch is electrifying. I can barely breathe.

He moves his mouth along the skin of my throat, not touching, just his breath leaving a fleeting path that makes my panties damp and my body flame. He blows against the throb of my carotid artery, and then he pins me against the wall.

I'm so turned on that it's impossible to think, to breathe, to do anything but melt and drown in him.

He's too hot.

I can't stand it.

He's tracing the thin strap of my dress with his fingers, and I ache for his mouth on my flesh so badly. I want him to peel the top down and—

I make myself stop.

This man's a monster.

He's covered in someone else's blood. Someone he murdered. And I saw it. Maybe not it exactly, but he was crouching by the body, a shirt around the victim's neck. He's fucking shirtless. It's not difficult to put the facts together.

And here I am basically begging for him to kiss and strip me.

And then his words register.

"What the fuck does that mean?"

"What does what mean?" he asks. "You went off into some blissful little world. Maybe dreaming of my lips on yours, or me tasting your pussy?"

"Don't be disgusting." Oh, crap, I want that.

No, my body might, but I don't.

"You said I'm not going anywhere," I say. "You're going to keep me captive?"

He doesn't answer. Instead, he moves in again.

This time he touches my throat, running his fingers over the sensitive skin. Little sparks leap under his caress.

"You witnessed a murder. A murder that I committed. How can I let you go?" he murmurs. "You'll tattle like the brat you are..."

"I didn't see shit." I sniff.

He grins.

"Just look down a little further." He gestures down his body to his cock. "And you'll get to see everything."

"Let me go."

"Why should I? You're in my house."

"You dragged me here. Some might say kidnapped." I try to escape, but he's too strong. He doesn't hurt me, but he uses his weight to hold me there. "Let me go, Ilya."

"Look down, pretty Kira, and all you see is yours." He leans in, and my heart starts to stutter. "Some might say it's just for you. Homegrown."

"You're a pig."

He laughs softly, his hand gently stroking my cheek. "You've always liked me."

His touch is a torture of the cruelest kind. Because of course he noticed my massive crush back then. But that was another lifetime. And I force the words. "I was a kid."

"So was I, but we're not kids anymore."

I'm about to shove him away when something stops me.

We're not kids anymore.

He knows of my old crush, and he likes me now, enough to get hard. Because I looked and... oh my God... he's huge. Not that I have experience, but... I can use his attraction.

"Realized how much you want me, Kira?" he asks, a silky taunt in his voice.

Something snaps.

I'll use him.

For my job.

To be his downfall.

Whatever it takes.

4

KIRA

I grab his face and pull him down to me. Then I do the dumbest thing I've ever done in my life. I kiss him.

Out of all the acts I've committed to get a story, this is the wildest, the absolute pinnacle.

And it's worth it.

He tastes so good. Dark and warm and deep, like everything I've ever imagined sex to be.

Ilya breaks the kiss, staring down at me. One hand's on my clavicle, the other on my throat, high up at where it meets my skull.

For a moment, he just stares. "What the fuck are you doing?"

"What does it look like?"

"Inviting trouble," he whispers, and closes the gap, taking my mouth.

This time, the kiss is more decadent and thorough. He delves into my mouth, taking all there is and giving me more.

I push up against him, rubbing on that massive hard-on like I'm an expert. The kiss turns more passionate. And what started as a way for me to trap him shifts into something bigger, more potent. Something that traps me, too.

Because each time his tongue slides over mine, I want more.

It's so good.

I've kissed guys before, but that's about as far as it's gone. No one's ever set off the fireworks or unleashed the hounds in my blood like this.

Ilya is nuclear.

When he steps back, I throw myself at him again. But he won't let me get the upper hand. He takes control as we slam into the wall, mouths and hands everywhere, fueling the fire inside me. I try to touch him, but his hand is there, sliding up between my thighs, and my entire body goes into freefall.

His mouth finds my throat, and he starts sucking, licking, biting. I'm in overload. I can't breathe; I don't want to. I just... I want...

"It's not fair," I say.

"Nothing's fair in lust and war."

My knees buckle, and he takes me down to the warm tile floor. The hiss of the shower and our harsh breathing blend together into a hypnotic song.

"You're naked and I'm dressed," I cover.

"An easy fix, Kira." He kisses me again.

I pull at his hair, and he rolls us over, our limbs tangling as we hit the wall again, me on him, thighs spread as I rock myself against him.

Ilya's eyes glitter with a hot feral light as he laughs, his hands coiling in my hair, pulling me toward him as he bucks up against me.

He's so big and hard it feels like biting into steel as I sink my teeth into his neck. His lips are softer, but that just makes me bite harder. He doesn't seem to mind. In fact, he groans with a low pleasure, then he bites back, rolling us again as he lands on top of me.

I wrap my legs around him and he rocks down into my body, rubbing against the silk of my panties, sending little thrills dancing under my skin.

Each little thrill acts as a momentary orgasm. My body tingles, crying for more. I scrape my hands down along his back, over those hard smooth muscles, and down until I grab his perfect, firm ass. I dig in my nails and he pulls my hair, yanking back my head to sink his teeth into my carotid artery.

He's sweaty, stained with blood.

And I don't care.

Ilya starts to tear at my dress, and we roll until I'm on top. He pulls it off, tossing the fresh rag aside so he can remove my panties. With a fevered desperation, I help him until they're gone.

He rolls us again and he's there, nestled between my thighs. He dips a hand down. "So wet for me, Kira."

Parting my folds, he dips a finger in and then it's gone, replaced by the fat, flat head of his cock.

What the fuck am I doing?

"No." I gasp, the words ripped from the depths of me, from my soul.

But as we lock eyes, I feel an undeniable pull toward him. I've never wanted something or someone as much as this and him in all my life.

"What? Not wet enough? I can change that. If you need to drip, I will make you drip."

He doesn't give me a chance to find my voice, it's there, somewhere, inside of me, but I can't reach it, and he kisses and bites his way down, little nibbles on my skin that send me higher and further away. And then his lips are between my thighs, stroking a path from my clit down.

"You really are gorgeous, Kira. Even more gorgeous than I imagined. This body you've grown into... fuck... and it's all for me."

His palm smooths along my thigh, pushing it until I start shaking with pleasure. "What—what are you doing?"

I can feel his breath against the wetness of my pussy, his nose nudging up, fingers stroking on my thighs. He uses his shoulder to push my legs further apart, to hold me down.

"What do you think?"

Ilya licks me, along my slit, delving just inside and unleashing a vibrant world of sensation. I clench my jaw to stop a scream at that intimate touch. It's so unbelievably moreish that I get light-headed.

He settles in between my thighs, his fingers higher, parting my folds as he starts to lick and suck everywhere.

Well, everywhere except for the part I ache for him to touch most. He avoids my clit, even as I grasp at his hair, trying to tug him up to the prize.

"Patience, little one," he mutters, before pushing two fingers inside of me.

A scream escapes my lips in a flutter as my toes curl.

"Oh my god..."

"You're so fucking tight, baby girl. Tight, hot, wet. Perfection."

He starts to move his fingers in me, turning them to rub something that makes waves of electric delight sweep through my body. I'm so wet and slick there's no resistance. I've never felt anything so damn good in my life.

And then his mouth closes on my clit and I can't hold back.

"Oh my fucking God."

He laughs against me, his deep tone sending shivers and reverberations through my flesh.

The soft strokes of his tongue, the tug as he sucks, and the scrape of teeth that adds a delicious, slightly painful, dark depth, all coil into one spring until I can't breathe anymore. Can't think. Just feel.

But even as I struggle with the intense pleasure he's giving me, Ilya keeps moving his fingers, harder now, deeper. The licks and sucks and bites grow more intense, taking me into a different realm.

I'm greedy. I fight him, wanting more, my hips moving, hands tugging as I try to get him deeper, to go at me harder.

Then, somewhere in the swirling pool of sensation, something grows and spreads out, making everything in me vibrate on a different level.

"Oh...oh...ohhh..."

I can't form a word as Ilya hits a stride. The beat he plays on me, in me, stays steady as it unspools a deeper pleasure, one that starts to rise up before it crashes, sweeping me away.

My hips arch, and he finally releases me.

I'm only vaguely aware of how my body grinds on him as that sensation takes me over. It hits me that I'm about to orgasm.

Everything shakes and throbs as I clench onto his fingers. Then, I shatter.

When I float back into this world, onto the warm bathroom floor, I realize I'm naked, and so is he, and we-we almost had sex.

What the hell have I gotten myself into?

I roll from him and curl into a ball. "Your floor's warm."

"Heated."

I can't tell a thing from his tone, but regret and disgust rage inside of me. I pushed into him, asked for more, begged maybe not with words, but with my body.

And hell, it was divine, amazing.

Something I shouldn't have done.

He trails a hand down along the curve of my side. "Looks like I was wrong."

"What do you mean?"

Ilya laughs softly. "You didn't end up cleaning me up. Hell, you made me a whole lot dirtier."

A dank, dark, filthy shame hits me hard, and I fight the weight of it, pushing up and shaking his touch from me. "That was..."

"The best fucking orgasm of your life? A nice morsel before the main course?"

I shudder and reach blindly for my dress, but something big and fluffy hits me instead—a towel. I wrap it around my trembling body and clutch my clothes to my damp skin as Ilya gets up, offering me his hand.

I ignore it and push myself away. "Do you have any booze?"

"I'm Russian. What do you think?" He's silent a moment. "There's a fridge full of it in the kitchen. Grab some while I shower."

The door to the shower clicks open and then shuts as I avert my eyes, not needing more stimulation by catching an eyeful of his naked form sluiced with water.

I swallow, mouth dry, and scurry out into the open plan of the penthouse.

"He's giving you free rein," I mutter, tossing the towel aside and slipping into my ripped clothes. "It's a good sign."

I pick the towel back up, fold it, and place it on the found wood dining table.

"It means he's not suspicious... anymore."

I look around at the understated wealth.

I'm not really sure what else I expected. Mounted bear heads? Black leather, steel, and dark wood?

This is light and—I don't care.

Right now, I need something to calm my nerves. I also need to leave. I've been compromised in the dirtiest way possible.

Deciding to combine the two, I storm toward the elevator, through the open kitchen where I catch sight of the wine fridge. But I need more than just wine. I veer off, out of the kitchen to the living area, where I had earlier spotted a well-stocked wet bar. In a small act of rebellion, I choose an insanely expensive bottle of Japanese whiskey.

"Fuck it. I'll take this with me. It's the least he can do."

I stalk over to the elevator and my heart sinks. There's a passcode, like whatever he used in the garage, and no matter how much I press the buttons, it won't light up.

"Asshole."

I glare at it. Fuck. I'm actually stuck. In here. With Ilya.

"And with nothing to show for it," I sneer, "... yet." Holding up the bottle, I unscrew the lid, then take a swig straight from the source, fully aware that it isn't how someone treats a thousand-dollar bottle of booze.

In the distance, I can still hear the shower running. I clench my fist.

"Do not picture him in there," I tell myself. "He's your enemy, remember?"

Right.

I poke around, sipping the booze and quietly plotting his demise, something that's turned into pure fantasy, because I don't think I can take him like this.

"Besides," I whisper, "where's the fun in that? Bringing him down's much better."

That way, he lives through his humiliation, his fall from the top, knowing it's me who cut him down.

A weird satisfaction spreads through me—not just from plotting, but from the pleasure he gave me, the pleasure he wanted to give me.

I'm going to bring him down. He might be hot, he might know how to give me the best orgasm I've ever had, but I hate him, and I'll never, ever forgive him for the pain he's caused me.

But I can use him. He got me good, making me show how I want him. But I can turn that around... pretend to be his fake girlfriend. That's what it seems like he wants, after all.

Right?

Of course. He made that clear enough.

It's brilliant; I can get in deeper this way—at least, that's what I tell myself.

When I hear the shower turn off, I gulp down more of the whiskey and then select a bottle of expensive wine, locate the opener, and remove the cork.

The wine glasses are easy to find. I pour two glasses, downing one and then refilling it and drinking more of the whiskey.

I can drink most men under the table. But Ilya doesn't know this, so if I pretend to be drunk, he might let his guard down.

"What are you plotting?" he says behind me, that smooth deep voice sending shivers down my spine.

I turn expansively, ready to sell the lightweight drinker, when everything in me turns molten.

Ilya stands there in nothing but a towel, water trickling down from his hair over that broad expanse of his tattooed chest.

His hips are narrow, he's shaved, and he doesn't look like a monster. He comes up to me, his dark brown eyes sparking as he takes me in.

He smells like bergamot, rum, citrus, clove leather and unsmoked tobacco. It's a heady scent, yet something that teases the air and invites me in for a closer, more intimate exploration.

"Like what you see?"

His words strike me hard.

Because I do.

Like this, cleaned up, Ilya is like a tatted prince charming.

And the base, unthinking part of me is here for it.

5

ILYA

"Do you, Kira?" I whisper, my mouth close to her ear, her scent like delicate, sultry fingers across my chest.

She smiles up at me, an invitation if ever I've seen one. But only if I don't look closely.

If I do?

There's no invitation at all, just a euphoria brought on by the bottle of fucking top-shelf whiskey she's helped herself to. My gaze travels past her to the bottle, and the expensive wine.

"What's not to like," she says, a slur to her voice as she trails the neck of the bottle over my bare chest, all the way down.

I grab her wrist. The bones are delicate, her skin smooth and alive with a heat that draws me in.

Earlier, still high on the killing, the fight, and seeing her, primal hate and arousal pulsed through me. The thing in the bathroom, where I'd have fucked her senseless, I figured was part anger, part need to humiliate, part pulsating desire borne of the blood and death in the alley.

But her here? Now?

Nothing's changed.

"One day we're going to finish what we started, Kira." And I'm not really sure if it's a promise or a warning.

She presses against me, a dangerous thing to do, no matter how much she reminds me of her brother—that bastard, Mikhail—Kira's still an irresistible young woman. All grown up. Legal.

Very, very legal.

But that doesn't change the facts. Her brother betrayed me and got me exiled from Russia. She must wear that guilt like it's her very own. Rules are rules.

"You should remind me," she whispers, swaying as she leans in to lick my chest. "of what it is we need to finish."

I hiss a breath.

Her tongue is wet, and it arouses me in all the right ways, awakening my passion, need, hate, and raging desires. My arousal is hard and ferocious. I want that tongue on my cock, her lips wrapped tight around me as I slam into her mouth, to the back of her throat.

"There's fire and there's lava, Kira. Flames that flicker a candle into life and flames that burn forests to the ground in minutes." I stroke a hand through her hair, coil it and lift her head. "Be careful which you choose to play with."

"Maybe I want to see a fire."

I take the bottle from her. "Not this kind. I'm the bad kind, Kira. Once you ignite me, you might not be able to put me out."

She takes a step and stumbles. I place the bottle on the table next to the towel, and she bumps into me, swaying.

I frown. There's tipsy and there's this. "You're drunk?"

"You're perceptive," she spits.

I sigh. "Drunk fucking girls are not attractive, Kira." Or guys, but they don't tend to try and get in my pants. Instead, they stupidly start fights. I'd put a drunk man in the ground before I got into the pants of a wasted girl. "Go drink some water."

She reaches past me and grabs the bottle, taking a deep swallow before I take it off her again and set it aside. "You don't wanna play?"

"Drunk isn't my scene. Come to your senses and then maybe we can talk."

Kira wraps around me and tries to get the towel off. I take her hand, and she half-falls on me, breathing expensive fumes up into my face. "We got off on the wrong foot. So let's stay off our feet and get horizontal..."

Fuck, her sloppiness is cute and tempting. Or maybe it's her. She tempts. She's half limpet, half octopus, and all temptation as she rubs those sweet tits against me. And she starts peppering me with kisses—chest, throat, nipples—and my cock's so stiff I'm getting fucking blue balls.

But I untangle her from my damp body.

I might be a bastard, but I've got a code.

She comes for me, and I gently guide her to a seat at the table, away from my Japanese whiskey.

"But I want to kiss you," she pouts.

"No," I say, wondering what the fuck's got into me, "you don't. Not right now."

"You don't know." She reaches for the towel, and I move out of the way. "Take off the towel."

"Rampaging fires, Kira," I say.

Her frown is all theatrics.

There's something so...goofy and young about her drunken attempts to fuck me that it reminds me of the young girl that Mikhail and I used to be so protective over. She was so innocent back then. I look at her. Is she still? Despite her actions, there's a naivety to her that hasn't been washed away quite yet

"Don't you want me?" Her voice is so small; I sense the lingering innocence there, as if it's woven into her very being.

I want to corrupt it... But I also want to nurture and protect it.

What the hell's gotten into me?

"Life isn't so simple," I say.

And it isn't. She stopped me from fucking her. No girl does that with me, especially not after I kiss them. When I do that, clothes seem to shed, and all the treasures are on offer.

"It is," she mutters, swaying a little in her seat. "Like I wanted to do this after I got some courage, but now I don't."

Wait, did I kiss her or did she kiss me? I'm having a hard time remembering.

Fuck.

"Some might call that fickle," I say.

"And some might call you a cockblocker."

I start laughing, and she stiffens. Insulting Kira is something I can do, even after all these years. Vulnerable and drunk and innocent? Not so much.

"I'm not sure you can cockblock yourself." I get my phone from the kitchen counter and send a quick text.

She's followed me, all narrow-eyed and emerald-green with jealousy, the kind that comes from being drunk off your tits. Shit, she's a fucking lightweight.

"Whoever it is better be ready for rejection."

"I'm not planning to make moves on Semyon." I wink. "I don't think I'm his type."

"You—"

"He's my assistant, and I'm getting him to take you home."

She glares, having forgotten that burst of jealousy. And then surprise hits her face as the glare fades. "You're not going to take advantage of me?"

I almost laugh. Instead, I shrug. "Don't really need to, do I? I already got what I want."

But that's not true. I can admit I want her. All of her. It doesn't matter if I might have to destroy her, I want everything she has.

I could take her instead of punishment. That works. But

she'll need to give herself freely. What will it take for her to let me in? To let me fuck her like I want?

"That's a fucking lie—"

The private elevator that leads to the sub-basement dings. It blends with the wall and Kira gasps as it opens on the far side of the living room.

Semyon Perov stands there, hands folded.

As my assistant, slash second-in-command, he likes to call me 'sir' to annoy me, but he knows his place. One look at Kira and he just waits.

I nod to him. "Go with Semyon, Kira. Get home safe."

"But..." Those big blue eyes rise to mine, and there's something there I can't work out. Something...

I shoot Semyon a glance, and he doesn't move.

Mikhail was always so protective of her... but Mikhail isn't around anymore. And Kira always had a real knack for trouble —nothing outrageous, but she never knew when to quit, never knew when to back the fuck down.

Maybe I can use that.

I go to her, deliberately crowding, so she has to tilt her head back to look up.

Through all this, from the shit in the alley to me stripping her and eating her out, to her getting drunk and trying to seduce me, she's kept her small bag.

Not in the bathroom, of course, but she put it down, and it's here now, in her hand. I take it.

"Hey," she says, snatching at it. I pluck her phone, toss the bag aside, type in my number, and send myself a text.

I hand it back, making her touch me. "I'll be in contact. We're having dinner tomorrow night."

The firecracker I remember so well flares into life. All grown up, stunning and unbelievably fuckable, but that fiery little girl still spits flame in the center of her. "Says who?"

"Says me." I lean in. "And what I say goes."

This time I nod at Semyon as I slap her on the ass and give her a gentle push toward the elevator.

"Semyon. If anything happens to her, it's your life," I say.

He gives me a bland look. "Yes, sir."

Kira stands there, looking for all the world like she doesn't know if she should go or stay. And it's a hell of a battle. I can see her gaze snag on the elevator, then shift to me, dropping her eyes to my cock.

It's one hell of a battle and I'm fucking here for it. Desperate to go, longing to stay. It's fuel for my desire.

"Go."

"This way, Miss." Semyon hustles her politely into the elevator, and the doors shut.

I sag against the back of the large cream sofa. With her gone, the room's empty, like something important is missing. But at least now, I can breathe.

"Fuck. What the actual fuck am I going to do with Kira?" I pause, straighten, and go into my room to throw on some clothes. Then I rake my hand through my hair. "What the fuck am I doing?"

I pick up my phone, run a finger over the message I sent, the one that gives me her number.

She could be useful. By blood, she's tied to this life, with those who fucked me over, exiled me. I'm already seeking revenge—sweet, cold and delicious. By targeting the internal affairs of the Bratva back in Russia, those who fucked me, like her fucking brother.

I just wish I'd been the one to—

No. No matter how badly Mikhail fucked me over, he didn't deserve what happened to him. I should have been the one to end him. No one else had the right.

I pull up Valentin's number and call him. "It's a no go."

"Fuck."

Kira's fucking bastard of a brother isn't here, but Kira is, and just because Mikhail and I used to be protective is no reason to go down that route anymore.

"I had to kill him."

"We'll find another way, another in."

Like Kira? If indeed, this has to do with them. Or maybe I'm grasping at fucking straws because there's a part of me that wants to see her again.

I leave the bedroom and head for my computers. "He was scared shitless."

"You can be scary," he says.

"Not," I say, "of me."

Valentin's silent; then, he exhales and a chair creaks. I know he's in his study. That fucking chair's a dead giveaway, creaking like a crone. "Want me to tell Andrei?"

"No, I will. I need to discuss some things."

"Okay. It's just a setback." And with that, Valentin hangs up. His tone belied his words. But there's nothing I can do about it.

Killing a bunch of Triad members, or me getting myself killed, isn't going to help anything. The first might exacerbate. The second...

Let's just say I'm more useful alive.

I start to pull Kira up on my computer, but then I stop. I could do a quick search or a deep dive; it wouldn't take long, but I hold off.

Maybe not knowing's more fun. I mean, Mikhail will never know what I do to his little sister, but it would still make me feel better. Getting payback on him and corrupting and using Kira would be fun. Therapeutic even.

Fuck. Or maybe I just fucking like her.

Who the hell knows?

The only thing that's certain is I need to see her again.

6

ILYA

The next day...

I sit with my legs crossed, fingers tapping a beat on the armchair in Andrei's old office at Club Silo247. He had to take care of an order or something equally annoying.

My mind's on the situation at hand, both of them.

For the first time in a long while, the girl wins out over work.

Still... fuck. Kira Zhirkov, like a ghost from the past, and maybe a link to the problems in our Bratva's yard. Not to mention the constant ache that no amount of jacking off seems to help.

Last night, she threw my accent back in my face. I have my reasons for keeping it, cultivating it. Reasons she won't understand. Or maybe she will, maybe—

"Ilya, what the fuck happened?"

Andrei saunters in and takes his seat. The hard lines of his face reveal the force of his iron fist. His eyes show his fairness.

But some mistake that for weakness.

Exactly once.

Then they end up dead.

I like a man like that.

Blowing out a breath, I spread my hands. "Fucking Lev met the fate of snitches everywhere."

"But didn't talk?"

"Oh, he talked. A lot of bullshit." I sit up and lean forward. "He was a lot more scared of whoever's behind the murders than he was of me."

Andrei's eyes narrow as he grasps the implications. "We're the scariest fucking thing to happen to Chicago in decades. You'd have to be stupid... or have some power behind you."

"A combination of both is my thought."

It hasn't all been blue balls and lust. The Lev shit's been turning in my mind too.

"But still, you didn't get anything?"

"I don't think you, me, and Valentin would have been able to. When I say he was scared, he was basically shitting himself." I sigh, "And yes, I'm fucking surprised too. Normally they talk."

"Normally."

The whole situation is odd, and in our world, odd equals danger.

But if we're in so much potential danger, why can't I get my mind off Kira? Shit, for as much as I hate her family, I'm not sure I can knowingly put her in any kind of danger—at least, not in danger that doesn't directly involve me.

Suddenly, I look up. Andrei's frowning. "Sorry, boss."

"I asked if there was anything?"

Her taste was definitely something. I force my head back to what he's asking. "I think he wanted to die rather than say a damn thing."

I can't get her into all this, not when I don't know the full extent of the dangers. What I do know is already bad enough. Even if Kira is Mikhail's sister...

Then again, she might not play. Even if she wants to. And she does; last night proved that. But last night she also said no. And when I texted her this morning when and where to meet me tonight, she never responded.

I don't expect her to.

She'll be in too much turmoil to do that. And it makes me suddenly want to smile.

"Ilya, is something on your mind?"

I don't miss the deadly tone under the quiet. "Nothing to do with this. Just something very pretty and probably trouble."

"I never thought I'd see the day... is the great mind of Ilya Rykov finally taking a back seat to his dick?"

I just give him a look. He gives me one right back and reaches for a bottle of vodka from a small hidden fridge. I'm betting it goes back to his single days when he'd pull strings of all-nighters. I should know; I have a whole setup so I barely have to leave my computers when I'm deep in the work I prefer.

He pours two shots and slides one over.

"I asked if the body will cause any issues."

"Triad territory. There won't be a trace."

We raise our glasses and toss the contents back. Then Andrei puts the glass down and leans in.

"I get it, Ilya. Trust me. But I need you. Your big brain. And I need it to be sharp like a blade. This threat is becoming beyond serious. Our associates and underlings are increasingly worried about being tortured and killed by this mysterious assailant."

I flick a glance at the Pakhan. "This big brain can operate on many levels and remain sharp."

"See that it does. I don't like people fucking with what's mine."

"The mission is in good hands," I assure him. "I'll get to the bottom of it."

"Good." He eyes me. "You know, there's no shame in sticking to your strengths."

"You chose me because I do what needs to be done, not just what I like. Fieldwork isn't my natural habitat, but that doesn't make me any less deadly."

"I know."

His phone rings, and he glances at it, then sweeps up his cell, waving me out.

"Ilya?"

"Yes?"

"Keep me updated."

I leave, knowing I lied. The lie won't interfere with my work, or the quality, or even my ability to remain scalpel sharp when needed. But I'm not focused on the job right now.

Instead, my mind has only one thing, one thought:

Kira.

I leave and drive home, stripping off for a shower because I'm taking fucking Kira out, whether she answers my texts or not. While I choose my suit, I send Semyon out on the job to find information for my next move.

Someone, somewhere, will slip, and my second-in-command has a knack for networking—and keeping track of them all. He can turn chameleon and move through different societal groups, something that comes in handy.

He can also turn deadly with his fists, knife, and gun, which is also handy.

With that done, I give over to the dangerous urge that's beating in my blood, like a drug I need. Kira.

Fucking Kira.

Because she isn't just beautiful; she's tied up in threads of me, a past that shaped my life.

I settle on a three-piece suit in slate, and choose a tie that has pinstripes in black. I purposely put on a sapphire ring too. It's the same color as her eyes.

Thing is, I've always liked her. Back then more like a sister, because she was too young and innocent for any other kind of relationship. Now, though, we're both adults, and she's unavoidably gorgeous and covered in a sinful scent. My sinful scent.

I smooth the tie into place and button the vest as a surge of old anger rushes me. Damn it, Mikhail. I should have kept you far from the Bratva.

Those threads pull.

There are wounds...

Screw it. I'll defile her to get back at Mikhail for what he did. Or shit, maybe I'll indulge because I want to.

There's something about her that makes my cold, empty chest tighten.

And I'm not sure I like that.

I scowl at my reflection as I slip on my jacket.

"Something about her," I mutter. "We'll see how I feel when I see her again."

I've booked us a meal at a swanky new restaurant. It's classy, expensive, and low-lit.

When I arrive, I get a drink at the bar, the place redolent with almost architectural displays of lush and elegant flowers. I decide to play a game while I wait.

Kira will be punctual... *after* going back and forth all day over whether or not she'll turn up. I think she'll be on time and wait to walk in a few minutes late. She's either going to dress upscale or frumpy. I haven't decided which.

But I'm going to find out because my watch just ticked over when she was meant to be here.

That's when the door opens.

I almost drop my drink.

"Holy fuck."

If Kira wanted my attention, it's worked. I can't tear my gaze from her.

She's wearing red. The dress is pretty, the wrong side of short, and the silky material's painted on. The neckline plunges between her breasts, and from the man staring almost bug-eyed at her ass, I'm going to guess it's fucking backless too.

Black stockings and stacked heels make her legs seem miles long, and there's a gold bracelet at her wrist, a cute black bag, and a gold choker on her elegant throat.

Her black hair is pinned up.

She's dressed to the nines and a little too slutty for a public place.

She looks like a modern-day courtesan heading to the king's boudoir.

And every fucking man in the place is stripping the scraps of material off her.

She's not wearing a bra, and I'm doubting she's wearing panties.

I want to gouge every male eye that's glued to her from each man's head.

A surge of heat, sharp and biting, courses through me, and I toss back my drink and rise slowly.

Looks like Kira needs to be taught a lesson.

7

KIRA

Ilya stares at me through narrowed eyes, and it's a jolt to my system.

He also steals my breath as he rises slowly, his gaze fused to mine for long beats.

Everything about him is stunning,

from his height and build to the way the slate suit fits with absolute perfection. His dark-haired beauty turns heads—masculine beauty personified. I'm betting there are more than a few damp panties in the room.

Ilya looks like he fits seamlessly into this world of money and status. Legit status. Even with an air of danger, he manages that.

He takes me in and doesn't smile. Instead, he shifts his gaze from me, sending death glares to the men in the room. Men I didn't even notice staring at me.

It's something I usually do. Something I know because women need to be aware of lurking predators. But this time I didn't notice a thing.

Every sense I've got was and is focused on this man.

Now, though, I feel them looking, touching with their gazes, undressing me. I swallow because, in that second of awareness, I'm naked in this outfit that verges on red-carpet X-rated film awards night.

My back straightens as Ilya comes toward me with slow deliberate steps. "What the fuck are you wearing?"

"What the fuck do you think?"

He leans in, his lips almost touching my skin. A shiver of desire runs right through the center of me. "I think you're playing with the wrong kind of fire again."

"You think, do you?"

"I can do that, Kira. And if I wasn't here, some of the less scrupulous wolves dressed as docile sheep would rip you the fuck apart."

"Maybe," I say, "I'd like that."

"And maybe you're adding button-pushing to your dangerous little repertoire."

Thing is, I'm grateful he's here. Kind of. He's a barrier between me and them. But who or what's the barrier between us?

What the fuck was I thinking, wearing something so tight, so revealing, so not me?

I know what I was thinking.

"You said dress up for dinner, so I did. I figured this would be to your tastes."

He flashes a nasty little grin as we're led to our table in the back, nestled among large floral displays, an air of intimacy about it. "I like what's in it. But the outfit? It doesn't seem to be you."

Ilya pauses as we're seated. Then his hand skims along my thigh for a breathless second. "Or maybe I'm wrong, and that makes me the luckiest man in here."

The hand's gone, the touch so fleeting I almost wonder if he touched me... except I can still feel the caress.

I wore the slutty dress to entice Ilya, to draw him in... and maybe to make him feel jealous, the way I did last night when he texted his right-hand man. That wasn't an act. It was real. And I want him to see he doesn't own me, that I'm desirable—but now it feels silly.

Silly and stupid and confusing, and not just because I'm suddenly teetering on the edge of vulnerability, but because he's clearly being protective.

In his own, scary, threatening way.

There's something there, in the middle of that silliness, a confusion that feels kind of nice.

I haven't felt protected since my brother left and my father died. For years now, it's just been me, fending for myself, all alone in the world.

"Do you feel lucky?" I ask as I flip open my menu.

But he puts his hand on the page. "Let me order?"

"Misogyny went out of practice."

This time, when he smiles, there's no agenda, just pure amusement. It transforms him into something spectacular. "So I've heard."

I stare around his hand at the menu, and some of the prices peep out. "You get one hall pass. Order away."

"Ox heart and tripe good for you?"

I narrow my eyes. "Delicious."

He leans in, lips skimming my ear. "And what would you do if they had that?"

I turn, our mouths way too close, our gazes catching.

"Make you eat it."

"Chicken."

"Now that I'll eat." And I laugh. Actually laugh.

His smile is low, loose, and one of the sexiest things I've seen. "Don't disappoint me. Chicken is the gruel of meats."

"And if I was vegan?"

"You're Russian. You wouldn't dare. Like black bread and vodka, being an omnivore is in your DNA."

I'd forgotten how damn smart he was, how quick. Way back when, sure I crushed on his pretty, pretty face, but I crushed harder on the book smarts about him. His intelligence he never bothered to hide.

"A potato vegan?"

"Potatoes are the meat of the earth."

I laugh again.

The wine arrives, and it's delicious—buttery, light, with hints of grassiness teasing the tongue and a final burst of citrus. It pairs utterly perfectly with the first course of green apple jus and crisped sashimi.

"This is sublime," I whisper.

"Just as you are."

He says this so softly, I almost miss it.

"You've done well for yourself, Ilya."

The smile shifts a little as the next course comes—lion's mane mushroom pâté with buttered dill toasts. "What were you doing in that seedy part of Chinatown last night? It wasn't exactly early."

I hesitate a beat and force my hand to calm as I pick up my wine. After all, I expected something like this. "I told you—"

"You went around the back to see if you could get in? It's Chinatown, and a seedy part at that."

Shit. Shit. He's right. A smart girl wouldn't do that, especially not one who grew up here in Chicago.

So I shift it a little. "You got me."

"I do." His gaze moves over me. "Don't I?"

I ignore the loaded weight to his words. "Sometimes a quiet drink is what a girl needs after a hard day at work, and that place can get rowdy, but... truth?"

"That'd be nice, Kira."

Sucking in a breath, I spear a leaf from the delicate salad that just arrived. The portions are small, perfect for satisfying hunger without leaving you too full before the entrée. I spear another leaf, take a bite, and savor the bursts of fresh citrus and an extra lush flavor that awakens my taste buds. Despite the sensory delight, I force myself to look at him.

"Truth is, I was thinking about a drink, but I was walking home after work and heard a commotion. So I went to see if I could help."

I continue eating the salad and sipping the wine, aware of his gaze on me, as if he's searching for something.

Suspicion lingers in the air, even though he merely nods and takes a sip of his wine.

I know he thinks I'm either lying or not telling him the entire truth.

That's the problem with a man like him. He likes puzzles, likes to poke and prod and uncover the workings beneath.

I set my wine down and lean in, touching his thigh beneath the table as I shift closer to him.

"What are you doing, Kira?

His words are soft, lazy, and seductive. It takes me a moment to realize he spoke in Russian.

The sound ripples over me.

I look up at him under my lashes. "Flirting." It's the only way to distract him

He touches my cheek, the corner of my mouth, lingering. Then he shifts so our thighs touch.

Ilya hands me my wine. "What do you think of this place?"

"Beautiful."

"The food is exemplary."

"Do you bring all your dates here?" I can't stop the words from tumbling free.

That smile flirts with his mouth. I want to lick it off.

"Jealous?" Ilya's hand trails up my thigh, slowly as he skims his lips along the skin of my throat, up to my ear. "Only you."

The wine changes to red, and his fingers slip up my inner

thigh. My clit throbs wildly, and I can't help it—I part my thighs a little.

The gleam in his eye says he hasn't missed that move.

But I touch him too. Because it's part of the game of interest, of pretending I could be his.

Because I want to.

"Are you..." The heat in his eyes stills, and I veer away from my question about the Bratva. "Are you happy to be back here in Chicago?"

"Instead of my homeland?" Again, he speaks in Russian, and I stick to English, finding something hot about that.

A battle, something needed?

I'm not sure, only I can't help myself—just as I can't help the tiny little jumps each stroke of his fingers on my bare flesh above the stockings sets off.

"Yes," I say. "Instead of Russia."

"I'm not a fan of the circumstances." The flatness in his words slams shut a door.

I stroke my hand up higher, flirting with his growing cock, feeling the heat and steel and the amount of space it takes up.

"Well, we ran into each other again. What do they call it?"

"Stalking?" His smile takes the sting. "I think you mean serendipity. If you're thinking this is a happy circumstance."

I flutter my lashes, squeeze his inner thigh. "I do."

This is nothing more than a game for my job, yet his touch sends those tiny sparks of warm electricity through me, and I keep touching him, so he keeps touching me.

I might be addicted to those tiny shocks.

Oh shit, please don't let me like him.

"Keep that up, and I won't be much of a gentleman for long," he mutters.

I suck in a breath, saved as the main course arrives—wagyu beef on a bed of roasted, creamy parsnip mash, and a rich jus studded with peppercorns. Dishes of baby carrots, zucchini, purple sprouting broccolini, and slender French beans come with it in a fragrant broth.

Thing is, I'm not hungry. Not for food.

But Ilya eats, and I do too, our hands touching, flirting under the table.

Each time he edges higher, dangerously close to touching my bare pussy, I brush against his balls or shaft.

The only reaction is his harsh breath. "Fire, Kira. A great storm of fire you insist on flirting with."

"Maybe," I say, stroking over the head of his cock, "I'm in fire retardant clothes."

"You're highly flammable and pouring gasoline on yourself."

This time, when he touches me, I yelp. The only reason I don't call attention is because he feeds me the melting beef.

Sublime.

Like him.

I can't figure out why he's being so accommodating, so restrained, as if he wants to make a good impression. But Ilya's never been like that, not when I was a kid crushing on him, and not now.

What the hell is his angle?

Does he like me?

Panic wells as that little girl who desperately wanted to please him keeps poking her nose out, and I keep shoving her down.

I keep losing.

"The beef's spectacular," I whisper.

He slides his fingers up along my slit to my clit, and I moan. "I don't give a fuck about the beef, Kira."

Then he pushes a finger into me as he feeds me some of the vegetables, and I don't know which is more orgasmic. The food or him.

That's a lie.

I do.

Him.

Definitely him.

I wrap my fingers around his cock and squeeze.

That sends him over the edge.

"Get your bag, get up, and wait for me by the bathrooms," he orders.

I don't question him. Ilya takes his hand from me and a protest drops from my lips. I can't think straight as I get up.

I take one step from the table before he's there. I can't help it, I glance down, but his erection, while still there, has been tucked away.

"Ilya."

He doesn't answer, just takes my arm and drags me out of the restaurant and to the unisex bathrooms. These are the lavish sort I've only seen on TV. One-room affairs with low lighting, dark colors, flowers. and air smelling like roses and spice. He pushes me back into the door, locking it.

Before I can say another word, his mouth is on mine. I'm lost as I kiss him back, his lips and tongue working dark magic.

He kisses a trail down my throat, his hands everywhere, up under my short skirt, two fingers pushing into me as he starts to thrust, fingers turned to stroke against my clit and I lose my mind.

But somehow I grab hold and fight it. "Wait, Ilya, I'm not, I'm—"

"I warned you."

His belt comes off with a thwack in the air. And his fingers move in me, each thrust long, slow, and deep. I can't get away.

I don't even know if I want to get away.

"I fucking warned you about playing with fire, Kira."

He pulls his fingers free and wraps his belt around my wrists, tying them behind my back. Then he drops to his knees.

"I fucking knew you weren't wearing panties." He pulls my

skirt up with his teeth, exposing me to the air, and he licks a path, sucking hard on my clit.

I moan loudly, my knees buckling as unfettered bliss washes through my body.

"All for me," he says, holding me in place with his face as he parts my folds with his fingers to delve right back in.

I shudder, wanting more, needing to stop it, but I can't seem to find the words as he starts thrusting hard, dragging his fingers in circles. The sensation is so intense, like a thousand buzzing gardens of delight. He sucks and licks my clit, pushing me up to completion in spectacular fashion.

This time Ilya isn't playing. He's not teasing. He wants to reach the prize, and then... I don't know what, because each thrust and downward motion of his fingers, each lick and suck on my clit shatters me further until I'm unable to think, only feel.

He sucks hard, pushing his tongue against my clit as he does, even as he rubs that spot. It's too much, a crescendo of pleasure.

I cum hard.

But Ilya isn't done. He rises with a grin, unzipping and unleashing himself. He then turns me around so I'm facing the door.

"Wait—"

He starts stroking me from behind, using the belt to position me with my ass out so I'm open and exposed to him.

Panic starts, along with excitement.

"Ilya, please, wait—"

My phone starts to ring and vibrate, and I already know it's Mr. Calhoun. I know because I keep my phone set like that for when he rings, and the ringing stops me telling Ilya I'm a virgin.

I can't miss the call, and I can't answer it and blow my cover.

"Fuck no," he says. "No phones."

My bag's still on my shoulder, but he sweeps it off, reaching in to grab the phone. So I grab his cock.

My hands are still tied behind my back, but I straighten and start to pull his shaft, rubbing my fingers over him. He drops my bag and phone.

"Fuck yes," he says, one of his hands landing hard on the wall as he starts to thrust hard into my hands. "Like that, Kira... tighter... perfect."

He cums, and ropes of his release hit my ass as he grunts, shuddering.

When he's done, he kisses my shoulders and rubs his cum into me, then pulls my skirt down and undoes my hands.

On wobbly feet, I face him.

"I... I need to go," I say, my voice scratching.

"Where? You got another fucking date, Kira?"

I swallow hard, straightening my dress, aware that his cum is on my skin under my dress. I grab my bag.

"To make money," I snap, "we can't all make millions killing people for a living."

He strokes a hand over my cheek. "Billions," he corrects. "And you don't need money; I'll take care of you."

"I don't want you to take care of me." I narrow my eyes. "I don't need it."

"Really?" His face turns to stone. "What is it you do for money that makes you so fucking independent?"

My palm itches to smack him, but I keep it fisted by my side. "None of your business."

"Still feisty." He sucks my lobe and then feathers his lips over mine. "I love feisty."

He's turning me on all over again, and my entire body throbs. "I have to go."

I'm ready for a fight, one that doesn't come. He merely nods.

"If you want to go and miss out on the real fun, go."

He unlocks the door and gestures for me to leave, and my cheeks flare hot.

Ilya's wandered ahead, seemingly having lost interest, his dark head bent over his phone. But it's a ploy. He's focused on me, it's in the stillness, and I know he's full of suspicion because, apart from anything, that's him.

I go to him and half reach for his arm, but he doesn't look up. With shock, I realize I loved what he did. I loved touching him. I loved how hot his cock felt.

I want him to fuck me.

I want him to be caught up in me for real.

Shit. I'm in so far over my head it's not funny, but this is something I need to risk for my ambition.

That's what's important. Not Ilya.

So I turn, taking a deep breath, and I walk away as my phone rings again.

I wait until I'm outside before I answer.

"Hello?"

8

ILYA

"Thing is," I say, rubbing a hand over my chin in my kitchen as I pour a whiskey, "I find the whole fucking thing suspicious."

The outfit, the flirting. The... outfit.

Oh fuck, the *outfit*.

"Not to mention the way she responded to that phone call. Like her pimp or her lover was on the other end." I pause, down the drink and pour another. This one I set on the island. "I don't think she's some kind of call girl or escort. And her excuse for being in that alley in Chinatown stinks."

I shake my head and sigh, picking up the glass to take a sip.

"There's something there."

And I can't seem to put my goddamn thoughts in order enough to work it out. She's too much in the way. Kira in the almost-dress. Kira's hands tied behind her back while she gives me a hand job. While I use her hands like it's her cunt.

The fucking dress.

"Shit."

I take another big mouthful of the whiskey, barely registering the heat as it spreads through me.

"She fucking fogs my mind," I mutter, straightening up to

leave the kitchen before I change my mind and return for the bottle. It's a shit conversationalist, but it's got its uses.

"Thing is," I say to the bottle as I take it through the living room over to where my computers are set up, "between you and me, I've got a thing for her. That fucking hand job..."

It was some kind of American high schooler crap, and I was there for it. I used her hand to cum, and it was the hottest fucking thing I've done in a long time.

"I can come up with all kinds of excuses, some of them actually legit," I continue, taking a swallow of the whiskey as I sit in front of the screens.

As usual since this one-sided conversation started, I don't get an answer. I'm used to that by now.

"But the truth is, I don't want to know who the hell called her and made her run like she was summoned—" because it was a man, had to be "—because it might have to do with the shit that's been going on with my outfit. I want to know who my competition is."

I wait, but the world doesn't implode.

"Fine. I admit it. I want to know because I like her. I want to fuck her."

I finish the glass and start diving into Kira's more recent background. Online presence, history, arrests, whatever the fuck there is, but...

Something doesn't add up.

Last job she visibly had under the name Kira Zhirkov was at a coffee shop years ago when she was still a teen.

Maybe she turned to a life of crime. Maybe she's scrubbed herself from the internet to hide it all. But I doubt that.

So why isn't she here? Why isn't there even one social media post?

I'm a little shocked because Kira was always smart, excellent at school, and excelled in English and history. I remember because her father always bragged about it. Mikhail too. He was proud of his little sister.

And now she's around the age when she should be in college. So, why isn't she?

I do a light deep dive, but all I get in return is the obvious—like her topping her class in her senior year.

What the fuck? Can't she keep a job? Maybe Mikhail leaving.... and then her father's death... shit, maybe they did such a number on her that she lost focus...

My chest tightens and starts to ache. I rub it with my hand. Fuck me, is this partially my fault? Because no one but me convinced Mikhail to leave Chicago.

And when her father died...

She had no one.

She might still not have anyone.

"Fuck," I say, picking up the bottle and drinking from it. Right now, she might make me want to protect and provide for her, assuage the nag of guilt in me, but her father treated me like a piece of shit.

Her fucking brother betrayed me.

"I owe her nothing."

There's no black and white, no good guys. Just those who are loyal and those who aren't.

But...

I need to know more about her.

Everything.

It burns bright.

And I know a way to get answers. I pull out my phone and text her.

We're having dinner tomorrow night again. At my place this time.

She doesn't get back to me for minutes. ***Busy.***

I frown. That's suspicious. Isn't it?

So I type, ***Then I'll come to your place.***

She texts back. ***Do you even know where I live?***

Kira's forgotten who dropped her off last night. I send her address to her. Clearly, she needs to be reminded I have a far reach.

There's a pause until, finally, she responds.

Fine. I'll come over.

A smugness spreads through me. I didn't even have to push hard—

My phone starts to ring, and it's Semyon. "Tell me," I say, "something good."

"We've got another lead."

There's something in his voice that makes my guts go tight. I'm already on my feet, going for my gun.

"How bad is it?" I ask.

"Bad."

Twenty minutes later and I know I don't need the gun.

Instead, I stand in the weapon stash house in the hidden office.

The place was trashed, cameras smashed—those that were visible—and the word massacre is the only one I can think of.

"What the fuck happened?" My gaze moves from Semyon to two high-ranking members whose names have slipped my mind because they're of little importance compared to the injured guard.

Blood stains his uniform and the gash in his head isn't pretty. He holds his arm. Agony and guilt are scarred all over his face.

I zero in on him. "I won't ask again. Tell me. What the fuck happened?"

"I shouldn't be here. I should be dead. I deserve to be dead," the man says in Russian, and I grasp what his guilt is about.

He's telling me that not only did he not get to die fighting alongside his friends—like any good Russian is supposed to—but he didn't see who did this either. He doesn't have a description. He's useless.

And that means...

Fuck, I don't even have a culprit.

I look around, cursing under my breath. The cleanup crew has already gotten rid of the bodies, but something else catches my eye—or rather, the lack of something.

The weapons. "They took the fucking weapons..."

The firepower we store here is high-grade; it's worth a fortune. They're earmarked for distribution among our troops. If you wanted to hurt us, you'd have at least destroyed our stash along with our men.

But...

I look around again.

Whoever it was hit hard, smooth, and with precision—the kind of professional hit meant to burn.

They sent us a message.

One I'm hearing loud and fucking clear.

"Got something," a younger member of my crew says as he looks up from his laptop.

I go to him and look at the screen.

Footage.

That we weren't meant to see.

Unless this was an inside job...

That's an ugly thought, and it casts blame somewhere we haven't looked yet, inside the workings of our own Bratva.

But to turn on us like this is certain suicide. Andrei isn't known for his cuddly ways.

It also doesn't have the feel of an inside job. One of those wouldn't leave anyone alive.

If you do an inside job, it means you know me. Know Valentin. Know Andrei.

That means you fucking go big or go fucking home.

Now I'm thinking about Lev, about the fucking culprit taking and torturing our people. And from the sheer violence the footage shows, it's a message. A nasty, bloody one.

I glance at Semyon; he dismisses everyone and hands out orders, giving me the space to think.

When we're alone, I rub a hand over my chin, mind churning.

"They went straight for the men." I point at the screen.

"Anger?"

"No." I pause. "At least not like that. This is set up to look chaotic."

What have I been doing? Fucking mooning over a damn girl.

"They must have known we'd have another camera," he says.

"Maybe not. Were the wounds as horrific as the ones on those who've been tortured and killed already?" I ask.

The bodies were gone when I got here.

He hands me his phone. "A lead mentioned guns. He overheard it in one of the hole-in-the-wall Russian bars. Didn't see who said it but called me. I was checking out enclaves when we talked."

I scroll through the gore and blood in the images.

"It didn't take me long, and they were gone."

I hand him the phone. "Let me guess. Bodies still warm?"

"Yes, but—"

"They expected us. This was a show. Take your phone to Andrei and Valentin. Tell them I'm on it."

He nods. "The footage?"

I've rewound and I'm watching again, but the attackers are all in black, complete with balaclavas and... I frown and lean forward, rewinding it.

"This man..." There are three others who skulk past. But

there's only one who comes close to the camera, who stays in focus. One fucking suspect. "There's something about this one..."

"What?"

I shake my head. "No idea, but..." I copy it and hand it to Semyon. "Take all this to Andrei and Valentin. I'll be in touch. And set up the usual security protocol. Word, if it's out, is we're looking for an out-of-town rival. Make it run-of-the-mill, make it like we're taking care of it."

Whoever did this, I want them to feel thwarted.

As Semyon leaves, I watch the original copy again.

There's something familiar about the way this one motherfucker moves. Goosebumps break out on my skin.

I want this fucker angry, like I am. Whoever it is, they're fucking with what's mine. No one does that. Not anymore.

If I wanted to be tested over and over again, I'd have fought to stay in Russia.

Instead, I chose to take the exile and leave. Come here.

But America is my territory now, and I've fought too hard to have someone fucking ruin it.

My phone buzzes, and I look at the screen.

Every nerve ending jumps.

Kira.

It's an address. Nothing else.

My hackles rise.

Because one thing I've learned over the years, one thing that's helped keep me alive, is to trust my instincts.

And every single one of those instincts whispers trouble.

Kira's in trouble.

9

KIRA

I finally took shit too far.

Baltika is the kind of rough-and-tumble, red-walled Russian bar in the bad part of downtown Chicago that even Mikhail kept away from.

And yet, here I am, in over my head as men corner me.

I curse Mitt Calhoun's very fucking name... as well as my own lack of judgement for coming here. He sent me here as punishment for not getting anything from Ilya. I'm sure of it.

"Dress to impress."

That was his order.

So my lack of judgement led me down the path of another slutty dress.

After all, a hot number of a dress worked on Ilya; it should work on distracting someone into talking more than they should here.

And this one—a black number that's a little longer and with an actual back—has worked.

Too well.

"I just came here to have a drink," I push out, trying to wiggle free, "that's all."

These dangerous men aren't in the mood to listen.

"I don't think so. Not like you look, girl." One of them comes up even closer and sniffs my hair deeply.

It's a scrub-yourself-clean moment.

Fear pops up like bubbles all over my skin, and I try to keep it in check. These men are sharks. If they think they've got a meal, they'll sink in their teeth and won't let go until there's nothing left of me.

I toss my hair. "You should let me go. My boyfriend—"

"Pimp more like," one says, licking my face and breathing sour fumes over me.

My heart beats hard and fast as panic rises.

A hand slides up my thighs as another arm loops around my shoulders.

"Show us your wares, girl. No one comes in here like that if they're not looking for action," the man with his hand sliding up my thighs snarls.

The one with his arm around me gropes a breast. "Nice tits. How many men do you service at the same time?"

I twist away and stumble into the bar, but the bartender only casts me a look and then the men. He doesn't come down to the end I'm at. "I just wanted to talk to—"

"Baby, we talk," says one.

"With our cocks," says another, and they laugh.

A third man grabs at me, and I slip away, but a fourth takes my hair, tugging at the top. "Don't run, we're having fun."

The jovial nature of their words only thinly coats the malice and intent. And there are more of them behind, waiting to paw at me, to rip my clothes.

There's no way I could get anyone to talk here and now. There are too many.

I only hope Ilya got the blind text I sent from my bag, a skill I've perfected as a reporter. But who knows if I got it right?

"Let go," I say, right as the one who had his arm looped

around me does it again, this time heading lower with his hand on my chest.

"You don't want that, girl," he snarls.

I try to stamp on the foot of the one whose hand is pushing its way into the top of my dress, but I miss.

So I twist and press my legs together to stop another wandering hand.

If I can just get this under control for a second, if I can put them in their place and hide my fear, maybe I can get out of here.

"Look," I say, "I'm really not here for that. But if you want to talk, we can."

The one who has his arm around me tightens it. I think he's the ringleader, because every time he does something, the others follow.

He's probably the man I'm here to talk to.

"There isn't a need for words, not with what I've got planned for that pretty mouth." He swings his free hand in and squeezes my cheeks, hard. "How much does your pimp charge for you?"

My eyes burn with helpless rage, with fear.

These men don't care where they are. They've got a victim in their sights, and that's me.

And Christ... pimp? Shit, is that really the image I'm giving off? One of a hooker? Is that why Ilya dragged me to the bathroom the other night?

I try to get free, but every time I wiggle, they tighten their hold. And it's too hard to run with my thighs basically superglued together with sheer stubbornness.

The one with his hand in my top touches my nipple, and something snaps. I jerk free with strength I didn't know I had and grab a bottle from the bar to slam it into his head. It breaks, and he finally staggers away.

The others step back too.

Then he comes at me. Fast.

He pulls something out of his pocket and flicks it. And all my blood turns to ice. A knife pops out, deadly and sharp.

The others do the same.

I swallow hard as I back up. He nods at the men closest to me.

"Hold her. I'm going to teach this used-up cunt a lesson. Leave her the two-dollar-a-ride variety of whore." He sneers. "Ruin that pretty face."

I need to get out, run, but they have me cornered. All I can do is raise my chin. "You don't know who you're messing with."

My back hits the bar, and the other two grab my wrists.

"A whore past her use-by date."

Fuck. Oh, fuck. I look him in the eye. "I'm not a whore. You're messing with the wrong girl."

He laughs. "You don't look all that important, honey—but I bet your pimp tells you he's a big, powerful man—"

"I'm not a whore."

"All the better for us, but I'll tell you something for free, cunt." He looks me up and down. "You will be after we get through with you."

Terror streaks through my chest. I have no idea if Ilya got my message or not. I'm lucky I still had his number open on my phone after he'd invited me over for dinner.

But he's Bratva. Dangerous. And these men know who runs this town. They know the players. I yell in Russian, loud enough that if anyone can help, they will. "Ilya Rykov's my boyfriend, and he doesn't like others touching what's his. So let me the fuck go."

The leader sneers like he doesn't believe me. "I don't care."

He backhands me, right across the cheek. Pain stuns me for a moment. One of the others shoves me at his friend, who pushes me back, ripping at my dress.

But the rest... They don't move. I can feel their fear.

One actually grabs the leader. "Stop. I know the name Rykov."

"This Ilya is not one to be fucked with," says his friend.

Those two back off, melting into the small crowd, while the others all argue amongst themselves.

They don't let me go, but they don't try to hurt me either. Not for one second do I think I'm home free. I won't be until I walk out of this horrible bar.

"What's this about not fucking caring who I am?"

Suddenly, Ilya's low, deep voice cuts through the noise. "Because you're putting hands on my woman... and people have died for far less than that."

He doesn't give them a chance to respond. Ilya moves fast and fluid, a thing of beautiful power as he takes the knife from the leader and delivers a sucker punch.

I scream as another leaps at him, but Ilya sweeps out his legs and brings his foot down hard on the man's throat.

Some of the dumber ones come at him, others try to run, but he's a blaze of controlled fury and death as he grabs one man and uses him to stab another before slamming that man's head into the bar.

He grabs another two and cracks their heads together, twisting the first one's neck with a sickening snap.

Ilya leaves a pile of bodies, flinging anyone stupid enough to come at him away like a flea. He kills with violence, without compunction, and I can't shake the feeling that this isn't enjoyment, but rather what he thinks he needs to do to protect me.

Yet a scream builds in my chest, and when he starts going for bystanders, it escapes.

"No, Ilya, please, enough! Stop, please."

He has a man by the collar and his fist pulled back, ready to drive hard into the man's face.

But he stops.

Ilya stops.

Then he lets the man go, straightens his shirt, steps over a pile of bodies, and gently takes hold of my arm.

"We've got to stop meeting like this," he says, nodding to the bar. "Can I buy you a drink?"

I stare at him, and he takes my face in one large hand and looks, eyes narrowing.

"Shouldn't we leave? What if more come?" I try to pull away. "What about the police?"

"The cops?" He laughs and shakes his head. "No. They wouldn't dare."

"Then," I say, "other dirtbags?"

"I'll fuck them up them too."

He would. He'd do it without a thought, and like his life depended on it. But I can't... I can't deal with more right now. Besides, those who still stand—those who haven't run, that is—are staring like this is a free show and they were lucky to get front-row seats.

"No..." I put my hand on his chest, letting the steady, strong beat of his heart soothe something in me. "No, I don't want to be here anymore. I've had enough violence, let's go."

Again, he touches my cheek, and I realize it's where the now-dead man hit me. Anger flares in Ilya's eyes.

"Okay," he says, "but I'm taking you back to my place."

"Ilya..." I want to, I don't want to.

"Don't argue," he says softly. "I need to make sure you're taken care of and cleaned up. Those monsters hurt you, ripped your dress."

I breathe out, suddenly glad he's making me, because I want—need—to go with him. My resistance is shot.

"Fine."

There's a hint of a smile. "Like you had a choice."

The words should bother me, but they don't. He makes me feel oddly safe in his presence.

He leads me out of the bar as I press into him.

I'm finally safe. Sound.

That is, until he says one more thing that sends a streak of dread through me.

"Oh, and by the way, when we get to my place, Kira, you and I are having a talk. You've got some questions to answer."

Fuck.

10

KIRA

Ilya pushes a glass of booze into my hands. Japanese whiskey, judging by the complex fruit and caramel notes to it.

While I drink, he puts an ice pack wrapped in a tea towel on my throbbing cheek. Funny to think of him as a man owning something as mundane as a tea towel.

I go to rise, needing to move, but he takes one of my hands to replace his on the pack. "Sit and use the ice pack next to you for your cheek. I don't think you'll bruise, but let's make sure."

With a curious glance at him, at this tender side to the brute of a monster, the cold genius, I start to drop the pack. "I'm fine."

"I'll be the judge of that." He puts it back. "I'm not above spanking you for reckless moves, Kira. And it won't be the sexy, kinky kind of spanking either."

I open my mouth, then close it. Words fail me.

He cleans me up, rubbing a lavender cream into the places those fuckers grabbed, on the red marks.

"Lavender? Next, you'll break out the bubble bath."

A small grin lights up his face as he massages my skin, making me shiver with heat. "We'll save the bubbles and toenail painting for another time. Lavender's good for muscles. It helps soothe," he says.

An ugly, cold flame shoots through me, and I narrow my eyes. "Who told you that?"

He smiles at the bite in my voice. "One of my men's wives. She's into natural shit, but it smells good, and it's been sitting here, and I thought you might like it."

"Because I'm a girl?"

"Because you're a woman of taste."

He rubs it into my wrist, and I'm not sure if it's his touch or the product, but it feels better, like tension is seeping from my skin—a certain kind of tension.

"So, it's about time you start answering some questions," he says, bending his neck. "About those reckless moves... What the hell do you do for a living that drags you out, dressed like that?"

I jolt, almost pulling my wrist from him, but he doesn't let me go, just continues the gentle massage. My mind races as I try to come up with a good enough lie. But none come, so I go for pure outrageousness, something that a man like Ilya, one who grew up like he did, just might buy.

Narrowing my eyes like I'm daring him not to believe me, I say, "I rob drunk men."

"You're a thief?" He leans in, his fingers smoothing slow over my skin, sending ripples of honey-dipped sensation through me. "Of what? Money? Hearts? Virtue?"

"Virtue?" I go to toss my head, but a sharp burning pain shoots through my neck from a pulled muscle. Those assholes flung me around like a rag doll. "In a place like that?"

"You were there."

"You think I'm virtuous?" I don't examine the burst of sweetness from that thought. "I'm not."

"So, you steal money from drunks?" He lifts a brow and moves to my other wrist. "Not exactly an exalted career."

"I'm a survivor."

Ilya nods and strokes up my arm. He made me change when we got here, into an impossibly soft, old black T-shirt. He rubs under the sleeve, at the bruises and soreness there on my inner arm. "Are you planning on robbing me? Is that your long game here?"

"Got anything valuable?" I take a sip of my drink.

He takes the glass and finishes it, then refills from the bottle next to him, giving it back. "Depends on what you find valuable."

I shrug. "I find lots of things valuable."

Ilya doesn't answer for a beat. "Maybe the right things, since the monetary ones surround you in here and you haven't tried to slip anything in your pocket." He looks me over. "You've had a rough time. Tell you what, Kira, I'll give you the combination to the safe. There's money in there. A lot."

I consider him. "What would you do if I said do it?"

"Then I'd do it." He dips into some warm water that has an herbal scent as he lifts the cloth to run over my throat and face, like he's washing away the stench of those men. I move the pack as he does so. "I'm a man of my word."

"Are you?"

He starts to wipe down my legs, beginning at my thighs like he knows they touched me there. Or maybe he just knows men.

It's not sexual or even overly sensual.

What it is, is tender.

And it makes tears push at my eyes, hot and unwanted.

I blink them back.

"What about if I used it and stole?"

"Is it stealing," he muses, "if I give you the combination?"

"Maybe," I snap. "If I took all your money in there? All that purported wealth?"

"Then you're not what I suspect you are, Kira."

His words unsettle me, and I don't try to untangle them, just let them sit. We both know I'm not opening his safe, not even if his place wasn't full of expensive things. And we both know if I wanted to rob him, I'd have done so.

But there's believing my lie and believing I'm unworthy. I want him to do the first and not the second.

How the hell did this become so complicated?

Fuck. I close my eyes. My head pounds. I'm not sure if it's from the men in that bar or this... whatever *this* is.

I know I must have taken the wrong approach at the bar by flaunting. But then again, even if I tried to get a story in baggy jeans and an oversize sweater, chances are they'd have thought I was there to whore myself out.

And then there's Ilya. Hot, overbearing. Way too smart and complicated. A man who'll try and fuck me in an expensive restaurant's bathroom, who'll tie me up, who'll kill for me. And a man who'll both make all sorts of assumptions about me and yet treat me with the tenderness of a healer, a protector.

Without opening my eyes, I whisper, "What the hell do men want?"

"Open your eyes, Kira."

I do.

Ilya's frowning at me. "Is someone you like causing trouble?"

"Yes." Him. He is. "And you know it."

"Do you want me to teach you what men want?"

"Always the opportunist," I say. "You'll teach me what men really want?"

He grins, but his eyes aren't anything like amused. They're burning hot. "No. I'll teach you what I want."

I try to speak but nothing comes out. He knows I meant him. He knows it. For a second, I saw a flash of something dark, like he thought he'd have to kill his competition. And it excites me, even though I know it shouldn't.

"And what's that?" I ask, playing along. "What does a man like you, a man who has everything, want?"

"You."

He says it soft, emphatic, and it takes all the air in the room.

He doesn't give me a chance to respond. He takes the glass and the pack, puts them down, and then his mouth takes mine in a deep kiss. It sears my soul, sparking with the kind of heat that can transform, scar.

And yet, Ilya's gentle. I can't help it. That gentleness undoes me. I kiss him back like my life depends on it. He pushes his hand up my thighs, and I part them for him.

When he presses in against me, his hands stroking over me, I moan.

My whole being's alive, and I want him to take me. But I'm not sure what exactly to do. So I push him, gently.

He lifts his mouth from mine. "What? You want it harder, faster? You want me to make you beg? On your knees? You want to be tied up? Taken like a goddess? Talk."

Ilya pushes the shirt up to expose me, and he kisses my pussy, then lifts his head.

"Thing is, Kira, if you want to know what I want, it really is you. And I want it all the ways there are," he mutters. "That's what this man wants."

A kind of helplessness comes over me. "I don't know what to do."

His brows rise. "You seemed to in that bathroom."

"I know what to do, just not... the... minutiae. I..." I make myself look at him. "I'm a virgin."

Silence falls heavily, and he stares at me. "You're... what?"

"A virgin."

He shakes his head, and I swear his accent grows thicker. "And here I thought you might have been a prostitute. I mean, why else would you be in such a seedy bar, dressed the way you were?"

I narrow my eyes. "Like a slut?"

"You said it, not me."

It takes me two beats to get what he's saying.

There's sarcasm in his words, and he clearly doesn't think or didn't think I was selling my wares. But he said that and not anything about me robbing men. He never believed me; I see that now. He just wanted to hear what I'd say.

Ilya raises a brow, running his hand over my hard nipples. "So, out of interest, why were you really there?"

I try to scramble away, but he doesn't let me. "I told you—"

"Not buying you as a master thief." He puts his hands on my hips, holding me in place. "You're not and never were. We always knew where you were even when you tried to skulk, Kira. You don't have that in you. Try again. Go on."

I swallow hard. Shit. I pluck a lie from the ether. "Fine," I huff. "I rep for a liquor company. And I wanted to see the clientele, the kind of things they drank—"

"Cheap, shitty beer. Cheap, shitty spirits. Base level Russian vodka." Each word is met with a slide of his hands, up to my breasts, then to my waist, a tease of a touch. I ache for him to dive between my thighs.

I want to stop the conversation.

I want to find out what the fuss with sex is about. And if it's anything close to what happened in the bathroom...

A shudder passes through me.

"The brand can go upscale or down, it hasn't launched yet. That won't be until next year, so it's important to get it in the right places. See where it will best belong."

Staying on track is getting harder and harder to do as Ilya's big hands slide and dance over my skin.

Hopefully, he won't look that deep into this mythical booze. Or into my terrible lie. There's only one place I want him to look deeply into, and that's me.

Hell, I don't even want him looking.

Just doing.

Then I can go back to hating him.

Back to thinking straight.

"I have influence," he says, lips skimming over my belly. "In a lot of ways. A lot of things."

I look at him as an idea comes to me. I could use this with him too. If it works. If he buys it, that is. "It's also a little shady. The foreign investor's possibly linked to criminal activity."

"Hence the low places?"

"Yes."

Ilya slides his hands to my hips. "It must be a shit brand this... what kind of booze is it? Just booze?" He strokes his thumbs on the delicate, sensitive skin there.

"They have different things."

"Oh good," he says. "But all of those different things must be absolute prison-grade crap if you're trying to send it to dives like that one."

I swallow again, unwilling to let this go. "We just need a foot in the door, and most places won't let a woman like me in."

Not that I have any idea. I've never been involved in the liquor industry, but how hard can it be to fake it?

"Who won't let a woman like you in?" he asks.

"Fancy places." Christ, I sound ridiculous, naïve. Which, when I think about it, works in my favor. I can play that up.

"I just took you to a fancy place," he says. "They let you in."

"Only because you were with me." I sigh. "These people want to buy from a man. Not me."

"No, they don't." He sits back and smiles, then snaps his fingers. "I'll prove it. We aren't eating here tonight anymore."

"What?" I sound like an idiot. "Then where?"

He smiles. "Somewhere good. I'm taking you out again." He leans in, whispers, "Dress appropriately."

"No—"

"No, you won't dress appropriately? Or no to dinner."

"You said here." It's too close to a date if we go out again, and I don't like him. Do I? Not beyond that physical want.

"Two birds, Kira." He slides his thumb over my lips. "I'll prove my point and spoil the fuck out of you. Clearly, you've had it rough. It's time I change that."

I breathe in sharply. Is... is he serious? I can't tell. I know he likes to show off, splash money, I saw that. But does he mean that? Has he bought into my lies and now wants to spoil me? Because... I can't work it out. Or maybe I can.

He wants me. But there's something else there too, something that both thrills and scares me.

"I'm not..." I whisper. "Men don't treat me like this."

"Consider that changed. With me."

I reach out, fingers shaking as I cup his cheek. "Why are you being so nice to me?"

He doesn't answer for a long moment, like he's searching for the right words.

Then he speaks, and he's quiet, but the words are soaked in confidence. "Because you deserve it."

No, not confidence. Truth. His truth.

And it makes my cold heart melt a little.

I blink rapidly, and he leans in, feathering his lips over mine.

"You've had quite the time, haven't you?" he muses.

At first, I think he means my father. Mikhail. "Well—"

"What with trying to sell wine, experimenting with terrible clothing choices, and worse men to flirt with."

I frown. "I wasn't flirting."

"Not to mention your predilection for stealing from everyone you come across."

I almost laugh. "Except for you."

"Except for me. Now, you need to sleep." Ilya pulls back from me. "Forget dinner. I'll feed you when you're rested. Take my bed tonight."

He gets up and holds out his hand, and I can't help but

notice his erection. My mouth waters even as fear and desire streak through me in equal measures.

"Ilya ..."

"Alone," he says as I put my hand in his. "Tomorrow I might not be so patient with you."

"W-what about you?" I ask.

"I'm not sleeping in that bed, Kira. I'm taking the couch."

"But you're too big for the couch."

"If I sleep in that bed," he says, sounding faintly irritated, "I won't be able to keep my hands to myself. There won't be much sleeping. Understand?"

I want to ask him to come with me anyway, but I manage to keep my lips shut as he leads me into his room, turns on a bedside lamp, and plumps a pillow on the huge Alaskan king mattress. The colors are neutral, the bedding I think is linen, soft from many washes.

Shit. This man keeps surprising me.

I'm not sure what I expected. Silk? Satin? Big, bold blacks and blues, not... not this. The natural colors lend the room a calmness. And I'm pulled toward the bed.

But I stop, because the bed's so big that there's more than enough room for him too. With him nearby, maybe the horrible memories of what happened wouldn't crowd... maybe then, the cool touch of loneliness I've been suffocated by every night for the past five years would disappear.

I turn to Ilya, but he's gone.

With a sigh, I climb into bed and turn off the light, as confused as ever.

11

ILYA

"Just you and me, kid," I say in my perfect American accent, old-school style.

I give the crystal glass of amber liquid a look and down it. Then I pour another.

"You really aren't much of a conversationalist, but here we find ourselves again," I say. "Alone."

Again.

I flop down on the sofa, and stare at the glass, storm clouds brewing in me.

She's a fucking terrible liar.

But excellent at secret-keeping.

That last one, I'll give her that.

I could sit and drink and brood, and while I'm definitely going to do the former, I can multitask with the latter.

I finish the second glass and wander to my computers, picking up the laptop I don't have hooked up to the whole set up. I can do that if I want, but I like having something not linked to the bigger server.

Sending the footage to myself from earlier, I go back to the sofa and pick up the bottle, taking a swig. Then I turn off the

Wi-Fi and watch the footage, scrolling back to the one man, that one scene.

The way he moves.

It tickles something in my memory, something just out of reach that I can't get to.

And since this is going to be a long fucking night, I call Valentin.

"You don't have a life?" he says, growling the words in Russian.

I grin, knowing I didn't interrupt anything with his woman, but I was close. Because as much of a focused, insane motherfucker he is, the man's not about to give up a second of time with Yelena unless it's an emergency.

And I didn't call on the emergency number.

I called him. His new personal phone.

Something I still laugh about, even as I ignore the bite of jealousy beneath it.

I'm happy for him, but there's a part of me that wants that too.

"Did you see the footage?"

He mutters something I don't catch. "You know them?"

"I don't know." I frown. "There's something… familiar."

"We have enemies."

That's the point, isn't it? We have enemies. Always. Forever.

Except this one is… I don't know. It feels personal.

"I think we need to make sure it's business as usual," I say.

This time, he doesn't respond.

I take my time. "There's something weird." I have a swig of the whiskey and then play back that one scene where it captures the man completely covered, ninja-style, in black. "Something I'm missing."

"We hold off?" he asks.

I breathe out, all the anger and frustrations beating hard in me as I do. "Until I can come up with a viable lead that takes us somewhere then we need to, and not just hold off, it's got to be business as usual. Only the most trusted can know we're on alert. Everyone else—"

"Then," he says, "we don't tell anyone about what happened. Those that were there get told it's a hit that's been taken care of."

"Exactly." I appreciate he's on the same field as me, in the same fucking game.

"This is your show, Ilya."

"So," I say, finishing for him, "make it a short, sweet, triumphant tale of revenge, and not a drawn-out Shakespearean tragedy where they all die in the end?"

Valentin laughs. "There's the smart mouth I know. Do I need to talk with Andrei?"

"When it's time. He's got enough on his plate, and it's why he has us."

Why he has me in his top-level fold.

"Thoughts?" Valentin asks.

I'm way too aware of the sweet-smelling girl in my bed for my own peace of mind. But that fact, along with the knowledge I'm not getting to sleep any time soon, gives me the opportunity to work, fit pieces and see if anything clicks.

But I push that away and think about what he just said.

I shake my head. "You'd have to be a crazy level of crazy to try and fuck with the Bratva."

"And yet," he says, "they are. And whoever this is has people more scared of him than you or me or Andrei."

I sit up, letting the video play. "Hold on."

Switching to speaker, I get up and go to my computer setup and place a call to Semyon so Valentin can hear. It saves time.

"That guard," I say without preamble, "the one who was wounded. Where is he?"

"Home. You want me to bring him to you?" Semyon asks. "Take him out?"

"No. Valentin, the country estate? Is it being used?"

"Not right now."

The country estate is just that. Rural Illinois. A place that's old and on disused farmland. A veritable fortress—a hideout and a place to lay low. Somewhere to keep prisoners, and to torture them, if needed.

But I don't want that.

I take a sip of the whiskey. "Take him and his family, if he has one, there. Make it nice, an enforced holiday. He shouldn't question it, but I also don't want him unduly scared. Lock it down. If asked, it's for his safety and his family's."

Valentin adds, "If he has any."

Semyon waits a beat to see if I'm done. "You don't trust him?"

"I don't know." I pause. "Anything odd... *anything*, report to me, Andrei or Valentin. You coordinate."

"Yes sir," Semyon says, before hanging up.

When it's just me and Valentin, I go back to the living room and take another swallow of the booze.

"Playing games?" he asks.

I sigh. "No. I just want to see if something pans out. It probably won't. But when life gives you fucking straws, grasp them all."

He snorts a laugh. "Heard you went to town tonight. Over some young thing."

"You can fuck right off with that." I scowl at the bottle before taking a swallow.

"Who is she?"

"Just a girl."

"When a man says that," Valentin chuckles, "it's never just a girl." He pauses. "Do you expect something to come from moving this guy?"

"Not really," I mutter. "But he lives. So... we watch."

"I prefer a good movie."

"Watching one right now. Not big on dialogue, but can't have fucking everything." I play the video yet again, not sure what I'm looking for, but it'll come.

"Is there something standing out?"

I know why he's asking. And it's not to micromanage. We just need to end this shit sooner than later.

"Not sure..."

"Not sure means something." I can almost hear Valentin nod.

I play the video again. "Not sure means not sure."

But he's right. There's something, I just don't know fucking what.

I stare at the computer screen.

"Shit, it's the fact there's something familiar about this guy."

"Hold on," Valentin mutters, and I hear him moving, tapping away on a keyboard. "Familiar in what way? I don't see it."

"Familiar," I say, "to me."

That familiar thing... it's both distant and close.

But how? Why? Fucking who?

A player in the shadows who crossed my outfit back in Russia? There are some sick fucks out there. On all sides and operating in the world on their own.

What this isn't, though, is a maniac who doesn't know what fight he's taking on.

He does.

And, I think, it's one he absolutely wants.

Question is why.

"Just how many enemies have you got?" Valentin asks.

I pick up the bottle and take a deep swallow. "The usual amount. Two less than you. Fucker."

"Can I get back to my life now? I'm ready to spill blood and take names, but my woman just walked in the door."

I snort, that strange little twinge of happy and longing pulls at me. "You take names?"

"By ripping out hearts, yes." And Valentin laughs.

There's a woman in my bed, a fucking virgin... a virgin, so I don't know why my chest feels tight.

"Try and stay this side of sane, Valentin."

When I hang up, I keep watching the fucking video, trying to see something I've missed, but I don't. My mind returns to Kira.

A virgin.

I figured they were like unicorns these days.

But it fits.

I rub a hand over my face, a restlessness moving through me. She slides into places I didn't know existed, and maybe always did. But then she was a kid, and that felt more like family. This...

This is not little sister family vibes I'm feeling.

She isn't my sister, never was. Kira was just too young, and then, when on that cusp, too off-limits. I was way too driven to think about looking anyway. I had points to prove. Plans to follow.

Points and plans that were ripped apart by others.

Like her fucking brother, Mikhail. He got shot for his trouble. He didn't make it as far as me. End of the fucking story.

I get up, restless, and take the whiskey. "You're letting me down in the drunk department, too," I tell it. "I don't expect you to be much of a talker, but I do expect you to do your job."

Taking another swallow, I move across my penthouse to the big window, staring out at the glitter of the city. It's pretty, but it doesn't hold any answers. Shit, I'm so fucking restless. I wander into the kitchen, but there's nothing there I need.

Everything I need is in my bed.

And I'm talking to a bottle of whiskey.

Fuck.

I go to my room and ease open the door. The lamp's on, like she needed some light for comfort. And it has the unfortunate effect of bathing her in a golden soft glow.

An angel. My T-shirt twisted around her. She's thrown half the covers off.

Just enough to taunt and tease.

She looks so sweet and innocent there. It reminds me of that sweetness that was the willful, inquisitive little Kira. And that innocence, it still sticks.

It might have changed into something more mature, but it's still innocence, and not from her state of being untouched. Because I suspect she hasn't been touched much at all.

That thought grabs hold of my cock.

Deliberately, I move my thoughts from that.

Besides, she has the sort of innocence that would still be there even if she'd had a thousand men. Sure, I'd have to kill them all, but...

I laugh silently, fighting the urge that builds, that urge to touch.

Then the laughter fades as the hate that lives in her comes to mind.

It gives her a depth, takes some of the sweetness away. Gives it a bitter edge, like molasses.

Makes her that much more intriguing.

Can't lie for shit, though. It's like she's never spent time in a bar. Never seen an actual rep. They don't sell to the staff; they sell to the owners. And they come during the day, when it's not busy. Fancy places would love a pretty girl coming in. Jesus.

So she doesn't rob men. I already knew she wasn't any kind of call girl, and she definitely doesn't sell booze. Not wine, not a certain selection of spirits. Not even the name of the company. Just... booze.

I can also strike spy off the list because she'd suck at that.

Then what the fuck does she do for a living?

All that inquisitiveness that lived in her as a kid must still be there. She knew I was bad news before anyone in her family, including her brother.

Her fucking brother.

I'm thinking she has a real job, not in a shop or anything like that, but something she sees as making a difference. A doctor. Lawyer. Teacher. All those fit. She's too young to be the first two, and for all three, she'd need a degree. But she'd need to be registered under her real name to go to school.

She turns over, back to me, and she's narrow, delicate in that way someone unarmed and untutored is. I thought I could use her, but not anymore. Oh, I could. I just don't want to.

What I want to do is so unexpected that it almost makes me drop the bottle.

I want to protect her.

Keep her safe.

But not from me.

Because I want more.

I want to fucking shatter her sweet innocence. Take it, destroy it, make her mine. I want to protect her from the world and unleash myself on her, mark her.

With me, she'll be safe from everything.

Except from me.

It's such a fine fucking line that it makes the anger rear up in my gut.

She tosses that perfect little body back my way, and my roiling anger softens into longing. Her eyes flutter open. They go wide with fear... until she recognizes that the shape in the dark is me.

We look at each other, and her blue eyes turn warm, then hot, and she parts her lips.

Without saying a word, she lifts the blanket, inviting me into bed.

I set the bottle down and strip off my shirt, then my pants.

I'm in my underwear as I slide in under the covers. I'm not thinking. I don't want to think.

I want to feel.

Her.

We kiss, her mouth melting open under mine, her hands coming up around my neck.

"Ilya …" She drops tiny kisses on my skin, and then her gaze dips, and I know she can feel my erection.

I wait until she looks back up.

"Kira," I say. "Are you ready for me?"

"Yes."

12

KIRA

Ilya smiles. It's a wolfish smile, and it does things to me.

Things that should be illegal.

Any other time, on any other person, I might call it a predatory smile, but there's something about the light in his eyes that takes the darkness from that. It's there, I know it, but when this man looks at me like this, I'm lost.

He saved me from those men, took care of me in a way little me would've found romantic.

Now? I find it disturbing, wrong, yet so right—a different sort of romance. One that allows him to have that softness, that edge of romance without love. Or maybe it's the kind of romance that's grown up, full of blood and bone.

"Ilya," I whisper.

He slides a hand under the T-shirt I'm wearing to cup a breast, his thumb teasing my nipple. "Are you ready for your spanking?"

A dark thrill passes through me as I turn to him, my mouth seeking his. "Maybe I am."

"Then maybe I'll give it to you. If you're good."

Ilya plays with me, his mouth almost on mine, breath on

my lips, before he shifts, moving his head, making me chase the kiss he won't give.

Every near miss only makes something in me throb deeper, makes the longing grow bigger, until I'm a mess of wants and needs, and I don't know what to do anymore.

"Tell me you want it," he whispers.

"No," I whisper back.

He skims his lips over mine, again teasing, and I try to catch him, but he just nips my ear. "Oh, you're going to be fucking *fun*, Kira."

He kisses my neck, then slides my shirt up, pulling it off me.

"Beautiful." Ilya rises on tattooed arms, gazing down at my bare breasts like he's never seen anything so mesmerizing.

Or maybe it's that I'm just new enough to awe him.

Or he's just caught up in what he sees.

The last one makes my stomach dance.

He bends his dark head and sucks one nipple into his mouth, making me moan. My body sparks into life. Then, he turns his attention to my other tit.

Everything quivers in need. A pressure rises in my core. I slide my hands into his hair, gripping as he works his way across my chest.

"Harder, Kira."

Ilya tugs on my nipple with his teeth, and I gasp. He lets go.

"H-harder?"

"My hair. Pull so hard it hurts."

I... my head spins, and he bites my other nipple suddenly. I squeal, fingers pulling at him. He comes up, pulling at my sensitive nub as he rises. It sends a slash of pleasure through me. It's a good ache, a wild ache. Deep and tingling, and I know only he can fill it.

My back arches.

"Are you going to say it?" he asks, letting go of my nipple and kissing his way up to my ear. One of his hands trails down over my stomach until it's between my thighs. He spreads me further apart.

"Are you going to tell me you want it?" His lips finally feather over mine.

"I..." I don't know what to say. Except I do.

"You what?"

Before I can answer, his tongue dips into my mouth, and he starts fingering me, running my clit in slow circles.

Each time a little more pressure, a little deeper, until I'm almost whimpering.

He kisses me again, that flirting tease of a kiss, a little longer now, but nowhere near enough.

"I... I don't know what I want."

"You want me," he says. "You're just scared. But don't worry, I can be gentle."

"I-I don't want gentle," I mindlessly reply. "I don't think."

He's at my neck now, fingers stroking, scissoring in me, his thumb thrumming on my wet clit.

He smiles right there at the curve of my throat and shoulder, whispering over my senses.

"Close your eyes, and the answer will come."

I try to do as he says, but no thoughts will form in my mind.

"I... I don't know." I gasp. He's stroking into me, his lips tasting and sucking on my skin.

"Use your words, Kira."

My hand flounders down, touching him, feeling the sheer size, the heat, and the steel. I start to pull like he had me do in that bathroom. I'm rewarded with a low groan and a hard thrust into my hand.

"I was going to say—" My eyes flutter open as he works my pussy. "I don't know enough to know."

He adds a third finger into my tight little cunt. "Should hope not, being a virgin."

"Ilya, I haven't ever done what we've done. I-I've..." Oh,

fuck, this is humiliating. "I've kissed, gotten to third base—is that the one where—"

"Kira." He lifts his head, looks at me, and I'm caught in his gaze. "Are you trying to tell me you're basically a step away from being a nun?"

"Yes... no... I'm a failure." I bury my head into his chest, and he doesn't stop the thrusts of his fingers inside me.

Now, he stops, but he doesn't pull out. He merely looks at me. "You're not."

"If I do this wrong?"

"There is no wrong."

"I'm sure there is."

"Then I'll teach you.

But he isn't listening. He starts to slowly kiss me, down my throat to my breasts, suckling on one nipple and then the other.

"I..."

"Enough. Move your hand. Relax. I'll take over from here."

I do as he says, taking my hand from him. He descends down my body. Then, keeping his fingers pumping in and out, he starts to eat me out.

It doesn't take long before I explode.

"One for you..." he says, pulling back. "And one for me."

He's only gone for moments, and then he's back, between my thighs, and I can feel the flat, thick head of his cock as he slides it over me.

"Is this really happening?" I whisper to myself.

"You won't be saying that when I'm inside of you."

My body is hungry for him. I'm still coming when he starts to slowly push in.

It's an invasion like no other.

My breath catches. Despite how wet I am, it's a tight fit. Luckily, Ilya takes his time, easing into me slowly. It's a level of restraint I could have never imagined from a beast like him.

When he's fully in, I realize I've been holding my breath.

"Ilya." His name escapes from my lips in a long, quiet exhale that's followed by intense, almost painful pleasure.

I'm pulsating against him. It's a gentle contraction and a sweetness that echoes *his*.

"Legs around my waist, little one. We're going for a ride."

I do as ordered, and he begins to rock into me, slow and shallow. That morphs into slow and deep. Each time he pulls out, I yearn for him, and each time he pushes in, I'm not sure how he fits, and yet he does. With utter perfection.

"Are you good?"

His voice deepens, growing more breathless.

"Y-yes."

"No," he shakes his head. "Not yet. Give your body over to it. Relax. Then you'll truly feel it."

It's easier said than done.

Still, I start to adapt. The pressure builds, my eyes close, my toes curl. Soon, we're not going slow anymore, soon it's a wild rollercoaster of him taking me up high only to slam into me so deep I careen down.

Each time is more intense.

"More," I find myself begging.

"Are you sure you can handle it?"

Like he's some kind of gentleman.

"Yes," I pant, a fire building inside me. "Yes, damn you. More. Give me more."

"As you fucking wish."

Just like that, he starts to fuck me in earnest.

And I'm not sure I can actually handle it. But there's no going back now. So I bite down on my lip and take every inch.

Each thrust is harder and deeper, but I just claw at him, desperate for more. Because when I said more, I meant it.

Ilya's awakened something in me that I can't suppress.

"You're so fucking tight," he booms, almost completely

pulling out before slamming back in so deeply that I fall apart all over again.

My entire body erupts into a wild pool of bliss.

Still...

"More." The word pushes out from me. Ilya grins down. There's sweat on his forehead. His gorgeous, tattooed muscles shine under the low light. He's like supple living marble—a powerhouse of a man.

He looks at me like I'm everything he's ever wanted.

"I've created a fucking monster," he taunts, breathing heavier than he did after taking on that whole bar earlier.

"It's so like you to take all the credit."

In response to that, Ilya pulls out, and I catch a glimpse of his glistening cock, still so hard I know he hasn't cum yet.

I try to sit up to taste him, but he just grabs my hips and flips me.

"Ass up." He slaps me there. "Hands and fucking knees."

I go up on my hands and knees and raise my throbbing, needing ass for him. His finger runs between both cheeks. "You take orders better than I expected. Let's see what else you can take."

A moment later, a new burst of wild pleasure whips through me. Ilya sends that finger into my throbbing hole, then pulls out and stretches my wet lips apart.

"A fucking masterpiece," he says, and I can hear him licking his lips. "Just like the rest of you."

This time, when he slides his cock inside of me, it's about him. He starts to fuck me how he wants. With a primal hunger.

From this position, he somehow manages to get in even deeper than before. His hard abs smack into my tender ass. Each brutal spank sends a shock of painful ecstasy searing through me.

I lose my mind, grasping at the sheets until nothing exists

but his cock and my pussy. When that huge, stiff cock somehow swells even bigger, I gasp.

"Yes!" he roars, his big hands grasped firmly around my tiny waist as he cums inside me.

I follow right behind him, my pussy clenching as I milk every last drop from him.

When there's nothing left, I collapse, ass still in the air, until he finally eases out and gathers me in his arms.

"Thatta girl," he rumbles, kissing me with gentle passion, the kind that wraps around me like a huge hug.

I want to say something, but I'm not sure what, so I just kiss him back.

"Any regrets?"

Ilya smooths my hair as he rolls us over, tucking me into his arms.

Part of me thinks of how I could get used to this, all of it.

For a man whom I hate because of what he did to my brother, he's a buffer from the world, an oasis of desires met and peace.

Regrets? I mull the word in my head. I should have them. From giving this man my virginity like it's some antique gift to what really should amount to an act of betrayal against my family and his part in their demise. And yet...

"No, I don't."

He laughs softly against my ear. "Tell me that tomorrow when you're sore."

"I'm fit."

"Sex has nothing to do with fitness and everything to do with tiny muscles you didn't know you had, tiny muscles that remind you of the pleasure."

I turn my face into his chest, breathing in the headiness that's a mixture of his scent and mine. "We'll see."

"Yes, we will. Now, go to sleep, Kira."

"I'm not tired."

"But I am."

Ilya sweeps the covers up over us, then reaches out to plunge the room into darkness.

As he turns off the light, and I'm once more crowded by darkness, it's not lonely or full of the ghosts that regularly haunt me.

This darkness is full of heat and safety. It's entirely eclipsed by the man holding me.

It doesn't take long for me to start drifting off when I decide that tonight I'll rest and sink down into the calm safety he temporarily provides.

But tomorrow?

Tomorrow I'll go back to destroying him.

13

KIRA

Ilya isn't here.

I'm still in a tangled nest of bedding when I get up and stumble around, half asleep, looking for the bathroom. After I find and make good use of it, I collapse back in bed and fall into a dreamless sleep.

But something trickles in, maybe the quietness or the lack of his warm body, but I wake, and this time, I don't sleep.

The side of the bed next to my cocoon is cold, like he's been gone a long time.

And that...

Loneliness spreads along with uncertainty, and now I'm fully awake. Every movement in the bed makes the memories of my first time tumble back. Each little strange ache makes it all painfully clear.

Part of me wants to burrow down into the sensations of the sex. The pleasure, the thrills, the delights. Nothing else but that.

But Ilya is too there in my head, too much part of it. He's both a source of pleasure and of guilt.

Pleasure in the wonders of his body.

Guilt of betraying my family with the enemy.

I close my eyes, ignoring the rumble in my stomach. My experience with sex is limited to a boyfriend touching my breasts, wanting more, things I wasn't willing to give. That ended and...

Virginity isn't important, like it's hallowed ground or some kind of dowry for me. It's just, I never had the time, and that first boy... he would have been too much of a distraction from my ambitions, my need to be a success. That came from a need to distract myself from the horrors and tragic deaths of my brother and my father, those life-shaping moments that haunted me and still do.

All of that stopped me having a real relationship... until now.

Not that this is a relationship. Or anything real beyond the physical.

But... well, no one's ever piqued my interest quite like Ilya.

He always, always has—from my stupid childhood dreams of innocent things like holding hands, kissing, and fairy-tale castles to my uncertain teenage years on the brink of womanhood and wanting to explore the vague idea of sex. It's always been Ilya at the heart of these thoughts and desires.

Even... even though the hate and resentment and blame lingered, I think a part of me always knew if Ilya showed up, it would end here, in his bed.

I guess, though, there's enough little girl romantic hope in me that figured he'd stay with me after the deed. I thought he'd look at me and—what? Love me?

At the very least, I expected to wake up with him next to me, not me alone in a cold bed.

Sadness crushes down on my chest as I push back the covers and realize I'm naked. I don't want to wear the dress from last night and the only thing I have is his T-shirt. It's better than nothing, so I pull it on.

With a yawn, I wander out into the living area, but Ilya's not there. I frown, looking around, wandering into the kitchen area and then back out, feeling a little lost and way too much alone, when suddenly the main elevator dings and the doors open.

"Why are you up?" Ilya scowls at me, holding packages and bags in his muscular arms.

I glare back. "Why did you run away?"

"Kira, I live here." He transfers things to one arm, presses buttons on the elevator keypad, and the light above it goes off, signaling it's locked. "I didn't fucking run away."

He breezes past me to the kitchen and dumps everything on the island.

Happiness bounces in my veins, but I ignore it. So what if he's back? I decide to also ignore the sadness I'd felt at waking up alone.

Ilya starts to unpack one of the bags. "What's your problem anyway? Hangry?"

"No." I scowl at him. "You were gone."

He shrugs. "So were you when I went into the bedroom an hour ago or so. Stripped off the fitted sheet to wash the blood."

My eyes widen, and my cheeks burn. "It's not—"

He clears his throat, suddenly appearing uncomfortable. "Just spots. From me taking your virginity." Ilya turns and thrusts a to-go cup at me. "Coffee. Drink it. There's cream and sugar. *Very* American."

"Blood?"

"A few drops." Now he sounds like he's in physical pain. "Cold water wash, and the sheet's linen."

He says this like it's an obvious answer.

I know some girls bleed and others don't. It didn't hurt, just... he's so big and... There's something weirdly cute about his embarrassment and him doing laundry. A part of me wants to hug and kiss him. I don't. Obviously. I just stand there.

"Here are clothes. As good as you look in my T-shirt..." He

has a glossy cardboard bag with the name of an expensive store on it. I watch as he picks up one of my shoes and puts it on a stool, then slides a shoe box forward to the edge. "And shoes..."

My mouth twitches. "You've been... busy."

"You were... sleeping."

He picks up another to-go cup from the little cardboard carrier, takes a sip, sets it down, and starts to unpack a cloth grocery bag.

"Bacon. Eggs. Bread. Avocado. Lettuce and... a tomato." He puts them down. "American breakfast." He pulls out another bag and puts down a slab of black bread, cold cuts, a jar of pickles, and cultured butter. "Ilya Russian breakfast."

I go to put the coffee down and wince; those damn muscles I didn't know I had are pulling.

He takes me in, then he takes my hand, as well as the bag of clothes. "The one thing this place doesn't have is a bath, but let's get you cleaned up before breakfast."

"I'm not a baby." I try to pull free.

But he doesn't let go. Instead, he drags me with him to the bathroom and turns on the shower, blindly adjusting it while pulling me in for a kiss. A long, slow, seductive kiss that leaves me feeling limp, his to do with as he wants. And that's exactly what he does.

Ilya strips me of the T-shirt, and then gently nudges me into the shower.

The hot water's the perfect temperature and works wonders to warm and unknot muscles.

I look over at him, about to ask for a sponge since I don't see one, but I stop as he shucks his clothes. Even in my blissed-out state, I'm taken in by his perfect form—the broad shoulders, the narrow waist, his long, powerfully muscled legs, all those black tattoos that cover his taut skin. And his cock.

Soft like this, it should seem smaller, less significant. But it isn't. He's half aroused and already huge. It's so beautiful I'm tempted to take him into my mouth, if I can. If he'll fit. A wave of electric longing courses through me, reaching right to my toes and fingertips.

"Make room."

Ilya gets in and finds a soft sponge behind a row of shampoo and conditioner bottles. He soaps it up with his body wash that smells like him and, pulling me against him, starts to wash me.

My head falls back against him, and the water sluices over me as he cleans my thighs, my chest, my ass, and my pussy. He takes his time, his fingers massaging me wherever he touches. And even though he slides those fingers through my folds, he doesn't make it sexual. He doesn't do the things I want.

He does the things I need.

Slow and sweet with a gentle touch, he cleans me. It's sensual, I can't deny that, and by now, I'd be wet even without the shower water. But it's not like he's trying to turn me on.

Or maybe I'm just being naïve....

I sigh as Ilya turns me, and I'm plastered against him, his hard-on pressed into my stomach. When I'm turned around so he can clean my back and ass, I can't resist rubbing against it. I slide my hands down to touch him, but he grabs my wrist and holds me in place. Planting small kisses along the line of my shoulder, I struggle to break free from his grip.

Finally, he lets me go, and I take his cock.

He makes a warning sound. "Kira."

"What?" I tip my head back against him.

"Keep doing that," he says, a low groan sliding free as I stroke that wet, hard, silky erection, "and you'll be getting fucked hard against the wall of the shower."

His words bring delight through my sore body, even as my muscles ache.

I still can't believe he got that inside me. I want to see if he can do it again. And again.

Fuck being sore. I wiggle against him. This time he growls and laughs at the same time, lighting up parts of me I didn't know could feed off such pleasure.

"Maybe—"

"If we do that," he says, cutting me off, nipping my ear with his teeth, "I'm going to take you from beginner to PhD level sex without warning. And I promise you won't be able to walk for days after."

"Well..." I try to formulate the right response, but I'm now wondering what the hell PhD level sex is.

"Ah, Kira, I'm going to have fun defiling you, teaching you, exploring you."

"If," I say, "I let you."

"Who said a thing about if? Or let?" he laughs, biting my ear again. "Don't worry, I want to delve into you again and again, but you only just started. It's time to rest and recover for next time."

To my surprise, he gives me a gentle push, and we separate as he starts rinsing himself off. I do the same.

"Besides," he says, turning off the water, stepping out, and grabbing a large towel. "I'm hungry."

Ilya flips the towel over his shoulder, grabs the clothes he had on earlier, and pads off to his room. After taking a moment to gather myself, I follow, picking up the bag of clothes on my way.

He dries off and goes to his closet while I open the bag.

He's not gone for long before I hear a nearby phone start buzzing. For a moment, I'm worried that it's mine, but then Ilya appears out of the closet and picks up a ringing cell from the bedside table. His.

A scowl appears on his handsome face as he checks the screen. A black shirt slips over his muscular torso.

"Stay, eat," he instructs, the sexy, sensual demeanor gone. In its place is someone cold, efficient, and deadly. "I need to go, but my driver will take you home later so you can properly dress for dinner tonight."

I zip up the sweet floral dress he got me and frown. "We're still going?"

He grabs me, hovering his lips just above mine, and says, "I wouldn't miss it for the world."

And then he's gone, leaving me alone.

Again.

14

ILYA

In a way, the need to go to work, to chase up whatever lead Semyon's uncovered, is a blessing.

Being with Kira is… unexpected. She's got a way of getting under my skin, and instead of using her as a means to vent my anger at her brother, it's bloomed into something else altogether.

I rub a hand over my eyes as a driver takes me to my office, a place in a non-descript building where my servers are.

Shit. I can't fucking believe I had sex with my former best friend's little sister. My enemy's sister.

And I took her virginity.

I half-smile at that.

She was innocent.

Like untouched snow.

And I sullied her.

"Fuck."

I can't think about Kira right now. Or sex. I need to focus.

It's like Semyon can read my mind. He texts, and I look down at my phone.

ETA? Got something.

I text back. ***Minutes.***

When I get to the unassuming basement office that's equipped with more security features than a bank in the Cayman's, I step inside to find Semyon fully immersed in his work. He doesn't look up.

I don't blame him. The man's got a whole complex network of security footage up on the screens, and they're telling a story.

He's using a system I developed for tracking people and cars. It utilizes AI and facial recognition, and runs through sped-up real-time footage from various public cameras throughout Chicago... not to mention some private security ones.

Walking up, I study the middle computer and the five cameras there.

One runs that footage I know backwards, the others...

"Is that when they hit?" I ask in Russian.

Semyon nods. "I've been trying to track down the fuckers who massacred our people."

I frown. "Where did you get this footage from?"

I tap the screen. It's still at the stash house, that night, and Semyon isn't telling me anything new about what happened there. But I know he's angry. I'm fucking angry.

"The camera's further out."

"This is them leaving." He points at the images filled with cars.

"We don't know how many came."

"I count ten that leave."

He mutters an insult in Russian.

"Could have been more. We don't know, Ilya."

"We work in the certainties. There are ten who leave, so ten is what we have." I pause and look at him. "What about our friend in the country?"

"Here." He pulls up corrupted footage, but it's enough to see the ambush and our surviving guard fighting, going down, and being left for dead. "I talked to him, but... he doesn't know a thing."

"Pull up the entire day and evening in the area around the stash house."

He does it and glances at me as I sit, brooding, staring at all the screens. To me they're full of puzzle pieces. I'm looking for that one corner piece that'll make everything connect.

The rest? Not important.

But right now, I don't know what's important and what isn't, so... I stare at it, not really taking it in, letting it all work in my subconscious.

"Are you after something? I went over it, but nothing happened."

"I'm not looking for something to happen. I'm looking for the mundane."

"Like what?" he asks.

"Rewind."

He does as he's told.

"Again."

Once more, Semyon rolls back the footage, and I watch it each time.

"Fuck."

There it is. Right there. Under my fucking nose. I get up, hit pause on the computer keyboard, and point. "That car. We have ten cars pull up. Some come and go, but there are ten you have up, yes?"

He nods.

"And they all leave at the same time?"

"And go in different directions."

"In case we're filming." Clever. But it's not clever enough. Because I can follow the one with the distinctive gait. "Take down all footage of the cars, except for that one."

Semyon taps away on the computer. "Fuck. We lose him here."

It's a five block radius he's talking about. Countless garages, side streets, and warehouses that car could be stripped down in —more likely, though, there was a place to change cars. It wouldn't have been hard. This area is a hotbed of criminal activity. Not dangerous unless you're in the game, but it has a mix of both borderline artsy and dusty industrial businesses.

And security cameras here are high tech and protected.

Clever, yet again.

But thing is, this is where I shine. Not fucking breaking skulls or knifing scum on the streets. Not playing the way Andrei and Valentin love. I can do it. And I'm excellent at it. I've had to become a killing machine over the years, even before I was exiled from Russia.

But behind a keyboard, using my brain, no one can touch me.

There are better hackers who dedicate their lives to that. But I'm smarter.

This isn't a group of hacker geeks. These are organized crime groups. Or people dealing in highly sensitive stolen pieces like art and jewels. They have great systems.

And great systems always have back doors. I'm exceptional at finding those.

"I need to get footage from all the systems. As soon as I open and download, start running it. We're looking for that car.

On the ninth camera, Semyon says, "Boss?"

I look. "That's not just a one-block radius, but all those businesses and high-rises are protected. We can't go in manually; it's too big, and their system is too complex for us to break down if we get an outfit together. We'll tip them off. But..."

"I like the way you think."

"Keep flirting with me like that, Semyon, and I'm gonna start getting fucking ideas."

He snorts a laugh. "Don't think your pretty piece will be happy if I muscle in."

"Scared by a girl?"

I keep pulling up camera after camera, teasing through a time window with generous room on either side for error.

"She might look young and sweet, but she's clearly a little unhinged if she's dealing with you. Don't want to risk getting my balls cut off. I think I'll leave it at flirting."

I laugh. "You're missing out."

"If you want to share her..."

"Only if you want my knife slicing and dicing your cock." I warn.

"Have it your way." Then he asks, "You think this guy is the leader?"

I shrug. "If he is the leader, then ten to one it'll all come here..."

There he is.

The familiar walk. And there's something about it, something so dangerously familiar it makes my hackles rise, yet I can't pin it down.

Frustration makes me curl my hand. I count to ten.

The man goes down an alley that has unbelievably high-tech cameras, and he stops at a door. I'll be able to backtrack it with the car, to see where else the man went before the hit, but—

My thoughts stop hard.

The man punches in a code. And, as the door opens, he rips off the balaclava.

My stomach drops.

I know that face.

"What is it?" Semyon asks, but I barely hear him.

"Fuck."

"Boss."

"Do you recognize him?"

Semyon frowns at the screen. "Should I?"

"He's from the old country," I say. "An infamous assassin."

He gets it immediately. "We found the one doing all the kidnappings and murders?"

No fucking wonder Lev was scared out of his mind.

"Evgeni Kucherov," I explain. "Aka The Silent Butcher—The Butcher, for short. Fuck."

I'm being haunted by old ghosts still. And… Oh, fuck.

If they found out what I've been doing… sabotaging the Russian Bratva's computer systems… that's definitely something they'd send the fucking butcher to put an end to.

"We know where he is. And he's a big deal. Take him out and…"

"Andrei becomes even more powerful."

"All of us." It's not just tempting, it's the thing that makes the most sense.

We know where he is now. It's time to take him the fuck out.

"We can drive to that spot," Semyon says. "Or we take this to Andrei. What are your orders?"

We can do either. Both are the right thing to do. But it could also be a trap. Evgeni could expect me to come in with guns blazing. Then again, he might expect me to err on the side of caution. And then…

What?

Continue his operations?

Now I know who it is, I know what he wants. Me. Or, rather, to find out what I'm up to. But he can't, not directly… unless I come to him, alone.

I might give him what he wants. I can't let my past get in the way of my future. I won't let it affect Andrei and Valentin any longer.

I need to get to the bottom of this shit ASAP. I need to explore what's beyond that door.

"Semyon—"

Before I can bark out an order, my phone buzzes.

I look down at the screen. A scheduled reminder.

Pick Kira up.

A scowl twists my lips.

Dinner, with the lovely, gorgeous Kira.

... Or a fight with the Butcher.

Fuck. I need to make a decision, and fast.

But, then, I suddenly realize I don't.

The answer is already obvious.

I toss my phone down.

"Start the car."

15

KIRA

"Where is he?"

All I can do is mumble to myself as I check my reflection.

There's no denying it, I look good. Sure, it took a lot of time to get ready, but part of me was looking forward to this.

I never expected Ilya to be so late, and I certainly never expected to be so fucking bummed about it.

Maybe it's this dress I have on. His dress. Sad thing is, the prettiest and most expensive thing I now own is the dress he got me. And it is pretty—not hot and sexy, not slinky, or something a man might call slutty. Not that I care what a man might think. Except for Ilya—

"No, I don't care about his opinion either." But that's not true, and remembering that I want to destroy him is getting harder and harder.

Instead of plotting his downfall, I spent the past few hours putting on makeup, doing my hair, and preparing for our date tonight.

Thank goodness Mr. Calhoun didn't call. Because... shit. What would I do if he wanted me to go on another mission?

I'd have to decide between Ilya and work, and—

My door buzzes—right on time—and I rush over, count to ten, and press the enter button.

It's not Ilya, but his man? What is his name? Semyon?

I gather my bag and follow him to the car, and he drives me… not to Ilya's but to another luxurious building.

"Wait here," Semyon says.

A minute later, Ilya comes out, dressed in a beautiful suit, looking as good as ever. He motions for me to get out, and I grit my teeth, knowing why.

He wants to approve my outfit, and I… I need to play along. I might keep slipping up, but maybe if I keep away from sex, I can focus on learning whatever he knows. It's safer than doing what I did at home, which was start wondering where he was hours before he was scheduled to arrive.

This man likes control, so I get out of the car.

Ilya's eyes narrow. "What is this?"

"The dress you bought."

"This is for daytime." He sighs. "Not fancy dinners and heels."

Not for sex, he means. At least, that's my interpretation as I take in the disappointment.

Thing is, this dress might have cost him a fortune, but it's not sexy. It's not… slutty, not any of the things that have gotten me in trouble lately. And yes, it's basic in that classically classy and simple line way, but he's studying me like he wants to admire his meal before he eats it.

Me being the meal.

"I thought this was better. Less…"

"Fun?" He runs his eyes down me. "You are no longer a nun, Kira." He goes all pompous and formal, and there's dark humor in his voice that sends shivers down my spine. "Oh, sweet, young Kira…"

He touches my cheek with the back of his hand.

"Stop that," I say.

I swear he pretends to think about it. "No. Before, you were the sexy virgin; now you're a nun-like experienced woman."

"I hardly think one night makes me experienced."

"True," he says. "We'll make it a few more nights. Just to be sure. Build your repertoire."

"So, how are we going to prove I can sell my booze to high-end places?" I ask, trying to steer him back on track with my awful lie.

His mouth quirks at one side, but he just says, "We'll eat, and then we'll set up a plan. Nightclubs are always looking to cut corners, and I have a friend who owns some."

My heart ticks upward. He must be talking about Andrei, the Pakhan himself. Now, that would be a scoop. And by "friend," he means boss, because Ilya is Bratva. And the Bratva never lets their people go.

"But first, an outfit."

I look at him. "I like this one.

"Maybe, but I don't." He slides an arm around my waist and backs me into the car. Pressing against me, he murmurs. "I want something elegant."

I try to speak, but he's already sliding my skirt up.

"This isn't very elegant of you," I say.

"You misunderstand my definition of elegant," he responds. "I want the kind of elegant you wore the other night. Either outfit. Elegant enough I can almost see your ass. Elegant enough you can't wear anything under it. Elegant enough I can finger you if I want without having to move swathes of material. Elegant enough I can pull up the skirt or pull down the top and you're instantly naked and ready for me. That kind of elegant."

"You want me to shop at Whores R Us?"

He licks my ear. "Is that a place? I'd like to see it."

"No. And I'm not dressing like that for your whims."

"You will," he says, sucking on that earlobe, "because I like it. Because I've gotten used to it. Of course, I'll kill anyone who looks at you the wrong way, so you'll have to stick close to me."

"You'd be happy to kill again, wouldn't you?"

He lifts his head and searches my face. He isn't smiling. "I like the risk and danger it all represents. Nothing more, nothing less. I'll also protect you."

Like he did last night.

He doesn't have to say it. We both know it.

"In the car, Kira."

I scramble in, and Semyon drives. When it was just me, he took his time; now he's driving like a crazy person. I cling to the seat while Ilya sits calmly, unfazed, typing away on his phone.

We seem to be heading into a high-class shopping strip. I frown. "Where's the restaurant?"

"We're going shopping first, Kira."

"Why—my dress? You can't be serious."

"I am."

I stare at him as we pull up. I get it. Maybe he thinks I'm underdressed for the restaurant, but the dress is perfect, and I don't want to put any more ideas in his head. I don't want to seduce him again; it's getting too dangerous. For me. I'm too into him, I know that, but in this dress, I'm safe. At least, I feel safe.

But he... what? Wants me to dress slutty? Like it's an excuse to ravish and punish me?

"This is... this..."

"Women love this place."

He says it like he brings women here all the time, and as he gets out, I shove him, a burst of jealousy coming over me.

In return, he grabs my wrist and hauls me up against him.

"Careful," he murmurs.

"Women love this place? How many women do you bring here?"

"Only one."

I hate her. I want to gouge out her eyes, whoever she is. I glare at him. "Of course, there is. Let me at her."

He just laughs and pulls me closer, his mouth whispering against my throat. When he lets me go, I stand there. Christ. I can't believe I just said that. Out loud. He's my enemy, my... Shit.

He takes two steps, stops, and looks at me.

"One. You."

My legs threaten to buckle, and it's only his hand that comes around me that keeps me on my feet.

When we get inside the high-end store, I'm awestruck. I've never in my life been somewhere like this. It's like Disney World for grown women. Everything I look at is more beautiful than the last. I wander ahead while he stays back and talks to the manager.

Because isn't that what men do?

Let the woman pick and choose.

Not that I'm going to. I'm not about to let him buy me anything. But I can look and covet. And I do.

One dress catches my eye. It's a shimmery copper, down to the knee with a slit up the mid-thigh area. It's the exact kind of body-con dress Ilya wants. And it's stunning.

I look at the price tag and gasp. That's stunning too. Stunningly astronomical. And then I see a gorgeous purse.

Fuck. Purses. I've got a weakness for them, and this one is sleek, can hide a shit ton of stuff, and can be dressed up and down.

I almost start imagining it on my arm when I see the label. I know the designer. They charge upwards of forty thousand for a smaller bag. I don't even want to look to see how much this one is.

Fortunately, there's another purse nearby. I reach out to touch it, then I snatch back my hand when the price tag comes loose. I couldn't look away fast enough to ignore the zeros on it.

Almost a hundred K. Which is ridiculous. But it's so beautiful I want to cry.

"Take it," Ilya's commanding voice comes from behind me. I look around in time to see him pull out a breathtaking dress from the rack nearby. "This too."

I spin to fully face him, and he's holding out the same dress I'd just been looking at. Only this one's in a smaller size. On me, that size would be indecent.

I shake my head.

"That isn't my size," I note. "It's too small, would be way too tight. I'll get cold."

He frowns, looking at me and then the dress. "What is your size?"

I want to laugh. "At a store like this? I don't know. They have different sizes at this price range."

"Well, then take the whole rack. You can try each one on in the car. We need to eat and then be out of the restaurant before 8:30."

"Why?" Wait... What did he say? Car? I swallow. "First off, I'm not changing in a car, no matter how nice it is."

I try to get by him and put the dress away, but he corners me.

"Then let's go to the changeroom." He pulls at the top of my dress so he can see down it, and I smack his hand away. He puts it back, slipping his fingers over my covered nipples as he does so. "I can watch you change from in there."

My chest pounds, and I almost say yes, but instead, I grab the dress and slip away, ignoring the comment, even if it arouses me.

"No," I say.

"Okay." He grins. "I can watch you as you change out here."

There's a mirror on the way to the changerooms, and I stop. I'm momentarily distracted by the dress. It really is even more gorgeous up close. Up against me. Then I look again. Oh, Jesus. I can't wear it. It's way too small… but so gorgeous.

Shaking my head, I try to get back on subject.

"First, because it bears repeating, I'm not getting changed in the car or out here. And second, buying the whole rack would be absurd. I'm not letting you do that."

He shakes his head and smiles.

"Too late."

"Bullshit," I say, calling him out. "You haven't bought anything yet."

"Wrong," he flicks his chin, looking around. "I bought the whole store."

Looking over his shoulder, he nods at the eager manager. The manager nods back, giving thumbs up.

"You what?" I ask, my voice a little weak. I shake my head again.

"I bought the store, Kira."

My stomach drops as I look around at all the opulent designer bags and shoes and dresses. This is too much. It's beyond extra. I take this, and it's like I'm his. I'm not big, but I'm not a waif. I'm no teeny, skinny model waiting to get up on the catwalk.

And the price tags in this place. Oh. My. God. Some of these prices… Fuck me. I barely make enough to pay rent, let alone buy anything close to designer.

"Most of this stuff won't fit." I look at him, then down at what I'm wearing. "This is designer. It's good. It'll do."

And it will. He got me flats for it, just pretty colored kicks, but pair it with the heels I put on, and I'm ready for anything.

Ilya's eyes say different. He picks up the dress.

It's tiny. There's no way around that. It's too small.

He approaches and presses the dress into my stomach. I glare at him.

"It," I say, "Won't. Fit."

Ilya smiles, and it's one of heat and sinuous, deadly charm. "Then you can burn it for warmth. After you wear it. Burn it and the rest, because I've made up my mind."

"You're a bully."

He leans in, rubbing my stomach with the dress. It's a jaw-droppingly intimate move, weirdly hot for something so G-rated, and it makes my legs start to shake.

"Maybe," he murmurs against my ear, "a bully who bought you a whole shop."

"I'm not some superstar."

"You don't have to be," he says, licking my ear in a way that's anything but G-rated. My breath catches. "Wear the dress."

"You said I could burn it." My voice shakes almost as much as my knees.

"I did. But first? You're wearing it tonight."

I struggle to get a steady breath in. I'm drowning. If I give in to him and his seductive forceful will, I'm not sure there'll be anything less. "Fine, it's my shop, I'll choose."

"No, this one."

"It's too small." I reach for a compromise, even though I know he's too stubborn to budge. I dig my heels in anyway. Still, I try to soften that standing of my ground so he doesn't notice. What's the saying about flies and honey? I smile and point at another rack. "We can see if there's one in my size, right over there? I need something bigger, or else..."

"This. One."

Fucking hell. What's the point?

"Understood?"

"Fucking whatever."

I sigh and head off to get changed before he decides to come with me.

16

KIRA

The dinner is good, but I barely taste it from the few bites I manage.

We're on the entrée, and the restaurant is beautifully intimate, yet... it's nothing like the last time he took me out.

Was that only the other night?

It seems weeks ago. That's how quickly he's become ingrained in my life.

Picking up my wine glass, I take a sip when my phone rings. Ilya doesn't even seem to notice when I get up and excuse myself for the bathroom. With shaking hands, knowing the men are looking at me in my shimmery dress and spike heels he made me get, I pull out my phone.

It's Mr. Calhoun.

"Hello?"

"I need an update. Tate's on the ball, bringing in some juicy stuff. What do you have?" he asks.

My heart sinks. "I've got an angle."

"Which is?"

"You know the angle. I'm talking with him now."

He says something to someone, the words muffled. "Get on

it," he says to me. "And deliver me something juicy by end of the week, otherwise you're off the job and out the door."

Fuck. I close my eyes and lean on the wall in the hall outside the bathrooms. "You can't hurry a front-page exposé," I say, crossing two fingers behind my back.

"Thinking like an actual journalist." He makes an approving grunt.

"Thank you—"

"Kira, there's thinking and doing. I need you to do," Mr. Calhoun says. "More importantly, I need an update tomorrow. There was some activity out near some warehouses; people are saying shots were fired. Russians. Tate brought it to me, but if your Rykov is connected, maybe he's the better bet."

"I need to get back before he gets suspicious."

"Tomorrow."

I hang up, something inside me twinging uneasily from the conversation.

When I return, Ilya's dark head is bent over his phone, sipping whiskey instead of wine.

I slide into my seat, a little annoyed he didn't seem to notice me leave or come back.

I push my plate away. I think I had one bite of the seafood pasta in a delicate white wine, lemon, and smoked paprika dusted cream sauce.

"You seem distracted," I mutter.

He glances at me briefly, then goes back to his phone.

Screw him anyway. Maybe I will use him to get information. I can almost feel Mr. Calhoun's breath hot on my neck, and it pisses me off that Tate's made more progress than me, and he doesn't even have this connection to an actual high-up Bratva member.

Ilya's got to be high up. He's loaded, and he's the type to command, not follow orders.

"I said you seem distracted." I put my fork down and glare. When he doesn't respond, I shove the plate and cross my arms.

He finally looks at me. "I heard you the first time.

Irritation burns through my chest. "And you're not eating."

"Neither," he says, gesturing at my plate, "are you."

We stare at each other, and there's a spark that thickens the air, one of irritation.

And beneath that, there's a vibration of a different nature, one that makes my body hum.

I ignore that and go with the irritation. Just because he's a sexy piece of meat doesn't mean he gets away with all the bullshit he throws around.

If he wants a wilting flower, he can go hunting out the back of a florist for yesterday's rejects.

"I'm not hungry," I snap.

"Buy the fucking girl her own shop, and she's not happy. Women."

I lean forward. "Dress in the tacky dress the man buys because that's the only way he can get a girl to look like a high-class hooker. Men."

"Are you obsessed with the profession? I don't think it's as glamorous as you seem to think, Kira."

"I think," I say, reaching across the table, grabbing his whiskey, and downing it. "I think," I repeat, "that I don't like you very much."

"You don't have to." He shrugs. "You just have to like fucking me."

He's an asshole, honestly. Just because I've discovered this sex thing is something I love—with him—is no need for him to say that.

I slam down his empty glass. "And maybe I don't like that. After all, I don't have anyone else to compare it to. Maybe you're shit, and I need to experiment."

My face burns.

Now I reach for my wine, but he grabs my thigh under the

table, and I stop. He moves his hand slowly, gently on my skin, under the edge of the skirt. We both know I'm not wearing underwear.

"You're upset," he murmurs, all velvet. "Hangry? I'm paying. Eat."

"I don't want to."

He ignores me. "When was the last time you ate?"

"Breakfast."

He sighs. "We're not leaving until you crack a smile."

"I'm not in the mood to smile." I glare at him, trying not to melt at his touch.

"Maybe if you ate..."

I narrow my eyes. "I'm not hungry."

So does he. "Bullshit. You're always hungry."

"Unless you've been stalking me, how could you possibly know that?"

"It's true." He gives me a triumphant look.

I shake my head. "No. It isn't. You're thinking of when I was a child. I'm done growing; I don't need to eat as much."

"Yes," he says, "you do. And you will."

Waving down the waiter, he tightens his grip.

"What will it be, princess?" he asks, sounding like an ass.

"Nothing."

"That's not an option." His smile is tight, arrogant. "You're eating."

"Fine," I say, turning to the waiter. "I want one of everything on your menu."

The waiter looks at Ilya, probably thinking I'm a maniac, but Ilya only nods.

"You heard the lady." He waves his free hand at me. "One of everything. And two whiskies. Unless she wants booze? Do you want booze? That booze you sell?"

I swallow hateful words, and I blink rapidly, hot tears pressing at my eyes.

Ilya softens. "Some bread now, and two of the seafood specials you mentioned."

"I can order for myself," I snap when the waiter goes.

He leans forward. "If you order everything, be my guest. But you have to eat it all. If you don't like this, then order something else. But fucking eat or I'll make you get under the table and suck my cock."

I open my mouth, then snap it shut, because I think he would actually do that.

When the waiter comes with the bread and drinks, Ilya forces me to eat, slathering each warm piece of bread with the cultured butter... and fuck me, it does make me feel marginally better.

By the time the new entrees come and a second round of drinks, I've eaten half of mine, and I feel so much better. I hate admitting it, but I could get used to this.

What I have to do, though, is plot and scheme a way to get my story.

But my heart's lacking, and I keep coming back to one thing...

Do I really want to bring him down for the sake of my ambitions?

Ilya's not really one for small talk, and he's still distracted. I get the feeling that whatever it is, it's important. I keep going back to what Mr. Calhoun said about Tate's lead. What if it's that?

Eventually, though, Ilya does make an effort. He's charming when he wants to be, and I like his sense of humor.

So, when he orders dessert, I let him.

It's some passionfruit concoction that's insanely delicious, honestly.

When the bill comes, he says, "You can stay at my place tonight, but I need to go out and do some work."

I nod, and there's a very real part of me that doesn't want to be alone tonight.

Then again, if he is leaving me at his place, I can snoop.

"You sure I won't be able to convince you to stay?" I ask, trying to sound meek and innocent.

His eyes glitter with dark, delicious intent as he gives me a slow, burning look. "Let's see if you can," he says. "Try me."

17

ILYA

She's up to something. I don't buy coy or meek from her. Not for a second.

Never have, never will.

Innocent, yes. An air of naivety? Absolutely. But coy? Meek? Shy?

It isn't her.

Still... I'm not really sure what she wants. But I'm going to fucking find out.

"Come on, Kira." I take her hand and lead her from the restaurant to the waiting car outside. "Let's get you home and see if you can convince me to stay."

A less observant man might miss the fleeting narrowing of her eyes. I don't. As we drive through the city, she consumes my thoughts more than she should, even as she sits next to me, hands folded, a line of tension running through her.

"You don't have to. I know you're busy. I..." She slides me a look. "I should go home."

"No."

There are lots of reasons I say that. I want to keep an eye on her. Protect her. Find out what the fuck she's up to. I want to make sure she's out of my business and the hands of the Butcher.

But at the bottom of all that?

I just want her in my home.

My bed.

She looks down, like the meek little soul she isn't. And she says, "I don't want to interfere with your work..."

It's an opening, one I ignore. But I think about the man I need to go after.

Fucking Evgeni.

The Butcher is out there and hitting my turf. It means something, especially when considering the fact Lev was more frightened of him than me.

The fucking fact he changed his MO. I'd have picked that in a second if he'd gone about trying to get information, murdering for fun, if he'd done his usual.

The Butcher has that name for a reason. It's not because he likes to kill. He likes to carve bodies into cuts of meat, often from the living flesh. When they're already dead, he'll age them like beef and have the pieces delivered as a warning to whoever crossed him. He speaks through his work, hence the fucking silent part of the moniker.

If he changed his MO so I didn't pick up on him, it means he just might be after me.

Or someone from back home.

But I can't shake the feeling it's me.

Fuck.

"You're not going home, and you wanted to change my mind. So, change it," I say as my phone buzzes.

No movement.

Semyon and his crew are monitoring all the points we tracked the car to, and they haven't picked up on anything yet.

That means I have time to play this out with Kira. It's a delicious thought, one that makes my fucking pants tight.

We pull up, and I haul her out of the car and into one of my private lifts in the basement.

She stands there, seemingly withdrawn into herself, but I can sense the thick heat of awareness in the confined space enveloping us. Kira can fight it all she wants, but she wants me just as much as I want her.

Not that you can tell from a casual glance at her.

I punch in the code, and as the doors open into the living space, they automatically lock behind us.

She licks her lips. I follow that movement like a starved man.

"Convince me, Kira. I'm partial to lap dances."

"I just bet you are," she mutters, and I hide my smile. Then she takes a breath. "No, no, you go to work, and I'll go home—"

"I don't fucking think so."

Now the snotty brat appears, and she sniffs, saying coolly, "You don't want me wrecking your place while you're gone, do you?"

I step up to her. "You going to do that, Kira?"

"Maybe."

The coolness isn't something I buy, and she's not the kind to wreck a place. If she's going to search—*that* I buy, the inquisitive Kira streak runs straight down to the bone—she can. There's nothing incriminating here, and the computers are inaccessible to her.

I'm a careful man. Nothing I don't want an enemy or stranger to find would ever be at my home. There are personal things, but all the shit to do with Bratva life are on servers, and to access the servers, you need the codes. Wi-Fi won't do it.

Maybe this comes from years of fighting for every scrap, for being fucked over in so many ways; I should hang a fucking shingle for my ass.

I might not know my exact age, but I know her.

And she'll snoop.

But I welcome that. Maybe it'll show me what she actually does for a living.

I smile at her. "Go ahead. I'll wait."

"No, I'll go home."

"Like fuck you will. I want you to show me how much you want me to stay."

"I've changed my mind," she says.

I grab her, tossing her squealing, wriggling body over my shoulder. "And I've changed mine. I'm fucking sick of waiting for you to convince me. I'm fucking sick of standing in the doorway. So I'm going to take you in my bedroom. After all, you're not a virgin anymore."

She hits my back, and I ignore her. "Once removed."

"Twice, if you're counting."

Kira writhes so much her ass and hips keep brushing and bouncing against my head. She's that far over my shoulder. I grip her legs, sliding a hand high between her thighs, and she squeals again.

"No one's coming, so quit with the fucking noise, Kira."

"Let me down!"

"No."

She fights harder, scratching at my back and then hitting me with fists. At first, it's light, almost playful, but her wiggling is so much I tighten my grip. Then, I tighten it a bit more to show just how things might go.

Rough, hard, wild.

She starts to claw up my jacket and shirt to scratch and hit at me in earnest. "Let me go, you oaf!"

Her nails scrape so hard she must have drawn blood, because she takes in a sharp breath. I'm not complaining, though. It feels so fucking good.

Not just the light sear of pain, but the fact it means I can do what the fuck I want.

I really want to do what the fuck I want.

I veer to grab a bottle of whiskey because the idea of licking it off her is almost too good to pass up.

Then, suddenly, Kira starts biting.

Once. Twice. I barely feel it. When we get to the bedroom, I toss the bottle on the bed and prepare to place her on the mattress. Before I can, though, she bites again, this time so fucking hard I flinch.

"Oh, good. You're not made of stone." She twists, and her hand comes up to grab my hair, then she sinks her teeth into the nape of my neck and doesn't let go.

"God fucking damn it."

I let go of her with one hand, tighten my grip, and spank her. Hard.

She moans.

Oh, shit. She likes it.

Somehow, I pull her off me and dump her on the bed. I point hard at her, enjoying the view of her bare pussy because the dress has ridden up.

"You need to learn to listen."

I strip off my tie, jacket, and shirt, and kick off my shoes. To my surprise, she goes to do the same.

I come down over her, making her press against the bed as I put a hand on either side of her head and lean in close. "Did I say move?"

"N-no."

"Don't."

I pull back and observe her. Then I grab the dress and wrench it down the front, the delicate fabric tearing as I strip it from her. Before she can even gasp, I tie it around her head, gagging her.

"Much better."

She makes outrageous sounds, but I sit and pick her up. Laying her out over my knee, I spank her, bringing my hand down hard until her ass starts to turn a sweet, hot red. Each whack of my hand comes down in a slightly different spot. She writhes and moans.

I pull back on the makeshift gag as I hit her again and again, until she's whimpering and moving her hips up to me, offering her ass. I don't need to slide my fingers between her thighs to know she's wet. Her skin glistens with her juices.

I give her one more spank, and then I push my fingers up into her.

She screams, clenching around me.

I'm instantly rock hard.

She's like a vice. I want my cock in there more than anything.

No, not more than anything. I know what I want.

I pull my fingers out after she rides them to shuddering completion, then I whip the gag off. Using the ruined dress to tie her hands, I push her from me, down to the floor so she's between my thighs.

Her eyes are glazed, wild, as they meet mine.

I unzip and start to stroke my cock. "Ever given a blowjob?"

"No."

"Open your mouth, suck me in, and work me down to the back of your throat. Then up and down. It's easy."

"Given a lot of them, have you?"

I curl a hand in her hair and pull her into my cock. "I've had a lot of them, Kira."

"Just because I haven't given one, doesn't mean I don't know what to do."

"Porn expert, are you?"

She doesn't answer, just starts to lick me, sucking the head.

It's fucking amazing. She's feeling her way, has no real idea, but because it's Kira, it's hot as hell.

I use my hand to guide her, and she starts to suck me in, going deep. She gags and tries to come up, but I push her back down. The feeling of her throat on me when she gags is phenomenal.

Soon, I have her in a rhythm. And I know with a few more tries, my girl will be an expert. She sucks hard. My balls get tight, and sparks of pure hot pleasure flare into life, along with the pressing ache of needing to cum.

I groan low. I want to hit the back of her throat with my seed. I teeter along the edge, every fiber in me ready to let that sweet, vibrant release out.

Grabbing her hair, I pull her down. I'm on that knife's edge. She gags and coughs and tries to get up, and I'm almost there, I'm almost—

Fuck me. I pull her off, and watch her take in deep lungfuls of air.

She sags against me, but I'm not done, and I urge her up by her hair. "I want to fucking cum in you, Kira. Remember the thing about lap dances?"

She half nods.

"Get your sweet little ass up here and give me one."

I help her up, pulling her on me, and I push up into her.

She whines. "You feel so fucking good," she curses, almost angrily.

"Nothing compared to you, princess. Now move."

She does. And I let her undulate on me. She rocks and writhes. She rises and falls. She fucking squeezes me with the walls of her pussy.

And I don't stop her.

It's exquisite agony as she does her little dance. She's trying to get off is what she's doing, and she's looking for something that hits right. I hold off until she does. I want her to erupt.

Suddenly, she gasps.

We're both so fucking close.

It feels amazing. I'm being fucking strangled by her tight

hole, and it's a thing of fucking beauty. But she doesn't stop. Hell no. She goes harder. Rougher. Faster.

"H-help me, please. I want to cum."

I grab her hips and thrust up, deep, at an angle where I hit her hard against the G-spot and oh, fuck, I'm barely holding it together.

"Cum for me, baby. Do it. Now!"

"I..." she sucks in a breath. "I want to... I want to cum for you." She's starting to fracture, her words tumbling.

She offers to be mine. To serve. She asks me to take her hard and rough when I want. She tells me she wants me to cum down her throat. That she wants me to fucking eat her out over and over, and I can't take it. Her sweet filth's too much. My balls tighten, and I grab her hips, slamming her down hard so I can cum deep inside of her.

Kira screams out my name as an orgasm rips through her too.

We both climax together.

When we're done, I ease her off and untie her.

She lies on the bed, a boneless heap, and I want nothing more than to crawl up next to her, to take her all over again, licking and biting and teasing and denying her another orgasm until she begs me for it.

But I can't.

"Kira..."

"Don't let me tie you down," she says, slurring a little. "Go. It's okay. I understand."

"Tie me down, huh?"

Now that... that has possibilities. I kind of wish she would.

It's a pipe dream, though. Because I have to go and figure this Butcher shit out.

But while I have to leave, she has to stay. That nagging thought about his change in MO comes back. Chances are he's not thinking of me; he's thinking of another Russian exile. Fuck knows there are enough of us.

But I'm not taking that chance. Not with Kira. My place is the safest spot for her.

Well, the second safest. Close to me would technically be the safest, but if the Butcher's really after me, then I'm not safe, and that means she wouldn't be either. So I need to control when and where we go together.

But her being here? It's works, for now.

Suddenly, something unpleasant comes to me. Something I pushed from my head. The Butcher used to carve up an enemy's loved one. Often, he'd forgo the wife and take and murder the lover. He'd find the way to hit hardest.

Kira...

Somehow, he'd see her as my weakness. I need to protect her. Because... well, she might be. No one can know that we are together, that I'm starting to have serious feelings for her. No one.

It will put a target on her back.

I can't have that.

Not at all.

18

ILYA

"I expected early hours of the morning or last night, but it seems it happened under our noses," Semyon says, looking displeased.

I wait for him to continue.

When he doesn't, I cross my arms and switch to the cameras I hacked. This one is from the front of the building and the florist van.

"Things like this are both blatant and subtle. The florist has a warehouse there. Shipments come and go. Things for the store. Fresh market flowers. It's where they run their same-day shipping from." I stare at the image and rub my chin.

"Should have fucking known," he says in Russian.

I shrug. "They have a whole fleet of vans. But this car... you spotted it on footage I didn't ask you to look at." I turn, open a drawer, and pull out a gun. "It stands out."

"I went back over the course of a few days, and it was always the same workers. The same vans. Until it wasn't. Every once in a while, something fishy happens. They switch vans. They swap out personnel."

"And Evgeni?"

"He left in a different car. At the end of the block. Caught on peripheral from another camera."

The rabbit hole he navigated through is impressive. Not many have the brain or the patience.

"And you think the building is empty now?" I ask

"Yep."

"How sure are you?"

"Ninety percent."

"Good enough," I mutter. "I'm a gambling man. I'd have taken seventy."

He checks his weapons as I load mine. "We're going in?"

"No time like the present."

"Fuck."

I kick the ground as the overhead lights flicker.

"The fuckers didn't leave even a computer wire. What? Did they have an 'everything must go sale' and we weren't paying attention?"

"They took tables, chairs."

"Probably cheap pack-down crap. I'm more interested in computer hardware fire sales." I cock my head as I look around the empty bunker beneath the warehouse.

It's just Semyon and me. My driver's doing double duty as a lookout.

He might have a long ass shift because we need to go over this place like we're a fucking forensics team.

Grumbling between ourselves, we head back upstairs. That's where we start, now that we've scouted the entire bunker.

Upstairs is totally empty, not even the alarm hooked up anymore, just a pin code for the door that didn't take me long to crack.

"We're missing something," I mutter.

"Like what?" Semyon's studying one of the outlet sockets that seems loose.

"I don't know..." I look around, then something catches my eye. I go over to it. "This."

I didn't notice the piece of paper at first, as it's the same black as the floor, but when I pick it up, I see that it's an envelope. My skin crawls, and my blood turns to ice as I pull the thin sheet of paper out.

One word.

Ilya.

I recognize the handwriting.

And my stomach fucking hollows.

"Boss?"

I realize he's been talking to me, and I didn't hear a thing. Wordlessly, I show him the note.

"How the fuck did—"

"It's not from Evgeni. He doesn't leave calling cards. This is from the man who hired him." I swallow. "Boris Gusinsky."

"The Pakhan of the biggest fucking Bratva in Russia?" Semyon frowns.

"He wasn't always."

Semyon stays silent.

He knows I don't ever talk about my time back in Russia. About the betrayal that brought me here. About Mikhail and Boris and the Butcher.

Fucking hell.

I move off, lean against a wall, facing Semyon.

"Want to talk about it?" he asks.

"No." That's a lie. My mind is racing at a thousand miles per second, and we both know I like to talk my way through chaos. So, I open my big fat mouth and spill.

"The girl I've been seeing... I met her brother back when I came to America for the first time as a teenager. He fell in love with the Bratva life, and when I returned to Russia, he came with me. Thought the place was some romanticized criminal paradise. And honestly, it could have been. But the previous Pakhan, Ivan Orlov, was corrupt, even for the underworld. It's a different beast in the motherland. Fat with two-headed deals, vicious oligarchs, and betrayals. He was a monster, tried and true. He had to go, and so..."

Semyon meets my gaze.

"Mikhail and I, with the help of Gusinsky, were the main part of the struggle to overthrow Orlov. And we got close."

"Just close?"

"One day," I say, looking around this barren, abandoned place, "Boris and Mikhail seemingly teamed up to get me expelled from the country. I had no choice. Everyone had turned against me, and it was too dangerous to stay. I was told to go and not return. I had to leave. And now..."

"Your girl's brother and Gusinsky are coming after you?"

I shake my head. "Mikhail went down in a gunfight." Fuck. I hate all this.

He frowns, studying the slip of paper. "Maybe this Gusinsky doesn't know it's you coming for him. It's just a guess?"

"That paper's from the consulate. Extra thin. Cheap for internal shit. Russian-made." I push back from the wall. "He knows. Looks like they finally found out I've been sabotaging their operation in Russia from the states."

"This means he's here."

It's not an important point. "Maybe he is, maybe he isn't. He doesn't do dirty work. Not now that he's Pakhan."

No, what's important is that he's sent their most ruthless assassin after me.

Shit. Did I go too far by breaking into the Russian consulate? Is that how they found me?

Or maybe Kira—

I dismiss the thought as soon as it comes.

No matter her feelings about me, she hates the Bratva. Always did, just like her father. She wouldn't turn to one arm of the Bratva to hurt another. That would mean being indebted to them.

Fuck, if it's true that Boris is after me, it makes it more likely that the Butcher will know about Kira. I need to get back to her and make sure she's safe.

Taking the paper back from Semyon, I shove it in my pocket.

"Let's get the fuck out of here."

19

KIRA

"Damn it."

I stand in a room that should be an office. There are books, a desk, and a laptop thrown on it. But this is Ilya, a man who's always been gifted in computers and tech.

He wouldn't have just a laptop.

Fine, I'm snooping, but I have to. I need something, anything, to give Mr. Calhoun.

Shit. That thought makes my stomach knot and twist.

But I keep pressing on. This job is what I've worked for, and I'm not letting Tate steal the glory, not after everything I've been through.

The thought of losing whatever might be brewing with Ilya is something I can't let myself look at.

"He'll tire of me, and then what?" I whisper the words as I poke about. "I'll be on my own, without a job. Blackballed... isn't that what Mr. Calhoun said?"

Besides, a little snooping never hurt anyone.

There's a door I didn't notice, a pocket door, and I slide it open. Inside is a second sitting room, but what draws me is the computer system. A few screens. Sleek. And I'm betting this is hooked to a server somewhere, not regular Wi-Fi.

It's not my forte, but I know enough to understand that someone with this kind of kit is hardcore.

With shaking fingers, I move the keyboard, and everything comes to life. The screensaver is a rolling wave of blacks and grays, going from one screen to the next, like a lazy sporting crowd wave.

But that's it. When I tap a key a password box comes up. Shit.

I pull out the ergonomic chair and sit, trying everything I can think of. His name, the date when he left. The Pakhan of his Bratva. Then I frown.

"What if it's something to do with Mikhail? They were best friends, after all." And it's not something obvious.

My eyes blur as hot tears press at them. Frustration bubbles up, along with a bitterness that leaves an acrid taste.

Damn Mikhail. Damn Ilya. Why did he have to come to Chicago, take my brother from us, and essentially destroy my family?

Sure, he didn't put a gun to my father's head, but he didn't need to. Mikhail died because he followed Ilya to Russia. That might as well have been a gun to the temple.

The moment Mikhail left, my father knew it'd be the death of him. So did I. We were right.

I wipe my eyes as a few tears fall. And I make myself say it. "He killed them. It's his fault."

I repeat those words because Ilya makes me feel things for him I know I shouldn't.

"You're betraying them, Kira," I whisper. "And why the hell did you have to go to Russia, anyway? Huh, Mickey? Why did you have to die? Because then, Dad died, and I was all alone. I've been all alone since. So curse you as well as Ilya."

I suck in a wobbly breath and square my shoulders.

Feeling sorry for myself won't help. Without another thought, I start trying all sorts of Mikhail-oriented combinations—his name, his and Ilya's, even their favorite blood-fest action movie. I keep going until something occurs to me.

Mickey.

Did Ilya know Mikhail's nickname?

Either of them would do...

I used to call him Wally, but that was between us. Unless... had Ilya heard it or Mikhail told him? Because that would be something no one else would even piece together.

Wally brings back memories. It started as Mickey because, when I was really little, I struggled with Mikhail. And it stuck, until he introduced me to Disney movies.

As a kid, I was obsessed with not just the movies but also the whole history of Disney, and so I started calling him Wally because he was my Walt Disney—creator of magic in laughs and wonderful delights he brought to life through books, movies, and yes, treats.

And it's how I saw him, too. Walt ruled Disneyland, and Mikhail ruled our little sibling kingdom.

It stands to reason Disney is where I took my fake last name from, Arendelle—the name of Elsa's kingdom in Frozen.

I'm fueled now with an excited purpose. Excitement that quickly fades as I try and fail with each one.

There's nothing left.

Not unless I try Mickey.

It doesn't work. "Fuck."

I frown. And then I type **micky & ilya.**

Oh my God. It works. I'm in.

I'm about to see what's in here when the elevator dings, and I'm forced to quickly log out, almost falling in my rush to get out. Not that it matters. He'll know I was in here. Still, I grab a book and rush away, already counting down to when I can get back.

That will have to wait, though.

"Ilya?"

I don't see him immediately, and a part of me is glad.

So many memories swirl inside of me. So many conflicting feelings. Guilt for my betrayal. Love and sadness for my father. Love, anger, and sadness for my brother. And the mixed-up box of feelings for Ilya.

The man who essentially lured my brother to his death.

"Why are you reading a book on antique weapons?"

I look down. "Fun?"

Then I look at him, and my heart lurches. And it's not with guilt.

It's something more complex. He looks so impossibly handsome that those feelings, those mixed up, messed up feelings for him want to burst free.

He also looks tired, worried. Grim.

Despite my best efforts, I'm happy to see him, happy he's safe.

I shouldn't be happy. I shouldn't even be here. I should have cracked that password earlier and taken everything. Shit, I should have pumped him hard for information instead of having sex and expensive dinners.

But when he looks at me, concern is etched on his face... and I think it just might mirror mine. Because, try as I might, I can't pretend I'm not concerned for him.

Still, relief crosses his features as he comes to me, easing the book down. "Thank God you're okay."

"Why wouldn't I be?" I look up at him. "You locked me in your castle."

"Princess Kira." And then he kisses me, walking me backward, stripping me of my T-shirt and shorts of his until we're on the bed, kissing, touching. Exploring.

It's passion at its essence, red-hot and wildly intimate. The world disappears, as do all my memories, good and bad, until it's just us.

There's no thought of betrayal or using him. It's just him. It's just me. And this... whatever it is... is right.

For now.

He tastes so good, and it's a stretch to get him in, but the push and slide of his cock is like nothing else, and the groans and jerks and hisses of air from him are delicious. They make me feel powerful.

Right up to where he lifts me, spinning me, saying. "Keep your mouth where it is."

I do what he says, and suddenly, I'm upside down on him, his face at my pussy as he wraps his arms around my thighs.

"You have permission to choke on my cock, but don't you dare make me cum before I get you at least twice first. Understand?"

It's a threat, a warning, a promise all rolled into one.

"AAa?" I can't exactly say anything, with him filling my mouth to capacity.

"Isn't that the sound of fucking beauty."

Just like that, he starts to feast on me, licking, sucking, nibbling at my clit. And he pushes his tongue in me. I suck him hard and take him all the way to the back of my throat, choking myself.

He loosens an arm, slides that hand around, and pushes two fingers into me and one in my ass. I try to jump, but he holds me in place until it starts to feel good. Real good.

It quickly becomes a game of me trying to get him to cum so I can, too, because he's not pushing me to the brink—he's trying to push me over.

So I use my hands, too, squeezing the base of his cock, massaging his balls.

Suddenly, I feel a familiar swelling. His entire body lifts, and he erupts, thrusting so deep I can barely taste him as he cums down my throat.

Only one thought fills my mind.

Finally.

I cum, too, unable to stop the rushing storm of pleasure.

When we're done, Ilya pulls me into his arms and kisses me deeply. Then whispers, "As soon as I recover, I'm spanking you and taking you from behind. Hard."

"B-but I waited."

"This isn't punishment," he says. "It's a reward. I'll make sure you love it."

I shiver in anticipation.

Ilya keeps his promise, and when we're done with round two, he collapses next to me. I'm ready to pass out, but he gets up and pulls his boxers on. Without a word, he leaves the bedroom and comes back with a nasty, lethal looking gun. He slides it under his pillow.

"Uh, Ilya?"

"Yeah?"

"What's the giant gun for?"

"The usual gun things. Except this one holds a bigger clip. Custom made."

I bite back a retort. "I mean… why did you just put it under your pillow?"

"Safety."

"I promise I don't kick too hard in my sleep."

"Not from you, little one."

Leaning over, he kisses me on the forehead, then sinks down into his pillow, like there isn't a canon beneath it.

He's already asleep before I can ask any more questions. But that doesn't stop them from filling my mind.

What the hell have I gotten myself into?

Conflicting thoughts rage through me until I'm too

exhausted to contemplate them anymore. Finally, somehow, I manage to fall asleep.

If only that were enough to shut my mind off.

Dreams of the past fill my slumber. Mikhail is there. Mickey. Wally. Ilya shows up. They're fighting. Together. Bleeding. Then Wally's gone, Mickey, Mikhail—they disappear...

I wake with a start.

My heart is pounding, but an immediate calm comes over me. It's dark, safe. Ilya is asleep beside me.

That comfort soon becomes surrounded by dread.

So many thoughts chase and fight each other in my head that my heart hurts from being pulled in a thousand different directions. And even though I can't fight off the sense that I'm betraying memories of my family, I snuggle in next to the heat and strength of Ilya.

It feels like the only way to put the chaos at ease.

Fuck. How can something wrong feel so right?

I bite my lip. This is all going wrong—my plans, the revenge, even the story. I could have pushed tonight, and I didn't.

Thing is, when it comes down to it, will I have the guts to do what I came here to do? Will I have the courage to end whatever this has become?

Shit.

The truth is so scary I have to shut my eyes and hold on to Ilya extra tight.

Because I have no fucking idea what I'm going to do next.

20

ILYA

"Wally... Wally..."

I fucking freeze.

Next to me, Kira's deep asleep, clearly dreaming. A smile on her lips. It's not even fucking six a.m., and she's thinking of another man?

She can't help what she dreams, but that doesn't stop it from grabbing my attention. Who's Wally, and why the hell's she got him in her head?

There's one man and one man only that should be taking up the space in her dreams.

Me.

Jealousy cuts under my skin, searing along my bones. I throw the covers off and get out of bed. Kira's naked, her legs parted as she rolls on her back, flinging an arm.

Fuck this shit.

I'll make sure no other man enters her dreams. I'll carve my name on her soul.

Dipping down, I crawl back onto the mattress and get between her legs, nudging them apart. She stops talking and sighs in her sleep. I sink my teeth into her upper thigh before shifting to her cunt, licking it.

"Oh my God! Ilya!"

At least she knows who's between her thighs. But that doesn't mean I'm going to stop. If I haven't made it into her dreams yet, then I'll have to make a more lasting impression. That will start by showing her what it's like to wake and orgasm.

I make fast work of it, sucking on her clit as I push my fingers into her slick hole. With a gentle rhythm, I start to pump. Her thighs tremble around my ears. Soft moans wash down from above.

I can't tell if she's still asleep or not. It doesn't matter. The harder she squirms, the harder I go, hooking my fingers inside until her back's arched and her soft moans turn loud.

"Oh my god..."

Then she's awake, and I decide to change things up. I pull my fingers out and come up, thrusting into her, pushing her legs to my shoulders so I can hold her where I want to, so I can drill fucking deep into her tight, soaking pussy.

"Ilya!" Kira croaks as her thin fingers grab my thick wrist. Her eyes are still hazy from sleep, but I can still see them sparkle with excitement as an orgasm rips through her.

"I thought you might like some breakfast in bed," I grunt, slamming into her.

Kira's whole body seems to contract and squeeze around me. I roll us, so she's on top.

"Is that what this is?"

I look up at her, licking my lips. "Best meal I've ever had."

"You're crazy."

"You're not wrong."

She starts to get off me. I coil a hand in her hair and hold her there.

"Let me go," she says.

"Fuck no. My turn."

"I'll scream," she says, eyes flashing. And she looks for all the world like a girl who's trying to ask me to spank her.

But right now, I'm not interested in that. I've got other things on my mind.

Like filling her full of my cum.

"You already did," I remind her. I bite her lower lip, and she moans. "And guess what, Princess Kira? No one came. So…"

I'm still in her, and I reach down, rubbing her clit, teasing her, thrusting into her just enough that my engorged head slides hard against her G-spot and her eyes start to roll back.

I tighten my grip on her hair.

"I'm going to make you cum again. This time, when you scream, scream my name." I work her harder, thrusting into her a little more, and she starts to pulsate and contract around my cock.

Twisting her clit gently, just a touch to push her over the edge, she shatters. And when she does, she screams my name.

"Ilya!"

I pull her off me and then, using her hair, I pull her limp body up until she's between my thighs. With my other hand, I stroke myself, before grabbing her face and applying just enough pressure so that she opens her mouth for me.

"Good girl. No one else is allowed to fill your thoughts or your mouth." I shove my cock between her wet lips, down to the back of her throat.

And fuck, she starts to suck, to work me. I try to hold back, to enjoy the improvement in her technique since the first time, but the pleasure is too great and I only last a few minutes. I roar as I cum in her mouth.

This time she swallows and licks her lips clean.

"Harlot."

She laughs as I let go of her, easing her into my arms. "I don't think anyone's used that word for over sixty years."

"They should. I like it."

For a moment, I want to ask who Wally is, but I don't. Kira belongs to me, no one else. I'm the one who'll protect her, keep her safe. I'm the one who'll treat her like a princess and a naughty little whore. Not that she's a whore, but when we play dirty, filthy games, I like thinking that. It adds an edge.

Anyone else even dares to think or call her that, and I'll fucking slice off their balls.

After all, I already need to destroy what's threatening me and, by proxy, her. What's another few bodies if anyone's stupid enough to call her that?

Stupid enough to touch her.

With a sigh, I get up and shower. Kira is too exhausted to do anything but sink back into bed. I've got work to do, and despite all of these detours, there's no question that time is of the essence.

When I'm dressed, I return to the bedroom. Kira's still naked in my bed, and no, I'm not bothering to ask about this Wally. I don't give a shit about her old schoolgirl crushes. She's with a man now.

"I need to go out."

"Am I coming?"

"No. You'll stay here."

She pauses for a moment. "And if I don't want to?"

"I'm not giving you the option.

Her jaw clenches in a stubborn fit, but I can tell she doesn't want to leave the big, comfy bed either.

"You won't let me leave?" she says.

I give her a hard look. "I'm fucking serious."

"Why?" She frowns.

I can't tell her the truth. That would put her in actual danger. It would terrify her. So I just say, "It's for your safety."

"Well, I can't get out. There are codes."

And she's fucking smart. "Just stay."

Kira clutches the bed sheets. "And what about your safety?" Then her frown deepens. "Where are you going, anyway?"

I go to my side of the bed and take the gun out from under the pillow, double-checking to make sure it's loaded, even though I know it is. Cracking my neck, I slip it into my holster under my jacket.

"I'm going to take care of some business."

And then I leave, making sure I punch in the code on the inside of the elevator as I go.

21

KIRA

Goddamn it. I'm a prisoner in Ilya's castle in the sky.

And there's nothing I can do about it.

I grab a quick shower, and when I go to raid his closet, I stare with an open mouth at what's inside. Dresses and shoes. Not for him, obviously, but for me.

He must have been up very early to have them delivered because they weren't here last night when I snooped.

Flipping through the rack, I find that he's kept the dress he made me change out of. I throw it on, along with some delicate silk panties, and shove my feet into the cute flats.

"Might as well make the most of this," I shrug to myself.

With that, I turn and hurry through to the computer.

I hold my breath as I type in the password, hoping like hell he didn't change it.

But I get in.

"Yes!"

Excitement courses fast through my veins. As I go through file after file, that excitement grows. It's all in Russian, but that's not a problem. Thankfully, we spoke Russian at home, and I can read Cyrillic.

But…

"Holy shit. It's the motherlode."

I'm not being dramatic.

This is gold. This is a career moment. I could have it all. Bring people down.

It's a Watergate moment.

"Oh, fuck…" I open another file. "Holy fuck."

There are records of corrupt dealings, dirt on politicians here, dealings with top officials in Russia, and…

I swallow hard. My vision wavers.

Records of Ilya sabotaging a Bratva back in Russia.

"Why would he…?"

I stop myself. Why wouldn't he?

He's not a good guy. But maybe he's not entirely bad. Gray. Because what kind of dirtbag criminal would try to sabotage an entire country's Bratva?

Big, powerful groups like that make members who play by the rules extremely rich. Sabotage would mean danger. It would put him at risk of losing everything.

"Who are you, Ilya?" I whisper.

Complex —that's a word for him. Complex. And unexpected.

I keep going through it all, imagining stories with my name emblazoned on them because to let myself probe down into the unease I'm feeling is dangerous.

And the imagined stories are just that—imagined.

Right now, I'm not betraying him, if you don't count breaking into his computer, which—

A familiar name pops up in the files that chases all other thoughts away.

"Mikhail Zhirkov."

My brother.

Heart pounding, I dig deeper.

It's a host of reports and files, and—

"Oh God. No..."

I knew he went there with dreams of becoming Bratva and died, but...

"He became a Bratva leader? My Wally?"

Then my throat closes up because the file I just opened is all about his demise.

My hands tremble on the keyboard.

Mikhail was shot and disappeared... Code for killed. Anyone knows that. Plus—

My phone rings and vibrates.

I jump; it's the special ringtone. And... hell, I forgot Mr. Calhoun was expecting a scoop.

Luck or fate has just handed me one, but...

My finger hovers over the answer button. Do I tell him about everything I just found? It's like a holy grail for the paper, but it would also mean deciding to betray Ilya, right here and now. Fuck... I don't know.

I take a breath and hit answer. "Mr. Calhoun—"

"I've been waiting for your call, Miss *Zhirkov*," he says. I wince at my name. The implication is clear. I look at the time on the computer.

Wait a minute...

Waiting? He can't have been; it's still so early. But I keep that to myself.

"Mr. Cal—"

"Remember how I told you Tate had something?" he asks, cutting me off. I clench a hand on the desk as I hold the phone against my ear.

"Yes, Sir, but—"

"What he's got now is even better. Blow your damn head off good. Pulitzer good. And you?" he asks.

I drag in a breath. "I've got something better."

I cross my fingers.

"You don't know what Tate has," he says with a derisive

snort.

"Doesn't matter." I flex and unflex my hand, desperately trying to stay calm. "What I've got is even better."

He wants me to tell him, and even if I decide to do this, take all this information I've uncovered and use it, I'm not telling him anything until I've got an article. Because from where I'm sitting, the ball's in my court. If I tell him, he just might pack up the game, take that ball, and give it to Tate.

I won't let that happen.

"Is that so?" he prods.

"It is, and when I have it all in order, you'll be the first to see it, Mr. Calhoun."

There's a long, sharp silence.

"Well," he finally says. "I'll believe that when I see it. And Kira? If you don't come to me with that something better..." He trails off, and I close my fist, nails biting into my palm. "I'll replace you with Tate. The competition will be over. And I just might have you blackballed for wasting my time."

It's like everything implodes in that moment—hopes, dreams, a future beyond slinging food or pouring drinks. I fucking hate he's got that kind of power.

Maybe he's bluffing, maybe this is part of his process, but I get the feeling that he wants glory, and he's using me and Tate against each other to get it.

Even if that's the case, it doesn't change anything.

He has the power to kill my career.

"No, Sir," I say as meekly as I can, "I'd never do that. My job's my life."

"Really?" His sarcasm cuts through me.

"I'm not wasting your time, Mr. Calhoun. In fact, I just uncovered the motherlode of evidence. On everyone."

"Like I said, I'll believe it when I see it."

I lick my suddenly dry lips. "It'll take me a few days to verify certain aspects and make sure everything's covered. When we blow this open, we want to make sure it's documented."

He grunts. "You've got until the end of the week to hand me something."

He hangs up, and I instantly feel sick, sagging down in the seat.

I hate what I just did. Or said I'd do. In the end, all I really did was buy time for me to work out what the hell I'm going to do next.

For now, I keep reading. There's so much information here that I could bring down more than just the Bratva. There are—

My phone buzzes, and I look down. A text from Tate.

Just heard you found the 'motherlode' according to Calhoun. Of what? Crap?

With a scowl, I text back. ***Maybe you just want what I have.***

I've got great information, he shoots back.

Asshole. ***If your info is so good, why are you texting me?***

You know, he texts, ***if we work together, we could make this into something even bigger. All the pieces. The entire story.***

No way.

But he responds. ***Whatever you've got, I can help tie it all together with what I've found.***

I stare at the phone. Shit. Let's say I think he actually has something real, something I could use, and he's not just trying to find out what I have, I don't think I want to share. And hell, I don't even know if I *want* to tie it together.

Not until I figure out more about Ilya and my brother... and my true feelings about it all.

My true feelings about Ilya.

I definitely don't think I can trust Tate, but he's nothing compared to the men I've been dealing with lately. I can handle him. Right?

So Kira, want to meet?

I take a breath. Fuck it.

Sure.

Sure is what I'm not, but I figure at the very least I can take what he has and destroy it if I decide to protect Ilya...

That's when it hits me.

I'm locked in.

"Okay, genius. How are you getting out of this penthouse suite?"

Shit. I think I've got an idea...

22

ILYA

My fucking frustration levels are not insignificant.

All morning we've been out and about, searching all the expected hovels and dives and fancy fucking places, along with the unexpected ones. Places known to hide or be sympathetic to the Russian Bratva.

Some players are believers in the mother country, others opportunists for the highest amount to be made.

But there's no sign of him.

No whispers of the assassin or anyone new in town.

Worse, I reached out to contacts back in Russia, not just looking for news on the Butcher, but anything that might give me a hint as to what, exactly, the Russian Bratva know.

No one's hiding anyone, apparently.

And everyone I reach out to here and in Russia for any information on the Bratva?

Not available.

I can't get hold of anyone.

"Fuck," I say, looking at Semyon. "Any luck?"

He shakes his head. "No.

"Let's start at the beginning."

We head to the bunker, and he's frowning. I get it. It looks like it did yesterday. Empty.

He looks around. "We're here... why?"

"Why not? Always return to the scene of the crime."

"Ilya..."

I sigh. "Maybe there was something we missed."

"Like what?"

"Not invisible furniture..." I trail off. Maybe that's what we're looking for. Something that seems invisible. "Or something like that. Hidden but in plain sight. There's got to be a way they got in and out other than just the cars."

We start searching, both upstairs and down. The overheads don't cast nuanced light, and they're not harsh enough to show tiny imperfections.

So, in the basement of the bunker, I get down on my hands and knees, feeling the floor.

And that's where I find it. A spongy spot that looks like the rest of the black floor, but it isn't. It covers something beneath...

A fucking handle, hidden in plain sight.

"Got it. A hatch."

It's a hidden, modified trapdoor.

Semyon gets on his haunches and runs his hand over it. "If they have this, why did they even need all those cars? They could have gotten the weapons out this way."

"Contrary to rumor, I'm not their keeper or some kind of mind reader, so we'll have to find out the other way." I look at him. "By going down there. Back me up while I open it."

He stands with his gun pointed as I pull it open, easing it back.

I don't have a flashlight, but Semyon does, and I see it in his hand, flicking it on as I rise.

We don't need it. There's light coming up.

"I don't like this," he mutters when nothing happens.

Looking at him, I grin. "It's probably a trap, that's why."

My comment earns a glance. “You don’t do reckless.”

I’m halfway down the ladder, my gun in my hand as I say, “No time like the present.”

But really, there’s no other choice but to go down into what’s almost certainly a trap. There are times a stupid risk is what it takes to get answers. This is one of them.

I hit the ground silently, followed by Semyon. I glance at him, and he nods, knowing silence is the name of the game.

We look around and edge forward toward the bend in the tunnel.

The moment we turn, six men aim weapons at us.

I shoot two, Semyon another, and we both rip the guns from two close to us. I use my man as a struggling shield as I turn the weapon on the sixth guy who’s trying to hightail it down the tunnel. Then I take out the one I have, just as Semyon shoots his.

We let the bodies fall.

“That wasn’t so bad,” I mutter, as Semyon starts collecting weapons and searching the dead for anything that might be useful.

“I don’t think it’s over yet,” he replies.

He’s not wrong.

Someone else is here.

I look down the tunnel toward another bend, and there, a shadow flickers.

It’s familiar, the shape.

I’ve seen it too many times on video. I recognize it instantly. He’s here.

Evgeni. The Butcher.

He steps out.

There’s a moment that we’re face to face.

Gazes locked.

He’s dead and cold.

Mine is colder.

The Butcher sighs, disappearing around that corner.

Fuck that. I break into a run, my weapon ready as I approach that bend.

Suddenly, Evgeni rounds the corner, shooting.

"Shit."

I jump aside as a bullet narrowly misses my head, but he shoots again, aiming for the chest. I veer fast. It hits.

I stagger, and I know it was a clean shot to the shoulder. Bastard missed his target. I raise my gun and shoot until the clip's empty, dropping to make myself less of a target.

"Fucking bastard," I curse under my breath.

I reload, and as I do, I hear Evgeni yell out to me.

"Ilya, you ruin everything!"

"Come out and say that to my face." I get up and hit the wall, creeping along, gun at the ready. "Fucking coward."

"I shouldn't even be here. This is a fucking grunt's job," he says. "I should be out carving people up. So just fucking die already."

He steps out and shoots again, letting bullets spray in every direction. He doesn't know where I am—but that's almost more dangerous.

Shit.

He misses, and I don't give him a chance to reload. Gritting my teeth, I come at him, aiming and pulling the trigger.

Another bullet whizzes by me, but from behind. Semyon's shooting too. Together we approach that corner, shooting to kill anything and everything. But when we round it... nothing. Empty.

There's another turn ahead and stronger light. We make our way, pressing against the closest wall to the turn so it's harder for him to hit us if he tries to shoot.

But when we get there, we're met with the same thing.

Nothing.

We exchange a look.

"Stay," Semyon whispers. "I'll go."

Shaking my head, I ignore the pain and step forward, gun out, ready for the Butcher. But when I turn the next corner, he's gone.

The tunnel ends. There's only a door, and it's locked. I start to kick it down.

Semyon reaches for me, and I shake him off. "He's gone, Ilya."

"There's a chance I can still get him."

"Ilya, he set a trap. We foiled it. He's gone. Run away to try again another day."

I'm not paying heed to his damn words. I kick the door open, and it hangs on a hinge, splintered. There's a staircase going up. Ignoring the shout from Semyon, I take the stairs.

"Fuck! Fuck!"

He's not there.

The stairs take me to another door, this one steel. It's open, and when I burst through it, I'm on the street.

No one's there. Not one soul.

"Fuck."

Behind me, down below, comes a quick burst of gunfire. Then I hear Semyon's voice, lifting in triumph.

Someone must not have been dead yet.

Though, knowing Semyon and his meticulous ways, the moment I took off, he'd returned to make sure they were all very much dead.

I trudge back, each step hurting my shoulder like I'm being punched with a burning spear. I meet Semyon halfway.

"Trap or not," I say to him as we pass the bodies on our way to the ground floor, "too many people."

"Not enough for a real fight," he says.

I slide him a look. "Next time, I'll order you in an army and give you a pointed stick."

"A fairer fight."

I'd laugh, but I suspect it'll hurt. "They must have had something in here, in the tunnel."

"Whatever it was, they took it."

I nod and put my hand on the wall, needing to breathe. I don't miss the concern on Semyon's face.

"I've had worse," I assure him.

"There's blood, Ilya."

"Anatomy 101. Live bodies bleed when shot."

"You're wounded."

"I know. And I'm beginning to question your intelligence," I say, snapping because it hurts like a fucking bitch.

He starts muttering, and I leave him to it, slapping him away when he tries to look at the wound. I fucking know what a gunshot feels like. This isn't that bad. It just fucking hurts, is all. A stinger.

I let myself collapse to the ground, head against the wall as I take a moment to deal with the pain. Semyon's barking orders into his phone. When he reaches to help me, I wave him away again.

Gritting my teeth, I get back up and head for the exit, Semyon behind me.

"Where are you going?" he asks. "I've got our med—"

"Fuck that. I'm going home."

Because in that moment, there's only one thing that'll fix me, one thing I can think of:

Kira.

23

KIRA

I stare at it, a sense of wonder moving through me.

I found it.

It took me long enough, but I found what I was looking for.

Sometimes, being sent on boring jobs pays off. This is one of them. The job had been a report on corner-cutting in high-rises, where they didn't put a proper way out in case of fire or power outages.

The best places are to code, and even in something as highly secure and modified as Ilya's place, there's going to be a safety aspect. Though, I'll bet he sees it as an ace up his sleeve—a way to either get out, or get in, if needed when he's compromised.

But I doubt—

There's a sound at the elevator, a hum that comes with the small ding. It's not the main elevator, but the one his man, Semyon, used that one time.

My heart beats hard, loud, blood pounding.

I close the sliding panel and swing the shelving unit back. Then, I ease out of Ilya's giant walk-in pantry and hurry over as the elevator opens.

Ilya stumbles out, Semyon at his side.

"Get out," Ilya snarls at Semyon. "Now."

His head's down, and he's holding his arm weirdly against him. He's dirty, bloody, like he crawled out of an alligator-infested sewer.

Or a fight.

Semyon doesn't seem to take it personally. "Are you—"

Ilya snarls again. "I said—"

"You need a doctor." Semyon could be talking about the weather.

"I need shit."

"Got you, boss." He looks at me, and his eyes are lasers as he says, "call if there's a problem. Ilya knows the number."

Just like that, Semyon disappears back into the elevator. The doors close, and I rush over to Ilya, fear burning fissures into me as I reach him. All plans of getting the thumb drive from my bag, loading it with his secret files, and escaping out the fire door vanish.

I'm shaking as I hold him. He smells like sweat, blood, leather.

Like him.

And he's warm.

He's alive.

Thank God. He's alive.

I blink back tears.

"What happened?" I pull away, and he winces.

"Careful."

"Ilya, tell me what happened."

"Be Florence Nightingale for me. I got shot."

"Oh my God." Panic burns my veins, and I rush for my phone. "Ambulance. We need an ambulance. Fire that man for dumping you here."

He takes my phone. "We can't call. Gun. Shot. And I'm good. Clean shot. I just need help cleaning it."

Damn him, he's looking at me with a vulnerable light in his eyes that says *I just need you.*

"Ilya," I whisper, brushing close up against him, "tell me what to do."

He kisses me. It's tender, naked with a rough edge.

And he sighs, dropping his head against mine.

"Apart," I say, "from kissing."

"You want sex? Because I can, but you might have to—"

"Ilya." I cut him off, heat flooding my face as I ease away from him. "We need to get you clean, treated. You need to rest."

There's guilt nipping at me, guilt that I was... maybe not planning to sell him out, but I wasn't ruling it out either. Guilt I was planning to run. What if he'd come in, right after I'd gone? What if he'd been hurt worse and insisted on coming home instead of getting treatment?

I smooth my hands on either side of his face, the stubble and bones and muscle and flesh of him both soothes and skitters over my senses.

He came back for me.

To see me.

Not check up on me.

But to be with me.

He wanted me in his time of need.

I swallow as a reverence passes through my chest.

He wanted to be with me; I can feel that as surely as I can feel him.

Right now, I'm not going anywhere, except to the bathroom to clean him up. "Florence says get your ass into the bathroom," I say, gently tugging his hand.

"Doesn't sound like her. Sounds more Nurse Ratched."

"No," I say, "I'm trying to actually take care of you."

In the bathroom, I fill the sink with warm water and add some of his soap, and then I help him peel off his shirt. The only sound he makes is a small hiss of breath. Then I start to clean him.

His hard muscles are smooth, the ink mesmerizing. I can't help but wander away from the wound.

Ilya puts his hand on mine and holds it against his heart. "Princess, you aren't going to break me. You can clean the wound."

I lift my head and meet his gaze. "I've never done this before."

"Well, you're a natural. You have an angel's touch," he says. "And I've had more brutal wounds than this."

I can see the scars. I've felt them, but it hasn't registered until now just how many there are, all of them telling a story of his hard and violent life. There are scars from knives and old ones that look like cigarette burns. Also, a few puckered marks on one side have more scar tissue on the other.

And one that's neat and doesn't have an exit, down low.

"I was lucky. It missed major organs, but got lodged. That one..." He takes my hand and runs it over the mark. "I needed a doctor for."

He lets go of my hand and slides his fingers beneath my chin to raise it again. "This one is going to be fine. It just fucking hurts right now. Tomorrow, I'll be better."

"How like a man. Things don't work that way."

"They work how I need them to work, and if they don't, I make do," he says. "He didn't have a powerful gun."

He points me to the cabinet with all the wound cleaning paraphernalia: disinfectant, bandages, and the rest.

I skitter back when he slams a hand into the vanity as I'm applying disinfectant.

But he scoops me back in to where I was, standing between his legs. "I'm good. More, and then the superglue and the butterfly Band-Aids."

I do as I'm told, my heart and nerves leaping around.

"Now the bandage patch."

I rip it open and put one on the front, then I do the same on the back.

Then I take off his shoes and his pants.

"If I'd known you'd be doing this, I'd have asked for a light graze instead."

"A light what?" I help him out of his trousers, and then he's just in his boxers. Wrapping an arm around his good side, I walk with him to his room. He eases into bed.

"Graze. Wound. You know, instead of getting shot." He goes to arrange pillows and grimaces. I do it for him.

"You need something for the pain."

"I barely feel it."

Sticking my fists on my hips, I narrow my eyes. "Don't lie."

He closes his eyes. "I can't. I need to work. I just wanted to see you, rest a little, and then—"

"Stop."

I don't care if he means he'll go out or stay in and work; he needs to recuperate. Though, I'm sure a man like him, as tough and strong as he is, can force himself to keep going, he needs someone to force him to rest.

"Just take something."

He's silent for a long time, those dark eyes spitting fire as he takes me in, almost like he can sniff out what I've been doing. But then he nods to the bathroom. "I have pain meds. In behind the third medicine cabinet. Just Tylenol."

I inhale sharply. "You need more than that."

"I have a weak codeine prescription. One of those."

Turning, I go in. But I don't see any pills in that mirrored medicine cabinet. Then I spot something, a small indent. I push it, and it opens to a secret cabinet with medicine. There's a pharmacy in here. A tiny one, but there are more pills and hardcore wound management kits than I've seen in one place —at least, outside a pharmacy.

I reach for the one he mentioned and hesitate when I see a much stronger bottle of pain meds, ones that pretty much knock you out.

Thing is, I do feel bad for snooping, lying, the rest. But I need to escape. It's no life being under lock and key. Not that I think he's planning on keeping me here forever, but I need to see Tate like we arranged, even if it is just so I can learn what he has.

Because what if the information he's got could hurt Ilya?

I need to get out and stop Tate.

For Ilya.

I refuse to think about what that means. Refuse to contemplate what it says about my feelings toward the man I just helped clean and mend.

I'm going to stop Tate.

I just don't know how I can do that if I'm stuck here. Ilya won't let me run off, not even injured like he is.

Unless I do something drastic...

I close my hand around the heavy-duty pills and take two out. Then I pick up the weaker bottle of meds, and get him a bottle of water from his fridge. I go back to the bedroom and sit next to him.

"Open wide."

"I'm not a child," he says.

I pop the pills in while he's talking. "Drink, and no, you're not. You're being a baby."

"Fine." He swallows the pills with the water, and then he looks at me. "Lay with me?"

"Fine."

I snuggle into his arms, careful of the wound as I stroke his chest until his breathing evens out. He'll know I've gone if I go through the fire door. The elevator's ideal. But to get out, I'd need a passcode.

What if it's the same as his computer? For a tech-savvy guy, the password's weak on the computer, which means not many people come up here. And I'm wondering if he has the same code for the main elevator. The other? I doubt it. That's probably both key and keypad operated. Others use that. Others he trusts. So that one's going to be complicated. But the main elevator?

Heart racing, I lay with him a few minutes more.

"Ilya?"

No answer. I ease away from him.

He's asleep.

And he looks like the boy I fell for as a kid.

It twists my heart. I kiss him, then head for the elevator. I've got nothing to lose and everything to gain going that way. I can say he revealed it during his pill-fueled delirium. But he'll probably still be out when I return.

Crossing my fingers, I grab my shoes and bag and approach the elevator. I punch in the password.

The doors open.

"Finally, some fucking luck..."

With a deep breath, I get inside, put the password in again, and press ground floor.

24

ILYA

I wake with a start and a shoulder full of pain.

But the first word that comes to mind isn't a curse. It's a name.

"Kira?"

She doesn't answer.

"Kira?"

The bed is cold next to me, and I've no fucking idea how long I've been out. I push up out of bed to find her, pulling on a pair of jeans. But the place is quiet. Too quiet. "Kira?" I call out loudly. She might have gone to the sofa, or the study, or the other bedroom that's never been used.

I don't know why. Maybe she was worried she'd hurt me or—

My head's fuzzy, but it clears somewhat as fear starts to creep in, along with anger.

She's not fucking here.

I grip the back of the sofa and think. Where the fuck would she go? How the fuck did she leave?

Oh, fuck, was she taken while I was out of it? "No. That's

ridiculous," I mutter. "How the hell could someone even get in here?"

I don't need to say the answer out loud. I don't want to. But I know. There are ways. There are always ways.

If someone's determined enough, skilled enough, or is backed by enough money...

Anything's possible.

The panic is crawling now, with little claws that prick the skin. I stumble around, looking for my phone. Somewhere in the distance, I'm aware of the sharp pull of pain from my shoulder, but I ignore it. That doesn't matter.

Only Kira does.

That fucking girl with the big piercing blue eyes and long black hair. The girl with the inquisitive streak that's miles deep and long. The sweet girl who harbors secrets and piques my interest on all levels. She matters.

And she's not fucking here.

"Kira!" I shout now, the panic in my throat making it feel raw and bleeding.

The panic is everywhere, devouring common sense, my foundation of ice, steel, and rock. The place where emotions don't exist.

My panic for her overwhelms everything else.

Because I know that no one's breaking in to take her and leave me breathing.

Anyone who has an inkling about me, whether friend or foe, knows if there's someone else here then I care. And me caring means I won't stop, even if I have to turn the world to ruin to get her back.

If I can't?

I'll burn it to ashes and take out every fucker involved. No one and nothing will be safe.

Anyone who knows me knows that.

They'd never dare leave me alive.

But though I know all that, the panic is overwhelming in its intensity.

"Where the fuck is my phone?"

Shit, I need it. I go into the bathroom, and there, folded, are my pants, ruined shirt, and, on top, my phone.

I snatch it up.

The bars are low, and it's still locked.

Shit... my fucking hand's shaking, and everything in my head except for the thought of her and the rising panic is edged with narcotic fuzz.

I find her number and call, but it goes to voicemail.

"You better have been fucking kidnapped," I growl.

I hang up and take a breath, heart beating about a thousand times a second. A couple drops of codeine shouldn't have knocked me out, and it definitely shouldn't make me feel like this.

With shaking hands, I run the cold water and splash my face, ignoring the pull and burn of pain from my wound. It'll heal. Clean shot.

The Butcher isn't a great marksman, which makes him dangerous with a gun because of wild-flying bullets. It also makes him way less dangerous, because the gun he had could kill, yes, in the right hands, but if it's a wing shot like mine, the wound's small.

"Kira?" I say the moment it beeps to leave a message. "You were gone when I woke. You're still gone. Shit. Let me know you're okay."

I'm not good with emotions, not the soft ones, the underbelly. But for the first fucking time since I can remember, I'm scared.

Not for me.

For her.

I go into my room and ease into a button-down shirt, then

head to my computers. I don't log into the servers. I want to access the cameras I have on the doors and in the elevators.

"Fucking little sneak." Some tension seeps out of me, along with that panic and fear.

Not all the fear, but some.

Kira wasn't kidnapped.

She somehow worked out the code—perhaps saw me? Maybe I told her last night and don't remember. Because I sure as shit don't remember much past swallowing those pills and having her warm, soft, sweet-smelling body on me. If I was that out of it, or fuck, she'd grabbed the wrong pills, I could have sung the Russian national anthem backward for all I know.

I frown and go to my room where she left the pills. It's a prescription I've used for bad pain, for when I need to push through, but I've never used this one.

I pop the top and count.

They're all there.

With my heart beating a low, slow dirge, I walk over to the secret cabinet. I keep it utterly organized, but things are pushed around. I expect that, I sent her to get me something from there. Something specific.

But right at the front is a pill dispenser, the bright, clear orange showing me how many are in there.

I don't need to count.

Those were from a very bad injury, one needing surgery. I'd been told to take them until they were done and get another prescription. I didn't. Pills aren't my thing, and I don't like the fog and the way these can knock you out.

I'd taken half, one at a time instead of two. Which left six in there.

There are four.

"Why the fuck did you give me these, Kira?" I ask the bottle, closing my hand around it to take it with me.

I put it on the kitchen island, but they're as talkative as the whiskey.

The answer eludes me. Just like her leaving here on her own and voluntarily.

She didn't look scared, just trying to go quickly and quietly. The only glances were toward my room.

If she was scared of anyone, it was me. Who she'd drugged the fuck up.

I want to know why.

I want to know where the fuck she went.

There must be an explanation. One that doesn't make me as angry as I already am.

It's not safe for her out there. So I need to gather myself, formulate a plan.

I need to find her.

Before someone else does and figures out what she means.

To me.

25

KIRA

In my head, a clock ticks. I've been away too long already, and I haven't even made it to meet Tate yet.

I check my phone. There's still time to finish this and meet him. But it's not him I'm worried about. It's Ilya.

He's awake and left two messages already. He sounds pissed off.

Especially in his first message. The second's more apologetic, but I hear that undercurrent. Along with something else.

It almost sounds like... worry.

For me.

That only spurs me on in my task at hand. I know this is the right decision.

I'm back at my apartment. The job seems to never end.

There's an old fireplace I use in the dead of winter, so I stoke it up and pile papers that I can't hide and don't need; papers that have all the damning evidence about me on them. Fake aliases. Connections to my brother and his dirty dealings. Things I'd rather forget.

I've got a safe deposit box, one that I inherited from my father. I make a small pile to take to the bank: passport, the drive, all the important paperwork that enables me to get paid under the name Arendelle. That stuff is forged, but I used a portion of my meager inheritance on it. The rest? It's still meager, but tied up until I'm thirty because my father believed in long-term savings and interest.

In that pile, I add the evidence, like my press pass, proof that I work for the paper.

There's a lot of that stuff, and it takes me longer to sort through what to keep, what to hide, and what to burn.

I know Ilya has my address. His driver's dropped me here before. He'll come looking eventually.

The back of my neck burns. What it—

"Stop it," I whisper, double and triple-checking. "It's not just about protecting what you do from him..." Because I don't know what he'll do if he finds out I work for a paper. Ilya will realize I'm investigating him.

I take a breath.

"I also need to protect any connection I have to him from Tate."

That means hiding all evidence I've already collated in the safe deposit box—evidence that could get Ilya in trouble—in case Tate decides to snoop around here.

I wouldn't put anything past him.

My phone starts to buzz.

Where RU?

God damn Tate. There's no way he's got information. He's probably hoping to steal mine. I go through my little apartments, checking and rechecking, and then I stand over the fireplace, making sure everything's gone as the flames burn down, now without fuel.

Not a scrap of paperwork remains. Everything else is in a bag to take to the bank, which I'm going to do now.

I decide to let Tate stew a little, considering I'm not meant to be there yet. But it's also so Tate to push and grow impatient.

He comes from money, which means he probably buys off a lot of people or pays for information. But it doesn't mean he's not hungry...

Once I do a final sweep, I lock up and head to the bank. I breathe a sigh of relief once everything's locked away safely. Even being in there brings my losses rushing back.

I didn't open the trinkets and photos and little things my father put in there. I didn't look at the photos of my brother or my mother. Or my parents' wedding album.

I simply put the things in and had the box locked; now it's—

My phone buzzes. Tate. Again.

???

Annoyance spreads through my veins, and I think about just texting back that I changed my mind. Because I know the lack of calls or texts from Ilya means something. He's not going to be sitting at home waiting.

His injury flashes into my head, and I gulp down the bitter taste of guilt from leaving him like I did.

My phone buzzes again.

Kira?

The urge to say no is strong. But then again, even if Tate's really after everything I've got, and if he really has practically nothing, I need to find out.

And so, I finally text him back.

Give me 10.

It takes me five minutes to get to the small shop. It's a pawn shop, closed down and dusty. My stomach flips and twists as my senses start to pulse warnings.

The door's open, and in through the back are voices. One American, the other heavily accented.

I start to back away when Tate suddenly bursts out, his face marred by a bright smile that's edged with something fevered and strange.

"Finally! Come on. This way. I have to introduce you to someone."

"My boyfriend's waiting in the car outside," I bluff,

He frowns at me. "You brought someone? Never mind, call him and tell him to come back later—"

"He won't do that."

"Well," Tate says, his smile bright but tight now, "he can wait. You'll see why we should work together. This way."

We both stand there until Tate comes up and hustles me, a hand firm on my back as we go.

For Ilya, I think. I'll find out what Tate has and then get out of there. I know there's someone else, but most informants want money. And they're scared. I don't have money, but I'm too deep in to back out now. I'll just say my boyfriend can pay.

That way, I can steal the informant, and if he has something, Ilya can handle him.

I take a breath.

I'm getting ahead of myself.

We step into the back of the abandoned shop, and for a moment, I don't see anyone.

"I figure," says Tate, "you hand over to me what you have on the Bratva, on Ilya, and I'll share my informant with you. Yuri, meet—"

"Ilya Rykov's little whore." He steps from the shadows.

No one needs to tell me anything about this thug. I've already got him figured out. He's Russian, big, his nose broken more than once. Clearly Bratva... or someone trying to get away from them.

I take a step back, but Tate's in the doorway.

"My source, Kira, is a former mobster turned—" He casts the man a look and shifts back a little, and I know he was going to say snitch, but he doesn't. "Turned informant."

The other man, Yuri, growls.

"For the greater good, against corruption and threats from

your boyfriend—who obviously isn't here. Because from what I've learned, Rykov's not the type to let his little girl go into danger."

"Is this danger?" I ask, knowing full well it is.

"This Chicago Bratva is rotten," Yuri says. "At that core is Ilya, who must, along with his evil compatriots, be wiped out."

I lift my chin and look up. "Of which you were one?"

"I did not know." The menace coils under his words like smoke. "If they were to find out I gave some information, they'd torture me. Kill me. I was going to disappear, but someone convinced me you might be the key I was looking for."

"Me." I throw a look at Tate. "What is this?"

Tate just looks past me. "Give me your bag."

"No—"

Before I can stop them, Yuri snatches it and throws it to Tate, who starts digging into it, ultimately spilling its contents. "I know you put things on a drive. Where is it."

"Leave my shit alone."

Yuri back-hands me so hard, a dull ringing pain spreads through my head as I hit the ground. The hot, salty taste of coppery blood fills my mouth. "Give it to him."

"I don't have anything." I think fast. "I lied to Calhoun."

"She knows things. Protecting her man. Whore." Yuri spits. Stepping forward, he kicks me, hard, making me curl up as the urge to throw up mingles with the pain. "I've been told, slut, that you're fucking Ilya. Girlfriend? Mistress? What do they say these days for free prostitution? Friend with benefits? It doesn't matter. I can use you to destroy Ilya."

"He doesn't care about me. I barely know him," I say as the man grabs me by the hair and flings me into a wall.

"It is Ilya. He's fucking you. He cares enough to keep his warm dick hole in one piece. Probably tight? I will make it loose. Maybe start there. Make it so, if you live, no man will want you again."

I stare at him, fear searing through my skin. Then I make myself look at Tate. "You can't..."

But he can. He's trying to get into my phone, and when he can't, he throws it. Then he takes out a penknife and rips apart my bag to see if I've got anything hidden in there.

He glances at me. "Talk. It'll be easier, Kira."

"No."

Yuri runs a hand over my breast, then he grabs a nipple and twists so violently, so hard I scream. He lets go and slides a hand softly over my belly. "Talk, or it will be bad."

I keep my mouth shut.

"I'm highly skilled in torture. Your friend here said I don't need my tools, but..." He gestures to a table with gleaming silver instruments on it. "I brought them, anyway."

He smiles.

If I wasn't truly scared before, that smile seals the deal. It's utterly terrifying in its lack of humanity.

But I'm not going to talk. Say the wrong thing, and it could mean the end of Ilya. And I can't. I won't.

Yuri punches me again, lower, just above the pelvis, and then he twists a ring on his finger and punches me in the face.

It takes everything I have to stay conscious as the black dots of mercy spread, threatening to take me away from the spreading pain that's both dull and sharp and everywhere all at once.

"You think it's smart to stay quiet, but it's not. It just prolongs this. You'll talk. Eventually. And you'll tell me everything I need to know. Every. Thing."

Tate's eyes dart to me, and I take half a step before Yuri shoves me into the wall.

"Please, Tate," I whisper. "Stop this. I know you can."

Blood bubbles, and it hurts to talk from where he cut my lip. There's blood dripping from above my eye, but I'm too scared to wipe it away. Yuri's gaze is on me.

"You know what," Tate says, "I'm gonna leave you to this, Kira. I honestly don't have the stomach to watch something like this. So yeah, I'm going to go."

He heads to the door, then stops, and for a brief moment, I think he's going to come back in and get me out of this mess.

But Tate doesn't even look at me. "Just make sure to get all the good stuff out of Kira and relay it to me so I can help you destroy Ilya in the papers."

He leaves.

I'm alone now with Yuri, and he points at me. "Stay the fuck there. Or it'll be even worse."

He turns. He's a big guy, growing bigger by the second as my fear intensifies. But I force myself to stay calm.

My brother and Ilya protected me from what they did when I was a kid, but I saw things. And my father... he made me hide when big men came and beat him, threatened him if he didn't give up money to the Bratva. If he didn't join.

He never did. My father was adamant. Give them a dime, and they own you. Maybe that had a part to play in Wally going off to Russia. Maybe it was greed. Back then, the Bratva here was riddled with corruption. Too many factions.

I take a breath.

Point is, I'm not a wilting anything. And in the past few weeks, I've learned some tricks.

Even if it's from the time Ilya threw me over his shoulder, and I bit and scratched. Or watching him kill. I've been hardened.

I look at Yuri, who's dragged a heavy wooden chair over to the middle of the room.

I don't think about the chair and what he can do to me on it. I don't think about the instruments of torture.

What I do is push myself to look at him without emotion.

Yuri's big and strong, but maybe not as strong as he once was. He used one hand on me. I observe as he shifts things about, again with his left hand. His right only coming up to do light things.

Did he injure it in the past?

A mobster's life isn't exactly daisies. It's thorns and landmines. He's not young. Maybe pushing sixty.

And he's got a limp.

I'm smaller, but I'm not weak.

He's not going to expect me to do anything. But I need to act before he touches those tools.

He turns to grab a roll of plastic and a bucket that sloshes.

I run at him and launch myself at his back, clinging and biting at his ear like I want to rip it off.

I know enough about street fighting to understand that small can be an advantage. In a situation like this, I'm a fucking limpet with fangs and claws. I dig in, drawing blood.

It turns my stomach, but I don't let go as he tries to throw me off.

He slams me into the wall, battering my much smaller body against the hard plaster until I fall. I wipe the blood and crawl out of the way, turning and using my leg to try and swipe his.

"Bitch."

I connect with his injured leg, and he totters, howling. Without wasting any more time, I scramble to my feet.

Stiffening two fingers, I poke him in the eyes, using my other hand to grab and hold him as I bring my knee up hard, clocking him in the balls.

He grabs me by the throat, squeezing with his left hand. Metal clinks. Something sharp slices into me, and he slams me face first into the wall.

I kick out, and he grabs my foot, twisting it. I don't fight it. I go with the twist, trying to bring him down.

He gets his gun, and I roll out of the way and jump up, punching it away as I knee him three more times in the balls.

It's the only advantage I have, so I'm damn well going to take advantage of it.

This time, his howl is inhuman. He collapses to the ground, rolling.

"Finally," I huff, grabbing the gun.

Scrounging the floor, I quickly pick up my keys, wallet, and phone, then stagger out of there.

I wipe the blood dripping from my head. My side throbs. Everything aches. Running is hard because pain lances every time I put pressure on my ankle.

I'm in bad shape.

A wave of black comes over me, and I fall.

It takes me way too long to get up. My vision wavers when I do. The pavement outside the shop slowly becomes wet and red with blood. Mine.

Back inside, I hear screaming.

I need to get away.

I need medical help.

If I'm going to survive, there's only one person I can go to.

26

ILYA

What the fuck is going on?

There aren't any answers, just the smell of smoke and a cool fireplace. Cool, but not cold.

I should be home, resting. Which is why I didn't tell anyone I was going out hunting for fucking Kira. And the Butcher.

Her place is a fucking mess, and the door was jimmied. By an amateur, so I'm counting Bratva out.

We'll do it with finesse or kick the fucking door in.

Amateurs don't last in our ranks. Even rogue elements or the disgraced won't hire less than stellar people. I know. I'm one of the disgraced. A rogue.

This isn't the work of the Butcher, either.

But there's not one document or photo or anything to give me a hint of where Kira is or who she's pretending to be. Or even what she fucking does.

Someone has smashed the shit out of her computer.

Either her or someone else.

But, I think, a smart girl like Kira wouldn't keep anything incriminating on a computer. She'd have a hard drive or use a protected cloud.

That's the least of my worries.

I leave. Running around is fruitless right now, and I keep my phone at the ready. I'm itching to call her again, but I don't.

If someone has her, I'd rather my name doesn't pop up. If she's up to something, my call might ruin it. And maybe... shit... maybe she doesn't want to talk until she's ready.

She gets a little time. A little.

And only because distance might be good until I find out more about why the Butcher's here.

I start easing into haunts I know, talking to different people. Most don't know anything, but one underground source takes me into his back room. A woman's waiting there. The man who led me in puts some homemade vodka, black bread, and rendered pork belly on the table. The woman sits across from me.

"Drink?"

"Am I Russian?" she says. No English is spoken here, and I wasn't introduced, so I don't ask her name.

I pour and smear some of the rillettes-like pork on the bread and eat. I'm not hungry but, I need fuel. I down my drink, as she does. Then she pours a second and prepares some bread.

"I didn't expect Ilya Rykov to be so handsome," she says.

She's blonde, beautiful. In another life, I might have taken a different approach. But my interest is focused on Kira.

"I didn't expect my press agent to downplay my looks."

She doesn't crack a smile. "What do you want to know?"

"Butcher."

She doesn't flinch, though I see the flare in her eyes. "I keep an ear to the ground. What I know is this: you're being hunted. And those hunting you are getting ready for war... if need be."

"They have weapons?"

She pauses. She knows what I'm talking about.

To my relief, she doesn't play games. She just refills our glasses, and we drink. Then we have bread and pork.

"First, I don't know anything else. There are rumors. Faint. Gossip more than anything."

"What do the rumors say?"

"They mention a place."

I nod. "What do you need for that information?"

This time, the corner of her mouth shadows in a smile. She reaches into her pocket and slides a photo over to me.

"Him."

I pocket the photo. "Talk."

She does.

The spot she told me about is a holding place for moving stolen goods on the outskirts of the docks.

I pull my gun, even though no one's around. I can't help thinking maybe it's all connected. Kira being missing, this fucker hunting for me, the weapons.

There's no one around, and as I creep up, I find the place empty, except for a few familiar-looking bullet casings on the floor.

"Fuck me."

What I need to do is—

My phone rings, and my heart beats like a crazed, caged animal as I pull it out.

But it's not Kira.

No, it's the Pakhan himself. Andrei Zherdev.

"Pakhan," I say, going formal.

"Really?" He mutters something. Then, "Ilya, I need you to come by for a meeting right away."

I return to my car and open the door, dropping myself in the seat as I stare at the empty warehouse.

Half my mind's trying to work out what's going on, the other half's plotting the demise of Semyon, who must have told him about the fight and me getting shot.

"ASAP, Ilya."

"Can't do that." I rub my eyes. "Busy."

His voice drops. "You don't talk, fucking Semyon won't talk. Rumors are everywhere, and I want fucking answers."

Someone's with him. Because that was almost a fucking whisper. I frown. "Nothing I can't handle, Andrei."

"Not good enough." He snaps the words.

"It's all I have right now. Trust me."

"You really need to come in and explain what's fucking happening at least. Last time I checked, you weren't in charge. Besides…" Andrei pauses. "Someone high up wants to meet with you, says it's urgent."

I scoff. "Higher than you?"

"Yes… in a way." He's very much not pleased. "Get your fucking ass here now."

"From Russia." I say this flatly.

"Ilya… just come—"

"No. They're trying to kill me. I won't fall into another trap."

I hang up.

Hanging up on Andrei is a death sentence. A 'hang-that-fucker-who-dared-such-a-thing-up-to-dry-before-torture' move.

And I'd fucking do it again.

If someone's here from Russia, which is all I can think of, they can wait. They can all wait.

I'll face a firing squad… After I find Kira and make sure she's safe.

If this is a trap and someone's playing Andrei, I'll fucking deal with it.

Kira first.

And then?

I'll set up a trap of my own.

The pain is growing. My shoulder's starting to throb again, but in that dull still-drugged-up way.

I don't have time for that shit. I have to find Kira.

I start at the library because I know it's a place she always loved—Mikhail jokingly called it the free babysitter; you could drop the kid off at opening hours and pick her up at closing, and she'd be engrossed in another book or at one of the computers, or pestering the librarians that knew Kira by name.

But she's not there.

She's also not a kid anymore.

Frustration bubbles up.

But I've got nothing else to go on. All I can do is visit all the places she used to go. The old movie theater is gone, where they'd play Disney movies on weekend mornings—a throwback to the old days of cinema. It was a beautiful building that showcased classics and indie movies, often overrun by kids on weekends.

Of course, now it's some high-end beauty store. Shit, I remember when she'd drive us crazy with Frozen, her movie obsession. Whenever that played, Kira was there. So was Mikhail. I went with them once. It was enough.

Funny. Kira was a likable kid. But she really didn't have friends. I've got the feeling it's the same now. Back then, it might have been her father trying to protect her from people like me. And now? Old habits? A wall? Or I just haven't caught a glimpse of it.

Most women will talk about their lives, their friends, all of that shit. Kira doesn't.

Next, I go to the little park where she used to play. It's a pretty park, with a nice playground and lots of trees around the edges.

We'd take her and watch from a distance, near the skate

park outside the sewer and big drain tunnel entrance where me and Mikhail smoked pot.

We'd dream of a better life; a future in the Bratva.

What did we fucking call the place? Avalon? Arden?

"No... it was Arendelle, like that fucking kingdom from that stupid movie she loved, Frozen," I mumble to myself.

Because little Kira would swan around the playground like it was her kingdom, and the smoke from the joints we smoked blew like hot breath on an icy day.

She didn't even know we smoked pot. Just told us we smelled funny and acted silly.

She was too innocent. Not anymore. It's a blessing and a curse.

I don't want to admit it, but how can I not? I'm fucking out here with a gunshot wound searching for a girl that walked away from me.

Not a girl.

Woman.

And... fuck it. I care for her. Maybe too much.

Scowling, I look around some other places, including their old home. But the building's a new block of apartments now, so I doubt she'd be there.

With a sigh, I go home, exhaustion and the damn drugs fogging my brain. I punch in the code and half expect to see her, but the place is empty, devoid of her presence.

Fuck.

I grab the whiskey and knock back three or four glasses of it, just to add to that fogginess.

Kira... What the actual fuck am I even doing?

I run a hand over my face. I'm lost, and I know it.

Care for her?

Fuck, maybe I even love her.

She consumes me in a way no one's ever done before. Eats

away at armor and curls up. I don't fucking know if Kira ran because someone forced her, is using her, or...

Is she betraying me?

I have to entertain that thought, no matter how ugly it is.

No matter how much the idea hurts.

Because this is all new for me. I don't understand the terrain.

And I'm a smart fucking guy.

But this thing, these feelings?

I'm as dumb as dirt.

Christ, I really think I might love her. I think I fell when I wasn't looking, and now it's not just a matter of keeping a sweet girl alive through the mess that's happening in my life, but the woman I love.

That shakes me down to my soul.

What if I lose her?

What if I tell her I love her and she doesn't love me back?

I pour another glass and down it, then put the glass on a side table as I go to the bedroom, taking the bottle.

Those two options are unacceptable. And if either one happens, I'll burn the world down.

Fuck, I'm so exhausted. The pills are still in my system. With a deep sigh, I put my gun under my pillow and lie on the bed with the bottle, fully clothed. Somehow, I drift off.

... Until the ding of the elevator wakes me.

Immediately, I've got my gun out, and I'm on my feet, swaying as I listen.

Silence.

Then, there's a soft knock at the door.

"Who's here?" I mutter thickly.

I get ready to kill.

27

KIRA

"Jesus."

One word from him, more a breath with voice than speech. But it anchors me, gives me a little strength as I sway at the bedroom door. I don't know why I knocked. My head pounds and everything aches. The mirrored insides of the elevator that I took from the garage showed a fucked-up mess.

I'm that fucked-up mess.

Ilya, though... god, he's so beautiful. I just want to touch him.

I want to go to him.

I don't.

The look on his face is hard, emotionless. Like he's looking at a stranger.

And it hurts.

"Ilya." Talking's hard because my lip hurts and my jaw feels like it's twice the size it usually is. "I... I didn't know where else to go."

Something in his expression changes, and a sort of madness comes to him, along with rage. He stalks up to me. "Who the fuck did this to you?"

My eyes fill with tears, and I shake my head. “Don’t be mad.”

“Goddamn it, Kira. I could fucking kill.” He puts his gun away and strokes his fingers over my face.

It’s so tender and sweet how he touches me. But I know he’s not just being soothing; he’s checking for broken bones, to see how bad the injuries are.

“Tell me who did this to you so I can cut them into pieces.”

Or, I think, get himself killed, and I can’t deal with that. I… I can’t. My feelings for him overwhelm, threatening to drown me.

Right now, I just need him.

But he’s leading me into the bathroom, a tenderness with an undercurrent of violent rage showing with each touch. He sits me down and hands me the whiskey.

“Drink. And tell me what animal hit you, cut you…” He lifts my shirt. “Punched you.” And he traces over the soreness on my stomach.

I look down and see the cut and the blooming purple bruises.

“Who the fuck did this, Kira?” Again, his words are soft, his meaning harsh.

“I don’t know. I went… I had… someone called—”

“Who?”

“A friend.” Calling Tate that leaves a bitter taste in my mouth. “They were in trouble, and I got caught up in it.”

He strokes my hair. “Tell me why I should believe these lies?”

“I…” I give a half sob and take a swig of the whiskey, wincing as it burns my cut lip. I welcome the warmth as it reaches my belly. “Please, Ilya, just be kind.”

“I am being kind. To you.” But he gets up and disappears into the bathroom.

When he returns, he orders me to take off the shirt and

pants I'm wearing. I'm thankful I changed quickly at home. I don't want to think of that pretty dress he got me blood-soaked.

Without another word, Ilya starts to treat my wounds, dealing with the cuts first. He's better at it than me. Quick, like it's second nature. Quick, but thorough.

He rubs arnica cream over the bruises, then eases off my bra and looks long and hard at my breast, where Yuri hurt me.

"Monster," he mutters, rubbing the arnica in there in a sweet massage.

His touch does double duty, burning over the top of Yuri's, and I know that Ilya's fingers and their magic will stay with me into the night.

"That feels better," I whisper, my shoulders sinking.

"Good."

Leaning over, he kisses me between the breasts, then he moves up to my throat and growls softly at the marks there. He kisses over the pain.

When he reaches my mouth, he smells of the arnica on my throat, and he growls again at the cut and kisses the other side of my mouth. "Fucking monster. I'll find out, Kira, and I'll make them pay. It's a promise."

"No—"

"I *will* make them pay." He gets up and goes to his closet, returning with a big T-shirt. It's old and soft and smells like him, and he helps me put it on. Then he reaches under it and eases off my panties. "I'm burning all the clothes you were wearing."

"You have a fireplace?"

He doesn't.

"I'll throw them in the garbage chute." Then Ilya nods to the whiskey. "Drink."

I take another swallow, and he pulls back the covers, motioning for me to get in.

"But I'm not—"

"You're tired; you can barely keep your eyes open. So just try and rest, sleep if you can, and if your head gets worse, call this number."

He opens a drawer and scrawls one down on a piece of paper.

I nod because he's right; I'm tired, and I want to rest. With him by my side.

Wait.

"Where are you going?"

"Out. I need to see my boss… and figure out who did this to you. Then I'll be home. I'll get your book for you."

It's dark, late, when he stumbles into the bedroom. I sit up, sleep vanishing, and turn on the light.

What I see shocks me.

"Oh my God," I gasp. "What happened? Who hurt you? Did your boss try and kill you?"

He's stripping off, bruised, and covered in blood. When he's naked, he goes into the bathroom and turns on the shower, then comes back and picks me up. He winces, but he clearly doesn't care about his injuries—the fresh and fresher ones.

Without talking, he carries me all the way into the shower, where he starts to clean me. No matter how hard I try to get a word out of him, he doesn't speak. His hands move over my breasts, stomach, between my legs. Everywhere. When he's done, he takes the sponge to clean himself, but I take it back.

"Let me."

I soap him up and run the sponge over his broad, tattooed back, down his torso to his ass. When he turns, I start with his cock, getting caught up in sliding my hand up and down it until he stops me.

"Not unless you want me to fuck you right now," he warns. His first words.

"Fine." I swallow.

"But..." He kisses my bruised cheek, "I fucking loved it."

As I clean him, I ask, "What happened? Did your boss—"

"I didn't see Andrei. I was so fucking mad I went out looking for answers, looking for someone to kill, but you gave me the wrong pills, and I'm a little weak, a lot distracted. I only managed to get into a few bar brawls."

"Ilya, you can't..."

"I can. No one's going to stop me. If I want to fight, I will."

I lean my head to his chest as his arm comes around me. "But that's not you. You never went out and jumped into a fight without thinking it through. Mikhail did."

"You followed us more than I knew."

"Everywhere." I half laugh. "I didn't have anything else to do. And... and he was my brother, and... and I liked you."

"I know."

My face burns.

He laughs, the rumble in his chest vibrating through me as the water comes down over us. "I... I'm so embarrassed."

"It was cute."

"You thought I was annoying." I look up at him. He takes the sponge and puts it away.

"Sometimes. But mostly it was cute. Now... you can follow me anywhere."

My heart flip-flops. The thought opens up the warmest possibilities in me, ones I know are pipedreams. Ones I don't have the strength to shut down.

"Come."

Ilya turns off the shower and dries me with a big, fluffy towel before taking care of himself. Then he leads me back into the bedroom and checks all my wounds and bandages, changing out the old for the new. I take the roll of bandages from him, and start to do the same for him.

We take care of each other in silence, and I can't help but think it's like a strange and delicious little ceremony that seals us into our world.

When he takes me to bed, I can't help but almost feel at peace.

At least enough at peace that I can slowly drift off to sleep.

Over the next few days, we hardly leave the penthouse, except for food and the occasional walk. Eventually, Ilya has a meeting he needs to attend. I stay in his place, knowing where the spare guns are and the hidden alternative exit.

I'm so paranoid while he's out that I go to the pantry and find a lock hidden under the shelves and engage that.

Tate doesn't call, neither does Mr. Calhoun. I can't help but wonder if Tate thinks I'm dead. I wouldn't be surprised if he was honest about it all to Mr. Calhoun. Probably would have earned him a pat on the back.

I try and care because this is my dream, my break to be a real reporter and not an intern.

I try, and fail.

Because is it worth it when my job means I have to betray Ilya?

One day, after returning from a meeting, he asks me quietly, "You're jumpy, Kira. Why?"

"You were gone."

Gently, he pulls me into his arms.

"It's safe here."

I hold him because he's the only thing that stands between me and the world. He melts those hard, cold places within me. "I just feel a little..." I search for the word.

"Lost? Vulnerable?"

I nod as he eases me back.

"You're safe. But I didn't think." Ilya strips down to his boxers, tugs off my shirt, and pulls me back into bed. "It's not pleasant, finding out that you're human. A man hurt you."

"I'm fine."

"You're not healed, so we'll stay until you are." He half-smiles, as though he answered a question, like I asked him to stay and not leave.

I put my hand on his chest. "I'm not healed? You were shot."

He kisses my fingers. "And you were almost killed, princess. If you're trying to tell me I can come and go, I know that. I just want to make sure you heal."

Or, I think, a little dazedly, he wants to be with me. But I don't say it. It's enough he's framed it how he has. It's enough he's here and just told me he's not leaving me alone.

He's offering to be my constant pillar as I heal.

Then I look down and back at him.

"Is there a reason I'm naked?" I ask.

He grins. "I like it."

"Of course you do."

"Come," Ilya says, "you rest, I'll lie next to you."

That's how time passes. And bit by bit, I feel better. When he mentions we're low on food, I suggest we go to the supermarket. A few days later, we go for a walk and then have dinner.

Everything's quiet and out of the way when we venture out. I think he's trying to keep me safe, make me feel better.

But what I truly enjoy is staying in. And, as I get better, along with him, we cook —two wounded birds, making one fully functional creature.

Soon, there aren't any more meetings, and I don't ask why. There's little point. Ilya doesn't open up in that way.

Most of the time, we're in bed or on the sofa. We don't have sex, and while I think I could, there's something... romantic... about him waiting. About him wanting me healed.

Something romantic about how he wants to be with me and not just for the sex.

It's heady. And the longer I'm with him, the more I wonder what I'm going to do when this ends.

Compared to when I first turned up, I'm so much better off.

After a light dinner one evening, Ilya says he has a surprise.

"TV?" I ask him.

"Let's get comfortable."

He pats his lap, leaning on the sofa, remote control in hand.

Familiar music envelopes me.

"No... Ilya."

A smile breaks free. It's the Disney theme tune. I sigh and settle in.

I curl up on him, pulling a throw over us as the TV presents us with a slew of Disney movies.

"You like?" he says after Moana ends.

I nod. "I love." And another Disney movie begins.

He's set it up that way, for me. I know it.

I don't know what day it is, and I don't care. I feel better, stronger by the day, and more and more... in like with him.

It might be love, but like is safer.

"You know, under all that machismo, you're kind of... soft."

"Smart. I know the way to your heart." He sounds pleased with himself. "Books on antique weapons and Disney movies. I think Frozen is coming up soon."

I can't speak because I'm worried I might cry.

When Frozen starts, I kiss his chest. "I love this movie."

"I know. You went through a phase where it's all you'd watch. Drove your brother crazy." He starts laughing. "Remember that park?"

"And the movie theater. It's gone now." I sigh. "You and Mikhail smoked near that scary tunnel by the skate park."

Right next to the proper park where I'd play.

"You were so damn scared of that tunnel." He smooths my hair. "We'd go in to be alone and talk."

"Away from me."

"I didn't say that, princess."

I lightly bite his chest. "You didn't have to."

"You still followed us up to it. And once you went in. You were so scared. I think Mikhail was proud. I knew you'd do it. Can't keep an inquisitive girl down."

I turn my face into him to hide my smile. How can I be so happy and sad at the same time? Feel my heart swell with emotion for him, the good and the bad? Though right now, the good's far outweighing the bad.

"We used to call it Arendelle." And he laughs again.

"After the castle in my favorite movie?"

"Hush and watch."

I do.

A few days later, when I'm nearly fully recovered, I put on a dress and sneakers. I can tell it's not exactly a dress he likes, because when he sees me, his lip curls.

"What is that?"

"Clothes."

He's dressed casually, working on his laptop while leaning on the kitchen counter, a hot coffee next to him. "It's a nice color."

"It's black."

The dress is just a loose A-line, something I can move comfortably in, something that barely hints at what's underneath.

He waves a hand. "It's... fine."

"I'm not going around naked or in skin-tight clothes."

"Pity." Ilya sighs, and he closes the computer, his expression intense. "But that reminds me, now that you're better, we should talk."

My stomach lurches. "Ilya, I—"

"Why'd you leave?" he asks before I can come up with anything. "Why'd you give me the strong pills? At first, I thought you made a mistake, but you put the bottle for the weaker ones by the bed. And there weren't that many in the bottle of the strong ones. So... why?"

I suck in a breath and clutch the island. I could lie, and maybe he'd accept that.

Maybe, but he'd know.

He seems to always know when I lie or skirt the truth. He hasn't once asked me about my so-called job, so while he might not know about the journalism, he sure as shit knows I'm no distributor.

So, I make a snap decision. Maybe the most dangerous decision of my life.

I decide to tell him the truth.

"Ilya, I-I'll tell you everything. Just promise not to react until I do?"

He looks at me.

"Talk," he says. "Now."

28

ILYA

I don't know what I expected from Kira, but I'm not sure this is it.

She talks in halts, bursts, hands clenched by her side as her face gets pinched and pink.

The hate for me, the blame for her family's downfall—she's pinned that blame right on me like some kind of fucking medal. But it isn't completely unexpected. I saw it when I first ran into her.

We both bubbled with anger, resentment. Me at her for her being related to fucking Mikhail, who I loved like he was my brother. Her at me for her brother's demise in Russia. And the erroneous blame she lays at my feet for her father's death. I know who did that, and I took them out. A small fry, a zealot for the cause back home.

She thinks her father died of grief. It was of poison. But I don't tell her. Yet.

I'll see how my anger goes at this fucking reporter shit.

The whiskey is there on the island, and I think about drinking it. But for now, I hold off.

A fucking little reporter.

"And you what, Kira? Wanted to sell me out?"

"I owed you nothing," she whispers, not moving. "My family died as if by your damn hands, Ilya. And you work for the people who stole my brother. You wove a story of how good it was, how—" She stops and shakes her head. "I didn't know you."

"So, for the greater good of the world, you were going to use me to bring down the fucking Bratva?"

She doesn't even need to tell me the Bratva tried to hurt her. Though, how she got away is beyond me. Even Kira's going to have a hard time holding out against them.

But against me? She's got no chance.

"Yes..."

Her gaze flickers, and I start to laugh. "No. You wanted to climb the ladder. You were going to sell me out for greed."

"I owed you nothing."

"All this time, even when you drugged me, you were working your angle. I wanted you badly enough that I ignored every single fucking red flag." Now I swipe the bottle.

"No."

I look at her. "No?"

"Ilya, please." She takes a breath, a step toward me. "Listen."

I set the bottle on the edge of the island. "Well?"

"Things changed, and I... my boss was threatening me. He knew our connection. It wasn't just getting fired; it was being blackballed." She doesn't look away, and I'll give her that. "There's another intern. Tate. He said he had information. Wanted to know what I had."

Now I open the fucking bottle and take a long pull. It's that or get my gun, and I don't know who I want to shoot. This Tate? The boss? The fucking assholes who hurt her?

Anyone but her. Because I'm furious. So fucking furious I take another deep swallow.

"You and Tate worked together."

"No, and fucking listen."

She outlines the texts. Tosses me her open phone. Through the cracked screen, I can read those texts from Tate. She tells me how she went home to make sure there was nothing Tate or anyone could use against me.

And then she fucking ignored my calls and went off to meet this guy.

"How did you get the code?"

Now her face flames. "Mickey. Mikhail was Mickey. You alone knew that. And... I put the rest together."

"Clever girl," I snarl. "And if I check my computer properly..." I tap the shell of the one I was using with the bottom of the bottle, "not this, but my other ones, I'll find log-ins when I wasn't there or passed out, won't I? Evidence of you copying shit?" I narrow my eyes. "I have all kinds of security you don't know about on there."

"Ilya."

Her misery almost touches my heart. Almost.

"So, this Tate. Did he do this to you?" I point the bottle at the places where the bruises fade, the cuts heal, and where, under her clothes, that slash from a knife is knitting back together. "Just so I know the amount of pain to inflict."

"He left. He took me to see someone who knows you, to get me to talk."

Not the Butcher. She wouldn't have gotten free from him. "Did you?"

"No. And Tate couldn't find anything on me. If he went to my place—"

"Someone did."

"—then he'd find nothing. I put it all in a safe deposit box."

If I weren't so furious, I'd find it amusing. "Who cut you up? Tell me now."

"Y-Yuri."

"Yuri Naidov? What's that fucker involved for?"

She looks confused, and it pisses me off. Does she even realize who the fuck he is? What's going on? The danger she's bringing the fuck down?

"I don't know—"

"Big, ugly, old. Limp. Bad arm." I did that. Should have done more. Like kill him back when I had the chance.

She nods.

Seems like I will again.

"I'm sorry, I was trying to get a story, and then trying to protect you and—"

"No, you're complicating things." Now I drink more because behind the fury is white-hot fear. For her. And it makes me go ballistic.

I glare. "While we're being honest here, Kira," I snarl, "You put yourself in the line of danger. There's a fucking assassin out there. He's killing people, after torturing them. And he wants me dead. To do so, he inflicts maximum pain. He'll torture and kill you to get to me. To make me suffer."

"But you don't care—"

"I fucking care, Kira. I don't want you dead. Grown men would rather be killed outright than face his torture. He instills fear, rightly so. And he knows I've been trying to bring down the corrupt parts of the Russian Bratva back home. Goddamn it, Kira."

"I..." She comes around and reaches for me, but I stop her with my cold stare. She flinches, but she doesn't back away.

"No. Don't touch me." I stalk over to the elevators and change the password. The computers she can play on. She's already been in, so she knows what's there.

Then I pull on my rarely used Kevlar, my holsters, load up on weapons and bullets, and send Semyon a text.

Kira trails me, keeping a certain distance, like she's unsure what I'm going to do. "Your punishment will have to wait. Until I get back."

"Where are you going?" She swallows.

I check my last gun before putting it in place. "I'm going to kill the Butcher, Yuri, and Tate. Maybe your boss. What's his name?"

She shakes her head.

I back her into the corner as Semyon arrives with extra security. "You protect him?"

"I don't want you putting blood on my hands."

"Too late. I'll ask Tate." Then I step back. "Kira? Until I return, you're my prisoner. Officially."

I turn and leave with Semyon.

"You want me to come with you?"

I just give Semyon a dark look. "I asked for this Tate fucker's name and address, not a babysitter."

"Help, not hand-holding," he says. "You're armed to the teeth."

"I'm not sure what the evening's got in store. But first, I'm getting information, and I need you to hit all the spots, see if you can find anything on Yuri Naidov: where he is, how long he's been here, who he's working with. And be very discreet."

"Always."

We part ways, and I head off to the apartment building that Tate is supposed to call home. It's a pity he doesn't live in the suburbs in a house. Or maybe that's lucky for him. Not that his luck is much at all.

This is a Bratva property. Thick walls.

I break in and climb the stairs to the third floor, then knock.

It takes him a few minutes to answer the door. He's on the phone. His eyes go wide, face pasty when he sees me. He tries to slam the door shut, but I kick it and barge in, slamming it behind me. Then I grin.

"Uh, Mr. Calhoun, I'll call you back."

He hangs up.

"Who was that?" I ask.

"Get out or—"

I punch him and take his phone. He falls, crashing into his coffee table.

Grabbing him by the collar, I haul him up. "You'll call the cops? Do it. I'll tell you who to ask for."

He whimpers, and I punch him again. Then again.

He drops, the table splintering, and I start kicking him until he's a bleeding, blubbering mess. I pull his hair, dragging his head up. Then I fucking punch him again.

"That was for Kira."

"Please! Stop! I'm sorry."

I let him go and step back, pulling a gun, cocking it, and pointing it point-blank at him. I could shoot him. I want to shoot him, but even I know murdering a journalist in the USA is bad business.

"Why," I ask, "should I let you live?"

I know I shouldn't kill him, but he doesn't, and belief and fear are powerful.

He snivels, "I'll give you anything."

"Information?"

"Yes! I can do that. Please just don't kill me."

The man's a complete coward; he'd give up his own mother to save his skin. But I still don't trust him. Cowards are never trustworthy. You need to make them think the truth is the only way they live.

"Tell me everything," I say, "and if you tell me what I want, then you live. But there's a caveat."

"Anything!"

"Move away, far away. Get the fuck out of town tonight. I don't care if you have to pay someone to pack, but I want you gone, and you never come back, got me?"

"Y-yes, Mr. Rykov."

"Good. Someone's going to be watching you until you leave. Now. Talk."

He does.

He spills his verbal guts.

And he cries the entire time. I think about fucking him up more when he doesn't give me much on Yuri, only a chance meeting because of some scrap of unlikely information he dug up.

It happens. I know. I've had breaks that have catapulted me to a victory short hand-style. But I want, need more.

I don't think this sniveling weakling has it, though.

But what's interesting is this: Tate found where my stolen, illegal stash is now being held. He thought it was the link that would net him me, and by stealing what Kira had, he'd write an exposé. Get me arrested.

I really think about leaving him hanging on to his life and calling 911.

But I don't.

I kick him once more, repeat my order, and leave.

Outside in the air, I breathe deep, then get in my car and pull out my phone.

If he got that tip, or just plain old worked his butt off to get that info, it doesn't matter. It's all a set up to take me down.

Is that fucking the Butcher's plan? Not to kill me but ruin me and my Bratva?

Maybe it's a trap to lure me to my demise.

I call Andrei.

"You better be calling with something fucking great," he says. "After your lone adventures."

"I think I've found the weapons."

The snark melts away. "Where?"

"The construction site, one of our legal fronts."

"We," says Andrei, "have a lot of those. Be more specific."

"The one that's been abandoned for months because of the problem with the pipes beneath the site." I tap an impatient hand on the steering wheel.

"Are you sure?"

"I haven't been there, but my source swears it. And considering he's a coward of a fool, I believe him." These are never words I say lightly, and the Pakhan knows it. "Send an army."

"An army?" He pauses. "You think this is a trap?"

"I don't give a fuck. Bring that army. We're going to settle this. Once and for all."

29

KIRA

"How long do I have to be here?" I demand.

I asked this before. A few times. And I'm back. Because I honestly don't know what to do right now. And I'm willing to do anything to keep back the fear, the bulk of it, even if it means talking to and annoying two big Russian guards.

There are only two men here, stone-faced, armed. And they make me nervous because of what they mean.

I'm Ilya's prisoner, and he's gone off to kill... or worse, get himself killed.

They're about as talkative as my toaster, but some fancy ones definitely talk more than them. I sigh, itching to leave. Instead, I stomp into the kitchen, pour a drink, and get myself some water too. I unscrew the lid of Ilya's fancy-ass water and take a swallow; then I pick up the whiskey.

"Mmm," I say, running it under my nose, "delicious whiskey."

I think about splashing it about, but really, it's not going to have any effect; it'll just smell like a bar in here.

One radios to someone, and the other doesn't look. "It's not vodka."

I go to the freezer in his giant fridge and pull out a bottle. It's expensive, and Russian. I shake a little, because my father had one for special occasions, the good and the bad. And once he came home, Mikhail had drunk a fair bit. My brother giggled as my father yelled at him, then put him on yard, kitchen, and bathroom cleaning duty for a month.

That stopped the giggles and started the moans and pleas.

Mikhail was thirteen. He never stole from my father again.

I wave it in the air. "Russian vodka."

"Please. We are working."

"You need to do what we say," the other says. They exchange looks. "What Ilya has told us to say."

I sigh and put the vodka back. I sip my whiskey. As a plan, it wasn't good. What was I going to do? Get them wasted and tie them up and make a run for it?

It's not like they're the only ones here watching me.

These two weren't the only ones who turned up. They're just the two that got the privilege of staying with me.

About eight came in, and I'm guessing they're guarding the exits from the outside. As it is, these two face the elevators, ready for whatever might come.

I shiver at the thought, and I'm back to being scared that they're here, that Ilya thought I needed it. Because, sure, I'm his prisoner, but I'm also his prisoner because he thinks it's the only way to keep me safe.

I finish my drink and pour a half one. Part of me wants to take the bottle, crawl into bed, and hide, but I'm not really that girl. The girl I want to be sometimes; it would be so much easier. But I'm not.

Poking and digging and picking at threads are things I need to do. Like it's in my DNA.

I go over to them.

And though their backs are to me, I know they're aware of every move I make.

"Do you think Ilya will be okay?" I ask, sipping at my whiskey. I take my phone and try to call, but he doesn't pick up. "He's not answering his phone."

"He is busy," says one.

"And not answering my calls." I sound like a spoilt brat. "He should answer my calls. One of you call him. Please?"

They don't look at me. "We're here to watch you, not talk."

"Or make calls for you. This is grown-up business." This one waves a hand behind him, in my general direction. "Go and do something."

I don't move. In fact, I take a step closer.

"Grown-up business?" I'm glad to have a reprieve, something stupid to cling to. I step closer. "I'm grown up. Or do you mean men's business?"

"Do not hover," one says without looking back at me.

I narrow my eyes. "I can do what I want in here."

"You are a prisoner."

I almost roll my eyes. He's putting on a thick accent when earlier his accent was pure Chicago.

"I'm under your protection," I say quietly.

Thing is, I don't want to be alone.

Because I'm scared.

And these two will do. Because out there in the world, I don't know what's happening. Ilya's on a mission, and I'm not under lock and key because of my work rival. It's far worse than that. There's the man, Yuri. And Yuri isn't working alone. I'm sure he does and has in the past, but Ilya went on about the Butcher.

Even the name... I shiver.

And Tate? He's a worm, but he doesn't deserve death. Even if he was going to leave me to my fate, I can't be the cause of his.

And another soul on Ilya's record.

I take a shaking breath.

If Ilya kills Tate, that's blood on my hands. I'm not being

some stupid little girl. I know who and what Ilya is. But that blood? It'll be on me, because he'll kill Tate for me. And I don't want him marked with a murder because of my mistakes.

"Please leave us to our job so we don't have to tie you up."

"Everyone wants to tie everyone else up," I respond, speaking in Russian. If it shocks him, he doesn't say a word. "Fine, I'll go. And I might, in some ways, be a prisoner, but I'm allowed to go where I want. Within reason." As long as it's in here.

The other one speaks. "We're here to keep you safe. Out there, it's not safe. Go into the bedroom or another room. If someone comes in, hide."

For a moment, I don't move, and the fear swamps me again. "Do you think someone's going to do that?"

The first one goes back to his normal accent. "We'll keep you safe or die trying."

"This place is impenetrable." I hope.

"Go," the man says.

I want to curse Ilya, but fear paralyzes the anger.

Mostly.

Because I know even if Ilya is clever, careful, and has some kind of god on his side, things happen. Like with Mikhail. And when things happen with men like them, they usually end up dead.

If I were going to break in somewhere, the bedroom's the first place I'd look, so I don't go there.

Instead, I creep through the study to the computers and shut the door.

Leaning against it, I take a moment, give in to the shaking, then I cross to the desk, set down my phone and glass and stare at the black screens. There's no screensaver, which means Ilya turned them off.

So I turn them on again and wait for the main computer to flash the password box.

He changed the codes on the elevators, but I've no idea about the computers. Or if they're somehow all connected.

The box appears, and I hold my breath as I type in the password.

By some miracle, it works.

I breathe out slowly.

The whole desktop is cleared; there's nothing to get into, and when I find a hidden file, it's empty. There's just one icon, and it's for the internet. I click, and it's just the regular deal.

Shit, did he do this because of me, or...

Or what?

Ilya always seems one step ahead.

I try some different things, but I don't really know how to access the dark web. And there's no browser history. So instead, I spend a few minutes checking the news, but it's the same disasters and gossip and wars. Nothing about the Bratva and nothing other than the usual corruption stories.

With a sigh, I get down to business.

Getting to my email account is easy enough, and there's all the usual crap. Not one email from Mr. Calhoun.

Which is strange.

My gaze strays to my phone.

He hasn't called, either.

But it doesn't mean he won't come for me. So I need to face that head on. I also need the job. So I type a letter to Mr. Calhoun. In that letter is everything I know. All about Ilya and what he's been doing, all about the Bratva, and a glossed-over version of what I copied.

No way would I give him a thing to go on where he could cut me out.

I also tell him about Tate's betrayal.

When I'm done, I read it.

Christ, it's like I purged something inside me. Like this is a confessional of sorts.

I could tell him I'm being held against my will, send it, and I'd be able to have him send the cops here to rescue me. Better, he'd turn it into a media carnival. And then I'd be free. Free of the bratva, free of Ilya. Maybe even free of my past.

"If I do this," I whisper. "I'd have the career of my dreams."

And lose the love of my life.

Something punches me hard, and I can't breathe.

The love of my life.

Ilya.

It's always and forever been Ilya.

How was I never seeing that before now?

"Oh my god. It really is that. I just don't have feelings or care for him." Of course, I don't.

I stare at the screen, not seeing a thing.

"I love him."

I am in love. Always have been.

My finger hovers.

There are two things I can press.

Send or the delete button.

There's no competition.

I'm about to press when shouts go up outside in the penthouse.

"What the...?"

There's a series of loud booms followed by rapid gunfire. I dive for the floor, jamming myself beneath the desk.

It seems to last forever. When the silence comes, I almost don't recognize it.

No one yells. No one comes for me.

With a shaky breath, I push myself up and make my way to the door. My heart's beating so loud now, the blood a din in my ears. It takes real effort to open the door and step into the rest of the penthouse.

First thing I notice is that I'm alone.

There's no blood, but my guards are gone. Rushing to the first elevator and then the second, I check them.

They're in both the same condition. They aren't working—as in, they're not even on. It doesn't matter, I guess, since I don't know the code, but...

The shouts, explosions. Gunfire...

But if there was an attack where is everyone? There's no enemy. No guards.

My mouth turns dry as I glance over at the walk-in pantry. The door's open. I grab a chef's knife from the magnetic strip and edge my way there.

Food and tins are everywhere, and the door's busted.

My legs wobble.

Both doors.

Breaking the fire door open would take serious power. Unless... unless they tried to get in and Ilya's men fought them off.

I don't know what to do.

One thing is for certain, though. I can't stay here. It's a death trap now. I'm a sitting duck.

Shit. Panic lances through me as I take my knife and step over the mess in the pantry. I slowly swing the fire door open. I get a glimpse. It's the strangest fire well I've ever seen. Then again, this is a Bratva-owned building. Ilya wouldn't live anywhere else.

I step out on the carpeted floor, and the blood rushes to my feet.

The hallway's full of bodies.

Dead bodies.

Shit.

I'm in real trouble.

30

ILYA

It's my own personal world war. And it's happening on Bratva turf. My Bratva's turf.

"Fuck me," Andrei shouts as he lands next to me. "You were right."

The fucker's crazy. He didn't crouch, didn't run that fast, just took his sweet time and took out a load of the enemy as he did it.

I'd be impressed, if I wasn't so furious at myself.

The sound of guns and shouts echo in the empty construction site. And I fucking hate it. Hate that I've brought this on, hate I was a little too reckless in my information gathering—something that has gotten me results I don't want. Like death, destruction, and a girl I'm in love with in danger.

"Right about what?" I shoot, hitting a few of the enemy, only ducking when they focus on us.

Andrei is furious. I feel that in waves. Not at me, but at the situation. At the fact someone dared steal from us.

"The weapons are here. Mostly untouched." He taps his ear. "Dmitry just radioed in. We'll move them out when this is done. Heat coming from the left. And behind. Move!"

We run, shooting, and leap over some more giant cement pipes. From here, we can see the room, and no one can approach from the back, not unless they're stupid as fuck. But the pipes aren't the best cover. I scout ahead and point to a better position.

Guns blaze as we take cover behind a low cement wall, now abandoned. Overhead, the bullets fly.

"You were right that we needed an army," Andrei says, rising to shoot and take out an idiot running for us.

"It's what I do. Piss people off so you don't get too complacent. And what the fuck are you doing here, anyway? I said send an army, not deliver it yourself."

A shadow starts toward us; I turn and fire at it. A man screams, and a gun skitters out.

"Good shot," Andrei says, taking out another group coming from the other side.

"I try."

Our men are fighting all around us. And it's an epic battle. Guns, knives, kicks, and punches. It's a full-on fucking war.

I should have known Andrei would be in the thick of it. Both he and Valentin can't help themselves. They thrive on this shit.

Whereas I go in to do what needs to be done.

This needs to be done.

"A general doesn't stay at the sidelines." Andrei says, reloading his weapon.

I cast him a look. "That's exactly what they do. Where's Valentin?"

"Taking care of other business."

He goes to join the fray, but I stop him. "Trap?"

"Our turf. And we're beating the fuckers back." Andrei peels away, guns blazing, into the fight.

I hang back. There's something missing here. Sure, they

brought us here, and our weapons are here, but I'm not after these assholes.

The Butcher. Where the fuck is he? Hidden somewhere? He's not the type to get involved in big battles. He likes control. The nastiness of torture and slow, protracted kills.

But if I can grab one of his people, then maybe I can find out where he is.

I circle around the back of the fight. When we came in, Andrei, Semyon, and I were at the forefront, leading the charge, coming in from three directions. We created a full-on assault, like we'd dropped from the fucking ceilings.

They were watching the front door, which we left alone.

It helped to know the layout of the land. We've all been here on boring trips to try and solve the mundane, legal issues.

But while the Butcher might be a lot of things, stupid isn't one of them. This set up is his. He wants me here.

He might not have known Tate would talk, but he must have allowed the fucker to live on the off chance he'd lead me here.

Which should mean he's not off hiding somewhere far away. He's here. Somewhere. Nearby, but not in the midst of the battle.

I turn, just as a man rises above me, finger on the trigger. I slam my hand into the barrel, and the shot goes wide. I kick him in the balls, and as he falls, I shoot him in the chest, then the head.

So much for me questioning one of the men.

I grab his weapon, and I hit the ground at a low run, taking out a few more on the way, and then I burst out through the door.

"Voi-fucking-la."

Like a death wish, there he is, crouching next to a bulldozer.

The Butcher.

Of course he's outside, like a coward.

He's loading a gun, a big butcher's knife strapped to his leg. We lock eyes.

"Got you."

I charge at him.

But he runs from me, shooting behind himself wildly. One bullet hits the Kevlar. Fucking thing hurts like a bitch, but I don't stop. I don't shoot, either. I want to take him down personally. I want a fight.

"You won't get rid of me that easy, you bastard," I roar.

He darts into a construction site next to ours, one with the same issues, and I chase him in. He's mouse to my cat, and I let him think he's getting away until I have him cornered.

"Drop the gun," I say. "Now."

He does, turning. "How are you fucking impervious to my bullets."

"You're just a terrible shot."

"I respect you, Ilya. You're strong, and smart. Almost as smart as me."

"I'm smarter."

He ignores me. "No one else would have worked out if I wasn't in there."

"You're not all that."

"Took you long enough to work out who was helping to slice and dice your people. When I teamed with that idiot, Yuri—"

"Getting slow in your old age, are you?" I ask, filing the information away. "Maybe I wanted you to show yourself. Didn't think you'd turned into so much of a cockroach."

"They're survivors," he says. "Unlike you."

"What's that fucking song? I'm still standing."

"On borrowed time." He spits the words. "The real Pakhan, the true Pakhan, isn't happy. So I'm going to fuck with your little outfit. Torture those players, destroy all you've built, make you all destitute. Isn't that how to hurt you here? Finances? The American dream, in tatters?"

"Isn't it everyone's dream?"

"I'd say," he snarls, "time in exile has changed you, but you've always been a capitalistic shit."

"And you've always been a sadistic murdering psychopath."

"I can't wait to destroy your Bratva and your false Pakhan."

"One thing at a time. First, you have to go through me."

"Yes..." Then he cocks his head. "No weapons?"

I hold out my hands, as does he. "No weapons. We fight."

"Should we play for your girl?" he asks, sending fury shooting through me as he backs away, stepping over pipes and bags until he hits a door. He shoves it and moves inside what seems to be a small room. I follow. There's nothing in here, which is perfect. I look around, a little on the small side, but doable. They must have used this as operations from within the site before all the issues hit. I move about until I'm in front of the door.

"You aren't getting anywhere near her," I snarl.

"Then we'll just gamble on life and death, then, I suppose."

"As long as it's your death we're talking about," I say. "Put down your knife and weapons. Now."

He makes a show of unbuckling the sheath for the knife. Then he pulls out a black leather case. "Scalpels, other tools." He grins. "You never know." Two guns and three more knives enter the pile. "Your turn."

I don't trust the fuck, but I make a show of dropping weapons he can see in the obvious places. The Kevlar is under a long-sleeved shirt, so I leave it on. Along with a few choice weapons. Not fair, perhaps, but there's no way this man is playing fair.

It doesn't matter. Right now, I could rip him apart with my bare hands for that suggestion about Kira. Hell, I'm going to attempt to do just that.

The Butcher raises his hands to fight me, and I know by his stance it's going to be dirty street fighting.

Fucking fine by me. "How about this? You get to take the first swing. I'll take the last."

"You think?"

"I know."

"We'll see." He takes one step forward when his phone rings. He stops and starts to curse, a hard look of concentration coming over his face, almost like whoever sent the message is far more important than me.

Suddenly, I'm desperate for the phone. I need to see who it is. But he pulls a gun right as I do, and we're pointing them at each other.

I'm a faster, better shot, and he knows it. But this close, there's a chance we'll hit each other.

"Fucker," I rumble.

He just shakes his head, pulling his weapon off me.

"I was afraid this would happen," the Butcher says, "That's why I have a backup plan. But don't worry, I'll be back to finish this. But..." He pushes a button on his phone and something begins to hiss. "You aren't the smartest. After all, I got you here, didn't I?"

"What the fuck are you on about?" I keep the gun on him, pulling the trigger a little too slow as he steps out, slamming and locking the door behind him.

My gun must not be working right.

Then I take a step and almost fall.

What the...?

There's a sweet smell in the room, and it fills up fast.

Oh. Fuck. Gas. My head starts to spin, and I run, stumbling to reach the door. I hit it, and my legs start to give way, but I clench my teeth, fighting the effects as I throw myself at the door to try and break it.

But each time I'm weaker, and more and more bursts of black appear in front of my eyes.

No wonder he didn't fall when he backed away from me.

He's been here. He...

I bang into the door again, but it doesn't move. And getting my thoughts to work is becoming harder.

I start to lose consciousness.

I try to fight it, try to get the door open, but the blackness claims me, and I fall into nothingness.

31

KIRA

"Move."

I mouth the word to myself from my hiding place under the kitchen island.

My eyes burn hot, vision blurry, and my chest is so tight it's like something's going to burst.

"Move, Kira."

But I can't.

I'm trying to be as quiet as possible. Being quiet, though, isn't the same as moving.

If I move, part of me whispers, I'll die.

"I can't," I mouth silently.

Yes, but if I stay, I'll definitely die, another part says.

So I need to move.

But my limbs refuse.

"You have to."

I'm the girl who chose journalism as a way to right wrongs, to vent and level my grudges against injustices.

I'm the damn girl who got a full scholarship to the University of Chicago. And the girl who threw that away because of her driving need to make something of her personal project of corruption in the school and to bring to light the personal corruption of the dean.

That got me expelled and landed me in a pile of shit, which had me scraping up low-paying jobs until I fought my way into the even lower-paying job of intern at Chicago Daily.

I'm the girl who stuck with it.

The girl who said, before all this, fuck you to the past, who paid for new papers to change her name after that less-than-stellar foray into higher education. Who had to deal with the dean wiping all trace of her scholarship from the record.

He threatened me with a bullshit reason of disgrace. I tried to shop that story, with my ejection from the school, only to find I looked like a disgruntled kid who wanted revenge because they didn't get accepted.

If I did all that, survived all that, I can fucking move.

I'm not the girl that hides.

I'm the girl that turned Ilya Rykov's head.

"But this is safe."

I shake my head, answer myself.

"For now."

No one's coming up that stairwell, and that means right now, it's safe where I am. But that doesn't mean this is how it's going to stay.

Maybe his men killed all the ones coming for Ilya. But that won't stop more from coming. Because his men… his men…

I push a hand to my mouth to stop a sob coming out. They're there, the sobs. So are the tears. But if I let one out, then they'll all come, and I don't know if they have an end. I can't afford to get hysterical.

His men are dead.

I have to deal with that.

"And you will be too, if you don't move."

I have to deal with that, yes. But not right now.

Right now, I need to get the fuck moving.

It takes me ten more minutes before I can actually put myself in motion. I pick up my knife and edge toward the door in the pantry.

And then I step out.

"They're just dummies, they aren't bodies. Just dummies."

I repeat this over and over again as I pick my way over the corpses. It's a long, hard slog. Because I know they were people.

But I have to keep up the lie. Not out of disrespect. It's just that I don't think I could do this—step over them, see them, wide-eyed, dead, some of the wounds—see all that and not pretend.

"Not real. Not real," I whisper, only looking down when I have to.

I move carefully, deliberately.

And I try not to breathe in the particular and stomach-turning scent of death.

I play that game until I reach a floor where I pass through a broken-down door, one that's been rammed in recently and with dedication. I step through it, and though there's debris, there aren't any bodies in this part of the stairwell. I look around on the landing. There are a number of floors below, but the levels here are written small, in Russian, so I know this has to definitely be the Bratva's private way in and out. I'm guessing for fast getaways. If they came up here, they could be waiting down below.

There's a door to my left. If I keep going down these steps, I'm going to come out where other men might be waiting. But if I go down through the door to my left, well...

I don't know.

And I won't know until I step through. There's a sign above it stating exit. Maybe to another stairwell because this building will have legit renters living here, ones who have nothing to do with the man on the top floor. Or elevators. A chance, maybe of getting out unseen.

Basically, I've got two choices: continue this way or open the door and see what's on the other side.

With a breath, I take the door, and I breathe a tiny sigh of reprieve. It's not quite relief, but close.

I'm in a hallway with apartments on either side. Just two doors. The one behind me closes, and it looks like the wall, but up the other end is an exit sign, past the elevators. I hurry over, prepared to maybe take an elevator. But they're both blank, no lights on them. A place for a key, and no code pad. Shit. Then again, what if they think I'll go for that exit?

Squaring my shoulders, I head straight to the exit door, pushing it open.

This time I step into the fire stairwell. I listen, but there's no sound, nothing coming from above or below, and it has a disused feel about it.

Perfect. It should take me down to the basement and garage. Best of all? It's body-free.

I take the stairs slowly, gripping my knife, scared of what might wait around every corner, just in case my senses have gone haywire. But there's nothing. No one.

It seems to take forever, but I pass the door marked 'basement' and take the short set of stairs to the next one. Garage.

I push open the door. I'm sure there's a second floor below, where that second elevator goes, but I don't know how to reach it.

This is here, though. So I'll take it. And it's the opposite side to where I would've come out if I'd taken the other set of stairs. I step out and look around, easing the door shut behind me silently.

It takes precious minutes for my eyes to adjust. But I don't hear anyone, although it creeps me out down here in the bowels of the building in a way I can't define, like every shadow hides something menacing.

But if there is someone here, then they'll be watching the other door. Right?

I see a path. It's a way out for people who leave on foot, and it leads to the shuttered exit. I start out across the dimly lit concrete, when all of a sudden something pops out of the shadows and grabs me.

Two men wrestle me into their grips.

A scream breaks free before one of them slams a hand on my mouth. I bite him hard, and he lets me go. I start to scramble, but the other grabs my hair.

I slash out with my knife and connect with something. "Cunt!"

He lets me go and punches me full in the face, sending light dancing and exploding as I stagger back.

The other man trips me, and I fall, hitting the cement, just barely managing to catch myself with my hands.

"Look at that, she's still got the knife," one says as he wrenches the weapon from me.

I kick at him and scream. "Help!"

"Be quiet," the one who took the knife mutters, kicking me hard in the ribs.

Pain blossoms. I try to breathe.

One of the men drags me up by the hair. "You're lucky we've got orders not to kill you, but that doesn't mean we can't have a little fun at your expense."

He shoves a hand into my pants, and I scream again just as someone snaps. "Enough."

"Sir—"

"Don't damage her."

Footsteps approach as an engine guns, and that same man says from behind me, "Put her in the trunk. I'll take the bitch from here."

32

ILYA

"What the fuck?" My mouth's full of cotton wool.

And I can't move.

The world is shaking violently. Something hits me in the face.

"He's coming to." Semyon says.

"Ilya? Can you hear me?" Andrei's voice now.

The floor beneath me is cold, dank, smelling of earth and concrete. It all starts to come back with each breath of clean, fresh air.

Gas-free air.

Fuck.

How the hell did I let the Butcher get the best of me? Trick me? Lock me in that room? This whole thing was one big setup to take me out.

While Evgeni would love to kill me for my crimes against the current Russian Pakhan, Gusinsky, he wants me to suffer. And he'll do that before taking me out. Shit.

I open my eyes. "Did you just hit me, Semyon?"

"I'll put a bullet between your eyes if you don't tell me what the fuck's going on." Andrei takes my shoulder and shakes me.

I try to push up, but pain lances up my arm. I look down. "This is not the way to get me to do drugs," I say, ripping the needle out as Semyon helps me up.

"You were locked in that windowless room for way too long, and the door's reinforced. Took five of us to break the fuck in, and we had to give you adrenaline to wake you up." Andrei shines a flashlight in the now-deep gloom of the construction site. "Had to cut the power too." He blasts the light in my face as I look at him. "To get to you. One more minute, and there wouldn't be a fucking you."

"I need my weapons."

Semyon starts handing them to me, along with the things the Butcher left. "I don't know how he had this here."

"A trap, and I fell for it," I mutter. "Fuck!"

Andrei studies me. "Obviously. It's how traps work."

"I'm smarter than that fuck. Look." I test my legs, take a few steps. There's still weakness, a wobble, but it'll go. "But I'm not hiding from it. I should have known it was more than a setup to take us out. Maybe that's why I asked for a fucking army..."

"He wanted you, not an army."

"And I nearly gave it to him."

"Glad you didn't. But why the hell does he want you so bad?"

I slide a look at Andrei as I shake off a helping hand from Semyon. "Long story. But it's part of why I've been trying to bring down the corrupt branch of the Bratva back in Russia. They're using the embassy to control people. To block us."

"There's more," Andrei guesses.

I sigh heavily. "I've fucked up."

"And how have you done that? Other than not tell me what the fuck you're doing, and not coming to see me?"

"Evgeni is brutal, beyond cruel. Maximum pain is maximum fun for him. It seems the current Russian Pakhan,

Gusinsky, isn't happy with you or me. You're too powerful, and I'm causing him trouble."

Andrei shrugs. "I know that."

I narrow my eyes. "Gusinsky sent the Butcher, Andrei. To fuck with you, and me. But it's a two birds one stone situation. Destroy your business—"

"Dmitry?" he commands.

One of his men comes by. "Find out everything on Evgeni Kucherov since he got here."

"We've already been working on it," Dmitry says.

"Work harder." Andrei doesn't raise his voice. "Now's the time to round up every affiliate and crush them. Send Gusinsky a loud message. And by clean up, I mean those doing business with the Bratva outside of us in this city."

Dmitry nods before heading off with a small group of men.

"He's not going to be so easy to get."

"That's your job. With backup—"

"No." I shake my head. "I don't need backup. He'll smell it."

"He'll have people."

"I'd be disappointed if he didn't."

"This is suicidal, Ilya." Andrei frowns.

I say, "No. It'll be his death."

"I'll go with him," says Semyon."

"No. You need to help Andrei." I look at them both. "He'll come after you and Valentin, all the higher-ups. He'll come after her..."

Kira.

My fists clench.

"I have to go. Me. Alone." I look at Andrei. "Semyon's got access to the servers. I shut down all connections from my computers already. Even if he could get on them, he'd see nothing. He's dangerous, but I can take him."

For her, I'd take on three armies. Four. I don't care how

many; I'd fight until death just so she could live. And I'm stubborn enough to hold on for that. For Kira's life.

"Ilya, listen—"

"I need to go alone."

Andrei studies me, then says, "Is she worth it?"

"Yes."

It's a tight nod, but Andrei gives nothing away.

"I fucking knew the Butcher would use this as a means for payback."

"Russia?"

"Yeah," I say to Andrei. "Russia. He lured me here to kill me when he saw he had the chance."

Or, I think, knock me out to take me for torture.

"How did he know about this place?" Andrei asks.

I shrug as we head outside, our scouts fanning out to make sure there aren't any enemies hiding. "It's easy enough to find out who owns the building they had the guns in. The real owners. If you're connected and moneyed."

"Fuck." Andrei breathes out. "And it's not overly hidden. But this place?"

"They built it. Both the sites are abandoned. Hindsight's a useless tool." I pause. "Though we know now he's after me."

Andrei and Semyon exchange a look, and all my senses go on high alert.

"What," I say, "was that?"

"Got word, Ilya," Semyon says. "While we looked for you."

No one says it, but me going off like that wasn't exactly the smartest thing. In fact, it was a page straight from the Andrei and Valentin fun and chaos handbook.

It was completely out of character. But I'm not myself lately.

And I know why.

Kira.

Suddenly, I swing my head to Semyon. "What is it?"

"Your place..."

A thousand gongs clang in my brain and reverberate ice-cold waves through me.

"The penthouse was ransacked," Andrei says, "and all the men killed. Whatever you were keeping there is gone."

"No."

"Your computer's destroyed, and—" Andrei stops. "Ilya."

"I don't give a shit about that. What's gone? Kira?"

I'm about to run when Andrei grabs me. "I don't know anything about Kira. But there was a message written in blood on the hallway walls."

"And what was it?" I ask quietly.

"ARENDELLE. COME ALONE."

He holds up his phone. Someone took a photo and sent it to Andrei.

My brain starts to tick.

"What does it mean?" he asks. "We'll get together another—"

"No. I know what it means."

Semyon and Andrei shout after me as I pull away and power out of the building to where my car is.

Nothing else matters now.

Nothing except her.

How the fuck did the Butcher know where she was?

My stomach sinks, turns, and sour acid fills my mouth.

I don't look back. I don't answer Andrei and his orders, and I don't fucking tell them where I'm going.

The Butcher's got Kira.

I know it.

"I accept your gauntlet," I mutter, gunning the engine and pulling away.

I'm no coward, and I am smarter than this fuck, but he's proven himself a worthy foe. I just can't let emotions get the better of me. Otherwise, he'll get me just like he did back there.

I won't let that happen again.

I'll control myself. I need to.

Even if it's easier said than done—especially when the girl I love is at risk.

I can't wait for anyone else.

I'm going in alone.

And I'll end it that way.

Alone.

33

KIRA

The ugly man pulls the blindfold off me, and I spit at him.

He just grins.

The motherfucker has already roughed me up, when he had me in the back of the van. To see what I was made of, he told me.

Whoever he is, I don't like him. The evil that radiates from his aura scrapes at my senses, making my skin crawl.

"You are pretty," he says. "Pity."

What the fuck does that mean?

I look around frantically, trying to work out where I am. I'm in a familiar tunnel, but the fear's too great to pinpoint it. There's something about it, though… But I can't waste my time on that. Instead, I test my hands and feet, but they don't move. He's got me strapped to a metal chair. And try as I might, I can't get free.

The stranger traces one finger along my cheek, mockingly gentle. "So pretty. Now." Leaning in, he breathes on my throat like a lover. It turns my stomach, hard. "You won't be. When I'm finished with you."

He licks my skin, and I slam my head into his.

Rearing back, he slaps me so hard my head whips back.

"Fucking little bitch."

"Who are you?" I demand. "Who are you working for?"

"Wrong questions."

"You don't know who you're messing with."

His eyes narrow. He doesn't like that. As if he thinks his reputation should precede him.

"You're a little stupid, aren't you? Didn't your silly little friend teach you manners?"

There's fresh blood in my mouth. I run my tongue over my teeth, checking to make sure they're all there. Nothing feels loose... yet. "What friend?"

"Your stupid friend who couldn't do a simple job," he says. "That friend."

"You'll have to be more specific. There's been a lot of stupid people in my life."

"My recruit." The man says this like he's the epitome of professional, the top of his game.

We're in a tunnel.

A stupid tunnel, like he's watched one too many Saturday morning old-school Batman cartoons.

He's also got a folding table in this tunnel, and I'd laugh at it all, really laugh. But I don't. Because it's not funny. What it is, is frightening, especially the flimsy table, seeing it so out of place.

The table is something so innocuous that it takes on an air of menace as he unrolls tools on it.

"Be more specific," I demand with as much force as I can muster. I'm pushing him, provoking, but if I can get him furious, maybe he'll make a mistake, and maybe I'll be able to get free. Or at least buy some time. "What recruit?

I don't want him to see my fear.

But he ignores me, going over to an array of items on the table. He runs a hand down them.

"Hey," I say. "I'm talking to you!"

His shoulders stiffen. I'm guessing he doesn't like his prey talking back. Well, that's just too damn bad. I'm all out of options. If I can buy enough time, maybe, just maybe, Ilya will come and save me.

And Ilya *will* come. Of that, I've no doubt. Ilya, for whatever reason, views me as his. He locked me in his apartment to keep me safe. To try and keep me safe. I see that.

Now.

"Ilya doesn't lose," I say. "I know that about him."

I realize my mistake. And veer in to correct it.

"At least," I say, "I picked up that much from the little I know."

"Be quiet."

"Imagine what he'll do to you," I say, hissing the words, "when he finds you went into his place and took me. Worse. You killed his men."

"I said shut up."

He picks up a leather strap and strikes me in the face. I bite down on the searing pain.

It wasn't hard enough to break the skin. "A warning," he says. "Just so you know who's in charge."

"Who are you again?" I ask as I try to work my hands free.

He strikes the belt on me again, this time over my breasts. The pain burns scars deep into my brain.

"Who. Are. You?" I push the words out. They're almost a scream, but I'm not about to give him the satisfaction.

The man pauses, looks at me. "Your boyfriend hasn't told you about me?"

He makes a disappointed sound, and horror starts to flood my veins. Oh, God. No. Ilya mentioned someone, the Butcher, and...and I think this is him.

"He did." He nods, smiling to himself. "Very good."

"You're insignificant," I say, hiding the quaking deep inside.

"Why would he say a thing? Especially to someone he barely knows?"

He laughs. "He told you. I saw the recognition on your face. And barely know him? I'll give you an ego boost, slut. He doesn't have whores in his lair unless he likes them. I can use that against him. Use you."

"Where did you learn to speak English?" I keep pushing. "The Supervillain school for idiots?"

"Shut up, or I'll shut your mouth for you. And you won't like my means."

"People skills aren't your forte, are they?"

He narrows his eyes and studies me. Like I'm prime beef. "And staying alive isn't your best one, little girl."

"I've managed it this long."

"Pure luck." He picks up a saw. It looks medical grade, and it freaks me the fuck out. But he puts it down in favor of a butcher knife. "Which has just run out."

I swallow as he approaches. I know he can hurt. He's already hurt me, roughed me up, just enough to knock me senseless and tie me up. Bring me here.

And now...

He's looking at me with a glint I hate.

He grabs my face. Turns it side to side. The Butcher runs the point of the knife lightly over my skin. And I know that even the smallest addition of pressure will inflict a deep cut.

But he changes direction, runs a line down the middle of my throat, pushing the point in a little at the dip where my clavicle meets, and then down, harder, cutting through the T-shirt, my flesh.

"Fuck!" I yell. It stings.

He smiles.

Poking a finger into the small cut, he digs in, making me gasp out. I clamp down harder.

"Delightful." His smile broadens. "I'm going to have fun with you."

This time, he picks up a switch.

Flexes it.

"Are you into pain, little one?"

I don't answer.

"It doesn't really matter," he says. "Because you won't be into anything when I'm done. I'd say tell me when it hurts, but it's all going to hurt."

He starts to bring the switch down on me. Hard. There doesn't seem to be a pattern, but he does avoid my face.

Not out of anything like decency, but because I get the horrible feeling he's going to save that for last.

At first, it all hurts at a high level, just below my tolerance, but he keeps it up, sometimes hard, sometimes soft, sometimes focusing on one place.

I can feel a slippery wetness on my arm where he's hitting. It's so painful it's almost numb.

Almost.

Finally, after a small forever, he puts the switch down and then grabs my hair, pulling it back as he begins to slap my face, harder and harder until they rain down like punches.

He finishes that by punching me so hard in the stomach that the pain rolls in nauseous waves through me.

"Yuri was good in his day, and a useful tool here," he says. "But really, there should be more marks. Some... real tenderization. Recruiting him worked. To a point. I guess it got me you."

I gasp and shake, trying to get myself under control.

"Getting you gets me Ilya. Win-win. For me."

I drag in a harsh breath of air.

"Ilya will kill you." I still don't know where I am or why it's so familiar. But I'm betting he's luring Ilya here.

Does the Butcher know he'll never win? No one can beat my man.

"He'll kill you," I snarl.

"No, he's not that smart," The Butcher says. "And you? Nothing. Just a pawn in a much larger game. Now shut up."

He puts the knife down and pulls on a glove with metal bits, then strikes me in the face. Before I can recover or spit out the blood that fills my mouth, he hits me hard in the stomach. He keeps it up, choosing places to hit. Then he sits back and nods in satisfaction.

"That's a warning, girl. Do not talk back to me, or I'll start cutting you into pieces."

Fear runs roughshod through me, but I spit the blood out of my mouth and raise my head.

I can't stand bullies. Can't stand people who wrong the weak. The innocent. And this man doesn't care who he hurts as long as it serves his purpose.

"Ilya," I say through swollen lips, my ribs hurting with each breath, "will come for me, and then—"

"I'm counting on it," he says, punching me again, this time in the ribs because he must have heard how I took in my breath.

I whimper; I can't help it. And satisfaction spreads over his face. Anger spreads through mine.

"He'll kill you," I whisper.

The Butcher just shakes his head. "No. I might have given him the chance before, but the stakes have gotten too high. My boss needs him dead and you alive..." He traces a line of one of my ribs and pushes, hard. I whimper again. "At least a little bit alive."

I cling to what I know of Ilya: his intelligence, strength, the anger, and his fighting prowess. I believe in him. He might not be able to save me, but he'll save himself.

That's all that matters. He's all that matters.

"You can't kill Ilya alone," I cough.

"Who said I'd be alone?"

My heart stops beating for a moment.

I'm a trap. That's what I am. A trap.

For Ilya.

"He's not going to come for me. You're wasting your time. But if you let me talk to him, I'll get him here," I say. If I can talk to Ilya, I'll make him hate me, turn, go the other way. And—

"Shut up, whore."

I'm hit again, then the Butcher picks up a long stick. He shoves it into my belly, presses a button, and a giant shot of electricity rips through me.

When he stops, I gasp, shaking, little ripples of the shock zipping over my skin.

"I'll up the voltage next time. I'm going to have some fun with you, I think."

He pulls out a pen and rips my shirt, exposing my entire arm, and he starts to mark it with small lines.

Now I can't help it; I'm crying, the salt of the tears making the cuts on my face burn.

It's a reaction, not the fear. From him electrocuting me. I want to spit and scratch and bite. I want to hurt him as badly as he hurt me.

But I can't move.

"Usually, I question, then start to slice, piece by piece." He comes in close and shoves something that smells like rubber in my mouth. I go to spit it out, but he pushes and holds my jaw shut. "Keep it there. That's a good girl."

I stare at him, eyes wide, and this time, he hits me with the prod, the juice higher. I scream and convulse, chomping on the bit. It doesn't seem to end until I almost black out.

He takes it away.

"But with you, I'm going to play before I cut you into pieces. I'm going to pull your nails and teeth, maybe clip out your tongue and cook it. I don't eat it, but imagine his face when it arrives by special courier, a gourmet meal of you. Considering you talk so much, it's a clever move, don't you think?"

I make sounds, trying to yell at him, but he holds my mouth shut. Then he gets tape and tapes it shut.

"Not so pretty now, are you?" He shakes his head with a laugh. "Of course—"

Just then, his phone rings.

"Always something," he grumbles, before answering.

He doesn't say a thing, just nods to himself, then hangs up.

Then he looks back at me and smiles.

"Show time."

34

ILYA

There's only one fucking thought in my head as I approach the storm tunnel near the park:

Kira.

This sadistic fuck's got Kira.

I need to push that way, as far from my mind as I can. It consumes, distracts, throws me off my game.

But it also fuels me.

No matter what happens to me, I'll save her. Because she's alive.

It's not just wishful thinking; I know she's alive. Not only do I feel it, I know. The Butcher. He wants me, and she's the key to get me back to him.

If he harms a hair on her, I'll....

I take a calming breath.

Oh, calm is the last thing I am, the last thing I feel, but I need to reach a place where I can work from logic.

He's fucking already beyond dead for touching her, for taking her in the first place, and I'm going to make him suffer.

First, though, I need him to talk. Because there are some questions I need answers to. Like, where the fuck did he get

Arendelle from? Her? Back when he no doubt had dealings with Mikhail?

One way or another, I'll find out.

Up ahead, I spot guards. Of course. Evgeni changed the rules to suit himself. Just like I expected.

I check my gun and count the guards I can see—at least eight, so there's likely to be a lot more.

"So much for one-on-one," I mutter, waiting for the man with the semi-automatic to find a place to smoke a cigarette. "Keep wandering away from the pack," I quietly goad him. "Be my fucking dinner."

I made sure to come in from the other side. Under a street lamp. Be seen.

The man with the semi-automatic comes close, lighting his cigarette. Others are looking for me. My advantage is that I know the area. Mikhail and I would come in from the side, not in front. The side, where I am now, is a good place to keep away from eyes who might be looking. Back then, it was the cops who'd sweep the park for punks like us.

As soon as he's that one step closer, bent to cup the cigarette as he lights it, I strike. Rising up, I grab him, slicing my knife across his neck just before I break it.

Quick, not so clean, but silent. I take the gun and his phone.

I move on, out around the edges. But that's where the advantage ends. From here, to the storm tunnel entrance, it's clear, which means I can see the men. The moment I step out, they'll be able to see me too.

Checking the semi-automatic, I step out. They instantly spot me, and a shout goes up just as I let loose a hail of bullets at them. They fucking drop. I charge forward into the mouth of the tunnel, but I don't get far before I'm jumped by other men who were waiting.

I can't use the gun; there's no room, but neither can they. It's knives and hand-to-hand. I use all my skills from the streets, from my time in the Bratva. Kicking the first man in the kneecap, I grab his howling ass and use him to take out three more. They all get a knife in the head. One drops a hand. I pick it up.

A bullet misses me, and I twist, shooting back. I hit someone, and they scream out. Another three men come at me, armed with knives, feet, and fists, all aiming to kill me. I take them each, one by one.

But every time a man goes down, another is there to take his place. They emerge from every direction—from outside, from deeper within the tunnel, from out of the fucking ground. It doesn't matter; I fight. I ignore each kick to the kidneys, each slam to the face.

I also ignore the wrenching pain from my still-unhealed bullet wound, and the wetness of blood from it.

A punch lands on my face, knocking me backward. I spit blood, ducking another fist and pivoting to land a kick into the nearest gut.

Someone grabs me from behind, and I throw him into the men in front, stomping down hard on his neck when he lands.

Wiping the blood from my face, I swing hard, connecting with bone, flesh, and cartilage.

Someone else has a knife, and he swipes me with it, cutting through my flesh. "You fucker!" I roar. Grabbing his wrist, I break it and don't let go. Instead, I use him to stab my next attacker.

I fucking fight as dirty as I know. I take more down. More come.

And they pile on. Each time I go down, I pull myself back up again, throwing them off. Blood from a cut on my forehead —I think someone kicked me there when I was down—gets in my eyes and runs down my face until I can no longer afford the time to wipe it away.

I'm surrounded. It's a nightmare game, and I'm losing

strength. A slam to the jaw sends me reeling, and someone kicks my legs out from behind.

I start to get up, but there's a gun pointed at my face. "Don't move, asshole."

Someone starts to slow clap, and the crowd of men parts.

The Butcher smiles down at me. He's got a cattle prod, and he uses it. The pain is horrifying, and I can't stop the seizures it causes, but fuck him if he thinks he'll get a sound from me.

Not of pain.

Not a plea.

When he's done, he crouches down. "Not so smart. She said you'd win, but... she's just a dumb whore."

"Fuck you, Butcher." Ignoring the guns, knives, and knuckle dusters that his men have, I focus on him. "I thought you wanted one-on-one?"

"Plans," he says, "have changed."

"Or your cowardice is showing."

The Butcher spits, narrowly missing me. "You dare say shit like that to me when all these men can't wait to end you? You're so close to death, Ilya, and you don't even know it, you fucking fool."

He steps back, away from the men, waving his hand at them as he goes. "Finish him. I was going to play, but... bigger fish, all that. Kill him. Now."

I clench my fists, trying to decide which one to go for first. If I'm going to die, I'm taking a few of them with me.

As I start to move, a shot rings out, and a man falls.

It's like slow motion. Bullets drive through the air and hit all the men, dropping them like flies. I can see the Butcher. He's frozen, eyes darting as the hail of bullets continues to come from behind him in the darkness of the tunnel.

I can't see who's firing, but it's not his order. That's obvious. The moment the bullets stop, the Butcher runs like the coward he is.

Whoever the shooter is, they've bought me time.

Did Semyon follow?

I don't have time to ponder the question. The Butcher's running, and I can't let him get away. These tunnels split and twist, and he'll be gone forever. So I push up, ignoring the pain, and force myself to run, taking off after him.

I stop. There are two tunnels, both with light spilling out. Clever. But I pause and listen, and when I don't hear anything, I choose the left one, like I'm being pulled that way.

I head down there.

And stop.

Falling to my knees.

Kira.

Head down, slumped, tied to a chair, with a table of gleaming fucking instruments at her side.

I make myself get up, using the fear. "Kira."

She groans. "Aaasn"

Lifting her head, I can see how bloodied, how beat up she is. And he's taped something in her mouth, the goddamned animal. I pull the tape and ease the rubber out. Her eyes flutter as she half focuses. The anger in me rises as my stomach lurches sickeningly.

I know what the rubber is for.

The fucker electrocuted her, probably with the same cattle prod he used on me. More than once, from the look of her.

That's not all he's done to her.

My chest tightens.

I'm going to fucking rip the bastard's head off. I pull off the Kevlar and wrap it around Kira, trying to cut her hands free. They're cold, and he'd clearly got them bound too tight... or maybe she's somehow tightened them in an attempt to get free.

I won't dismiss the latter.

But it's going to take some time to free her—time I don't have. She whimpers, and I brush her hair.

"Kira, it's okay. Just—"

A shot rings out, hitting the wall near my head, and I throw her chair down as the shooting continues. A bullet hits my shoulder, just above where I was shot last time. The next hits my side, narrowly missing my spine as I throw myself on her.

More shots ring out, and I try to turn while protecting her, but the next bullet hits me in the leg. I fall, hitting my face on the cold, hard ground.

Another bullet just barely misses. The next won't. I try to get up.

The need to save her consumes me. The pain barely registers.

I have to stay down as I shoot wildly, hoping like hell I hit flesh, that I hit the Butcher and kill him.

There's a small reprieve as I'm sure he's reloading. I take that time to topple the table, bringing it to stand as a barrier between Kira and the assassin.

Then I start crawling, away from her, leaving a trail of blood. These wounds aren't clean; I can feel it. One of those shots hit something that's making blood pump. I should get my shirt, get something, but I don't have time.

I have to get away from Kira because I'm the target, not her, and… where the fuck is he?

I can't see him. I wipe the blood that's running down my face. Suddenly, he shoots again, winging me and sending me spinning to the ground.

I'm losing a lot of blood, too much, but I'm not about to let the bursting black spots or the wooziness affect me. Using my left hand, I pull my gun, thanking whoever's in charge of this mess of a universe that I taught myself to use both hands, and I aim to where the shot came from.

There's a flicker of a shadow. I pull the trigger.

I miss, but he misses too. I keep crawling forward. He's not aiming now; he's shooting blindly at body height, so I have to stay down. I keep moving, pushing myself.

Then he slows with the shots.

No.

The Butcher's making a run for it. He's pulling back. I use all of my strength to push myself up, and I see him, back to me, running toward the opposite tunnel.

Before I can aim, another shot tears through the darkness, connecting with the Butcher's shoulder. He screams and falls to the ground.

I move fast because he's not dead yet. He's trying to get back up again. I race to him, pushing myself past my limits to grab him by the collar. Without wasting a second, I jam the butt of my gun in his face.

All the rage and fear for Kira comes out, and I lose it. I start punching him, smashing his head into the ground until he's pulp and making strange gurgling sounds. Then something breaks, probably his skull.

But I don't stop, even if he's dead.

I sit on him and fucking slam his head into the ground, over and over again, until I'm finally satisfied.

With a labored grunt, I shove him away and get up, wobbling on my unsteady feet.

"Kira..."

I'm about to turn and go back to her when an oddly familiar voice echoes through the darkness. One that sends tendrils of dark disbelief down my spine.

"Ilya ..."

I freeze.

That voice... I recognize that voice.

"No... It can't be."

I turn, but I don't see anything except for Kira. Someone's righted her chair, but she still looks out of it. I take half a step forward.

Then, a figure steps out of the darkness.

Every single sense zeroes in on his face.

"What the…" My fists curl, ready to fight. "You're supposed to be fucking dead."

"Did you really, honestly believe that, Ilya?" he asks.

I swallow a mouthful of blood.

No. Deep down, I don't think I did. Not where it really counts.

I stare at him. But just because a part of me always thought he could have survived doesn't mean he did.

Doesn't mean he's not a figment of my battle-wounded imagination. Or maybe I'm dead, and this is the afterlife.

"It's really me," he says, like he can read my mind.

And it is him.

Not my imagination.

It's Mikhail Zhirkov.

Kira's brother.

35

KIRA

My mouth tastes like rubber, and it hurts to breathe, like a pressure band is around me and getting tighter. I keep floating in the pain.

The delirium.

There were shots, and now there aren't.

Ilya was here. He protected me. Put something on me. Knocked me down and covered me from the bullets. So many bullets.

And then he disappeared.

Someone... gentle, strong hands... someone picked up the chair and touched my face. Familiar.

Not Ilya.

The world shifts, and I'm not focused on the aches and pains and heaviness on me. I'm not focused on the hands I can't feel.

The voices. I'm caught in the voices. One cadence I've gotten to know so well. Another a ghost from long ago.

How hard did I hit my head?

"...alive..."

The word stands out from their discussion. I look around the tunnel... until I see them.

My gaze catches on the beauty of Ilya. He's injured, bleeding, a mess, and still the most insanely good-looking man I've ever met. My heart picks up in a way that's got nothing to do with my injuries.

Then I blink to clear the sudden blur, and I focus on the other person.

And just like that, the bottom falls from my world.

No...

I bite back a cry. I'm dreaming. I have to be.

Or else Ilya's talking to a ghost.

Or maybe something in my head was knocked loose from all the abuse I've taken. I'm delirious, weak, beaten to an inch of sanity.

But...

But...

A whimper breaks free.

"Wally..." I whisper, my voice broken.

It is. Mikhail. My brother. He's not a ghost. They don't age and turn to real men.

Ilya's gaze darts by, and he takes a few steps toward me. Immediately, he starts to fall, but Mikhail's there, helping, like old times, like they used to do with each other. My brother and Ilya.

I don't understand. I don't think I can right now. All I know is he's here and...

I swallow hard.

My father isn't.

If this is real, it means my father died thinking my brother was dead.

Anger sweeps me. Love. Fear. I'm losing my mind.

But this isn't like old times. Ilya brushes him away. "I don't need your fucking help, traitor."

"You've been shot."

Alarm fills me at my brother's words.

"No! Ilya!" Again, my words come out in a whisper.

"Do I look like I care?" Ilya snarls at my brother. "I don't need anything from you. Ever."

"Right, and who do you think fucking saved your dumb ass back there? When those men were going to kill you?"

"My fairy fucking godmother," Ilya says, taking another step toward me.

But Mikhail moves in front of him. "Big bad Ilya, huh? I saved your ass back there, and here. I shot—"

Ilya rounds on him and grabs him by the front of his shirt. "Do you think I care? You betrayed me, you betrayed our future, and you tried to fuck over everything we built for your own selfish power. Fuck. I thought you were dead—"

"Bullshit."

"I did."

"There must have been a small part of you that knew."

"Because of you, that asshole Boris became Pakhan. He's ruined Russia. My *home*. And you're the one who put him there."

I start getting lightheaded, like the world's spinning. There's something warm wetting my thighs from beneath my top. The pain becomes distant. It's hard to keep my eyes open.

But I need to. I need to see my brother. I need to see Ilya.

I love him.

It doesn't matter if he loves me back.

I just want to tell him, even if it's the last thing I do."

"I said let go, Mikhail."

"You're as stubborn as ever. How the fuck do you think I found you?"

"You," Ilya says, "worked with that dead bastard."

"Come on... Did something happen to that big brain of yours? Why would I save you? We're on the same damn side."

"And I know that how?"

"Because Andrei knows I'm here. He showed me the picture of what the Butcher wrote on the wall. Look, we've got a lot to talk about, but we're not enemies." He pauses. "Not professionally... and I hope, not personally."

I make a small sound as I drift in and out, the words flowing through me, parts making sense, parts not, even though I can understand each word. It's like I'm only partially tethered to this plane and the strings are fraying.

I want to call out, but I can't. I can't seem to get my voice above a whisper.

"On your side. The same side, Ilya. Call Andrei."

"... I guess you did save my ass..."

"Thank you. Now if you're done bleeding all over the floor of this castle, maybe we should go to make sure the kid's all right."

"Wally," I breathe, just as Ilya lands near me.

"Oh fuck, Kira. Hang on."

"Hi Wally..."

Ilya's face appears in front of mine. "So this is the Wally you dream about, huh? I was jealous over him? No fucking way."

"You..." Mikhail says. "Maybe I'll shoot you, Ilya, for touching my sister. Hey, kid."

I want to say more, but I only manage to focus on Ilya, who seems to be weaving in and out. Sometimes there are two of him, sometimes one.

"It's gonna hurt," he says, "I'm sorry, but the plastic ties are too tight." Something metallic slides between my wrists, and they're free.

I cry out as pain and pins and needles and heat flood them.

"Sorry, princess." Ilya frees my feet next. "Can you stand?"

"I...I don't know." My throat is so dry I'm not even sure if those words came out.

Ilya wraps an arm around me. Even through the nausea-inducing sensation, I clutch at him, feeling the wetness spreading outward. He touches me there as he tries to help. I groan.

"Oh, fuck, Kira. You've been shot."

"Is she okay?"

"I'm not a fucking doctor," snaps Ilya.

"I... I'm... okay..." I say as I try and take a step. But the world spins, tips, my legs buckle, and I start going down.

Ilya holds me tighter as the world starts to close in, dim, until all that's left is him and my brother...

"I love you," I say to them both, finding an odd comfort in the words.

Maybe my little broken family isn't so broken after all...

From somewhere outside that encompassing darkness, I feel the heat and scent of Ilya, and I swear I hear him say something.

"I love you. I fucking love you, little..."

I think he says that? Or maybe it's wishful thinking. I think maybe my brother says it too.

The words wash over me again, and I sink into their warmth.

We're all here. Together again, like the old times.

Except this time, they're not trying to leave me behind.

And my secret crush is holding me just as gently as I always wished he would.

I can't stand up anymore, and I think... I think I have to let go. I can't hold on any longer; the darkness is too invasive; it crushes me down.

But this is the best way to go out.

Surrounded by love.

I finally let the darkness take me, until I feel nothing at all.

36

KIRA

I come awake in stages. The room has a strange smell, and the bed is small. I ache.

My head is filled with terrifying and wonderful dreams.

Horrors of being tortured, shot.

Joy that my brother is alive.

I open my eyes, and a different kind of joy spreads through me.

Ilya.

"You're alive."

"Careful," he says, stopping me from throwing my arms around him. "You have a drip."

I look down and see what's pulling at my arm. "I'm in the hospital?"

"Yeah."

I swallow and look around.

Sure enough, I'm in a hospital room. But that's not what I'm looking for.

My heart drops.

Mikhail isn't here.

It must have been a dream. How cruel.

"Ilya, I... I thought I saw my brother. I thought it meant I was dying too."

Ilya shakes his head.

"Mikhail is far from dead, even if seeing him is like seeing a ghost."

My back stiffens, and a flash of pain spreads through me.

I fight through it.

"He's alive?"

"It was his turn to make sure the property is secured. He'll be back soon."

"What... I'm so confused." I look at him. "Property?"

"This is a very exclusive private hospital. We thought it best you be somewhere on record. It's been put down that you were mugged and shot."

"But... police?"

"Your statement has already been filed."

"I really am confused," I whisper.

"Then let me ground you."

He kisses me.

It's soft, sweet, tender—a haven from my inner storm. When he lifts his head, he says, "Mikhail and I are taking turns patrolling."

"So... you're just doing your duty, being here with me?"

"No, this is me wanting to be with you." He kisses me again, and my heart soars. "I love you."

"I love you too." I'm so full of happiness I might burst.

"I need you closer."

"Whatever you wish, princess." Ilya gets on the bed and carefully pulls me into his arms.

It's pure bliss.

The door opens, and I look up. The man—because Mikhail's a man now—is holding a stuffed blue bear in a tutu, tiara, and metallic skates sewn onto its feet.

I stare.

Mikhail's there. Alive.

Breathing.

My brother's alive.

Mikhail glances from me to Ilya, then to me again. He steps in, and the door shuts behind him. "Did I miss anything?"

I look at him, still completely in awe. All I want is to hug him tight and tell him how much I love him, that all's forgiven—but it isn't. How can it be?

"Where have you been?" I say stiffly.

"Trying to get this life back."

"You missed so much..."

"So I see." His narrow-eyed gaze wanders over me and Ilya on the bed.

"No, you don't." Ilya meets my brother's gaze, sitting up. "You missed a lot." Then he turns to me. "Do you want me to go?"

I probably should ask him to step outside, but I'm not going to. I've lied and omitted so much of the truth with him that I don't want to do that anymore. If we're going to have a chance, any chance at all, then it means open books. So I shake my head.

He picks up my hand and kisses it.

I'm pretty sure it's a 'fuck you' to his old friend. And there's something so wonderfully new yet familiar about it. I can't help but grin. At least for a second.

Then all the years tumble down on me. I take a long, deep breath and let it out.

"You... Dad died of a heart attack, a broken heart." I swallow over my grief and catch a brief look between them. "What is it?"

My brother purses his lips. "He was killed, Elsa. I didn't know until it was too late... and keeping away from you seemed like the best thing. If everyone thought I was dead, then they wouldn't come after you."

I'm in too much pain to feel the full extent of what just hit me.

I turn to Ilya. "You knew all this? A-about my father? Mikhail?"

"Your father..." He sucks in a breath. "Yes, but I thought Mikhail betrayed me and..."

"I see." I hated Ilya then, and he hated us. The family of his betrayer.

My brother sighs. "I'm not being truthful, Kira. Back in Russia, I knew someone was sabotaging our systems. When I thought about it, there was only one person smart enough, ballsy enough, to do it. Ilya. I couldn't see how, though. But I stuck at it. And eventually, I dug up the hidden trail. It led me here, to Ilya, which led me to you."

"I would rather have been in danger if it meant spending all those years with my brother..."

He smiles. But it's a sad smile that hurts in my heart.

Ilya just squeezes my hand.

"Up until I uncovered the link, I hadn't wanted you to see the monster I'd become." Mikhail stares at the floor, then up at me and Ilya. "And I would have kept away, but I knew what was coming for you and Ilya, and couldn't just let you both die. So I secretly came to America myself."

"And now what? You'll disappear again?" There are holes, giant holes in this, but I can only focus on one thing at a time, and I don't think this is new to Ilya.

At least, not as new as it is to me.

They must have been talking while I was knocked out.

Mikhail rubs the back of his neck, squeezing the life out of the bear with the other. "I can see you love Ilya, and I want to work on getting my last remaining family back. That's both of you. Can you forgive me for leaving? I was an immature teenager... I didn't know any better. I do now." My brother's voice drops. "Can you forgive me, Kira?"

"You need retribution, is that it?" I ask.

He meets my gaze. "I'm not sure if I can ask that."

"Well, you can't just go," Ilya says.

"Don't plan on it."

"You're staying?" I ask, shocked.

Mikhail shrugs and eyes Ilya.

"We're either going to be very good together, or wreak havoc...then again, maybe being good together means wreaking havoc. It's going to be fun finding out."

Ilya shakes his head. "I can't believe Andrei didn't tell me you were here. That bastard and his secrets."

Mikhail half laughs. "He tried to set up a meeting. But you kept ignoring it. Probably knew you'd go ballistic, so he was—"

"You betrayed me," interrupts Ilya, "had me expelled from Russia."

"And now I'm in the same boat. After leaving like I did, revealing that I was alive after faking my death..." My brother shrugs, "it will make me enemy number one back in Russia... so maybe I'll just join your Bratva. How does that sound, old friend?"

Ilya snorts. "You'll have to prove yourself."

"I'm more than capable."

A small laugh escapes my chapped lips. "I see you haven't lost your confidence."

"Someone's got to believe in me."

"I... I believed in you."

"I know, sis. I'm so—"

"I thought you were dead. I thought..." I swallow.

"I was shot, Kira. There was a power struggle for leadership over the biggest Bratva in Russia...

"It turns out you won that struggle," Ilya says. "Hail the fucking king."

"But I was also smart enough to know that someone always comes for the king... not to mention, I realized I underestimated the violence and danger of being in the Bratva. Kira, it's even worse in Russia than it is in America. So, I played up my supposed death and made sure everyone believed it—both as a way to hold onto power and to keep myself safe."

He's twisting the bear now, and Ilya mutters something I don't catch.

"Then I started controlling the Bratva from the shadows. I even placed a puppet Pahkan—Boris Gusinsky—as the figurehead for extra secrecy."

He and Ilya exchange looks again.

"Ilya told me you're a journalist."

"Intern."

"Her boss would make good fish food," Ilya says.

"No more killing for me," I say. "I don't know what you did to Tate, but I don't—"

"Told him to get out of town. Guess he did. Your boss called."

Heat suddenly flames my cheeks. "I wrote an email to Mr. Calhoun. I didn't send it. I thought about it, but I... I couldn't, and—"

"I did," Ilya says, holding up his phone. "You used the internet on my computer; I set it up. It came through, and I sent it. With changes. And yes, she's brilliant." He looks at my brother, who nods. "Mikhail and I were talking. We're going to give you the tale of corruption, of how Gusinksy's Bratva tried to get into Chicago."

"So... no names here, just sources, and I use the paper—or a paper, since I'm no doubt fired—to break a story of corruption with a political-mafia bent?" I ask, my mind suddenly putting things together from a different angle, one that protects my brother, Ilya, and his people, but brings down the corrupt elements that have affected politics here and in Russia.

"I told you she's smarter than you, Mikhail," Ilya says, his voice full of pride. "Strap into your hospital bed; you're in for a ride."

My eyes widen. "My phone. I need it."

Ilya puts his on the bed. "We can record on this."

"You start, Ilya."

He nods. "Before Mikhail became the shadow Pahkan, I was helping him in the struggle to overthrow the previous Pakhan, Ivan Orlov. Boris Gusinsky, the current puppet Pakhan, was helping too. Together, the three of us got close... then one day, Boris and Mikhail seemingly teamed up to get me expelled from the country. I had no choice. Everyone had turned against me. I had to leave."

"I didn't know why Mikhail betrayed me, but Boris? The man's an opportunist, one with no loyalty, so..." He breathes out. "I had to come here, and luckily, Andrei Zherdev saw value in me. So when he offered me work in his Chicago Bratva, I took it."

"And you hated me for it," says Mikhail.

"You could have let me in on your fucking plans."

I hold up my hands. "Boys..."

My brother takes over. "Because of Ilya's expulsion from Russia, he held great animosity for the Bratva in Russia, and consequently, for me."

"Of course, I blamed you. Who wouldn't?" Ilya takes a breath, kisses my hand, and continues. "But I saw the absolute corruption; it's what we wanted to end, so to stick it to you, I began to secretly sabotage their systems from America in my free time."

"Like what?" I ask.

"Things like security systems, financial systems, computer systems, the usual," Ilya says, flicking a hand in the air.

My brother continues to torture the bear.

"What I didn't know was that Boris has also worked it all out. Or he was informed. And instead of tell me, his actual boss, he decided to take some action on his own and fucking be autonomous for once—you knew him; being seen as nothing more than a lackey was his biggest insecurity.

"We all have our places, and he was a reliable pin, not a lackey."

"Until he was," my brother says. "He wanted to impress me by secretly hiring the Bratva's most feared assassin, Evgeni, the Butcher, to go after Ilya in Chicago and destroy everything he held dear."

"And you let him," I hiss, practically ripping Ilya's hand off. "Why would you do that?"

"I'm here. I came when I found out. I might be a monster, Kira, but I'm not that kind of monster. I'm not evil. And you two are family."

"Why wouldn't he just tell you?" My voice rises. "Isn't that enough?"

"Boris's plan was to reveal all of this to me after it was done," Mikhail says gently, "in the hopes he'd get some more freedom or power or... I don't know... praise in response."

"Mikhail," I whisper, "How is this helping?" I try to sit up, but I can't on my own. Ilya raises the bed and rearranges the pillows behind me, making sure that my drip isn't interfered with.

Shit, I feel horrible; my eyes are heavy, and so is my heart. I ache, physically and emotionally.

I glare at my brother, waiting for him to respond. "Well? How is it helping?"

He shoots a glance at Ilya, who only looks back before fussing over me.

I know part of that is a 'fuck you' to my brother, but it's mostly for me. I can feel it in the tender, loving way his fingers stroke over me.

It makes me feel alive again.

A small smile appears at the corner of Ilya's mouth as he

notices the subtle press of my thighs. He raises a brow, and heat rushes my cheeks.

I'm glad I'm not a man because there's no way I could begin to hide my arousal under this thin hospital blanket.

"Well? I snap at my brother. I almost demand the poor bear he's trying to mangle, but I don't. It's like his emotional support plushie, and if the poor thing survives, I know I'm calling it Olaf, even if it is wearing a tutu with skates and a tiara. "You just decided to let Ilya fend for himself until it suited you otherwise?"

"I'm not helpless," Ilya says.

"He's not helpless," my brother repeats.

We both glare at Mikhail.

He twists Olaf the other way. "I liked it better when you two weren't in love, when you"—he points at me —"just crushed on you"—he swings his finger at Ilya —"and you tolerated her."

"Jealous I like her more than you? Because," says Ilya, "I do."

Heat rushes my cheeks again, and I can't help but smile.

"Asshole—you better love the kid." Ilya growls at Mikhail. My brother sighs and keeps trying to make two bears and says, "Boris didn't know that I still cared about Ilya. When I found out about Boris's plot, I didn't sit back and wait, Kira. I traveled back here to America and revealed myself to Andrei—"

"That sneaky fuck," says Ilya.

"—and I offered him whatever he needed or wanted to help save you both."

"What I don't understand," Ilya says before I can, "is the reason why you did this. You told me you're on our side, you did this for me. You said you'd explain. So do it now. To your sister too."

"I told you."

No," Ilya says, "the reasons why. Not what you did. Your personal reasons. Because I thought we were in this together."

These two men I love, two best friends, are muddling it out. But in my head, a story is forming, something I can use as a lynchpin. How two men, one Russian, one American, risked everything to bring down the Russian Bratva from the inside out. And, they did it at great personal risk, while paying greater personal costs.

My brother nods, strangles the bear, looks at Ilya, and says, "I had you expelled, Ilya, to protect you. Orlov saw the tides turning against him, and as a last-ditch effort to save his ass, he uncovered some ancient rule about how, if there were two possible Pakhan replacements—which, with our plan, was you and me—the two potential usurpers would have to fight to the death in order to decide which of them could be crowned king."

Ilya scowls. "You could have told me."

"I know you. Wrongs are things you won't let sit. So I fucking saved you."

"And took the crown."

"I had to, in secret." My brother takes another step with the bear he's mutilating, and looks at both me and Ilya. "Ivan thought using this rule might weaken his challengers enough for him to hold onto power. But I found out about this plan... And I also knew there was no stopping it. In Russia, Kira," he says to me, "the Bratva's run on ancient code and tradition. No one could oppose a ruling as old and codified as the one Ivan uncovered. Everyone would fall in line."

"It's true," Ilya says, looking at Mikhail. "You still should have told me."

"I would have to fight my best friend, and probably kill you. Ilya, you're stronger than almost everyone, but your talent lies in your genius intellect, while my talent's straight up killing and violent fighting." Mikhail pauses. "Sorry, Kira."

"So... you did betray him?" I ask.

Mikhail goes to sit on the bed, then gets up. "I schemed to

have Ilya expelled from Russia in order to save his life. But I never had the time to explain it and couldn't risk reaching out once I became shadow Pakhan."

"But you didn't stop any of the corruption," I say.

"It's not that easy." Ilya kisses my hand again. "These things take time, and it was slower without me, right?"

"Yeah."

"I saw you get shot, Mikhail. I saw you fall. You were dead..." Ilya shakes his head. "At least I thought..."

"I was shot, Kira. I was shot in a power struggle for leadership over the biggest Bratva in Russia... it turns out, I won that struggle—but I was also smart enough to know that someone always comes for the king... not to mention, I realized I underestimated the violence and danger of being in the Bratva."

"It's the Bratva," I say.

"It's even worse in Russia than it is in America," my brother says. "I played up my supposed death and made sure everyone believed I was dead—both as a way to hold onto power and to keep myself safe. Then, I started controlling the Bratva from the shadows. I even placed a puppet Pahkan, Boris Gusinsky, as the figurehead for extra secrecy..."

He trails off, and I try to sit up.

"Is that all?" I ask, sarcastically.

"That's the gist of it. Any questions?"

"Two things," I say. "Can I have my bear? And can you give me more details? This would make for the story of a lifetime..."

37

KIRA

"Between you and me," I say to poor, misshapen Olaf, who sits next to the new laptop Ilya got me, "they're driving me crazy."

Outside the bedroom, my brother and Ilya argue. I'm not meant to be up. Bedrest until I'm completely better, according to my boyfriend.

Speaking of the devil.

He comes in, like I summoned him, and swoops down, picking me up and taking me to bed, raining kisses all over my face, his hand sliding up between my dress so he can explore my instantly wet and needing flesh.

"Ilya!" I quietly squeak.

"Would you rather sit at the stuffy computer all day?" he jokes, stroking over my pussy with his warm, firm hands.

"Can you stop that? Mikhail's outside. He could come in." I try and slap him away, but we both know I don't mean it.

Ilya nuzzles my neck. "He wouldn't dare. I closed the door."

He pushes a finger into me, claiming my mouth as he starts to thrust, his thumb working my clit. I'm a violent, wild sea of sensations. My body pulls tight, and I start to move my hand below his belt. A familiar bulge greets me. But before I can start massaging him, he flings my wrist away.

"Oh no, Kira. This is about you. Not me. That can come later. But this, you, need to cum now. Doctor's orders."

"I think I like this kind of medicine," I pant.

"A dick a day keeps the doctor away."

"Speaking of dick..."

He bites soft on my lower lip as I reach back below his belt.

"No," he grunts.

"I want more, Ilya. I want the whole thing."

He laughs. "You want me to fuck you?"

I nod, pressing my face up to his as I look into his dark eyes.

"Yes," I say, "Please. Fuck me."

He gets up and adjusts his erection. "When you get your clean bill of health."

Then be flops back onto the bed.

"I'm better."

"The doctor will let me know. I don't want to pop a stitch or cause you pain."

I poke him and roll on my side as he grabs my laptop from the nightstand. "Says the man with multiple gunshot wounds."

"I'm used to it," he says like his words are logical, which they're not. "It's not the same."

"I'm better, and..." I roll into him. "I want you."

"We have a lifetime." Then he gives me a look that's all disgust. "Fuck. This is what you've done to me. Domesticated me. I hope you're happy."

"No one," I say with a giggle, "can domesticate the Great and Terrible Ilya Rykov."

"Maybe, but if anyone's up for the job, it's you."

I smile.

Suddenly, I realize how happy I am. It's the happiest I've been in a long time. Maybe even ever. The only thing that brings a bittersweet note is that Dad isn't here. But I like to think he knows. And that he's somewhere with my mother. The woman he lost to illness and never replaced, never tried.

Yeah, I like to think they're together.

Ilya leans in, kisses me, then yells, "Mikhail, get in here!"

My brother comes in, eyes everywhere, like he's looking for evidence of what we've been up to. But Ilya tells him to sit and hands him the computer.

"Read," he tells him.

My brother opens up the laptop, and I watch as his eyes scan the screen.

"You wrote this?" he asks, looking up at me.

I nod. "You're both sources, anonymous, but... I think it'll break the chain of command. And all the evidence that you both got me against all those officials..."

"This is brilliant," Mikhail says.

Ilya touches my cheek and gives a smile just for me. "I know. My girl really fucking is brilliant, isn't she?"

"What do you think?"

I dance across the top floor of the duplex, taking in its splendid features. It has everything: a private gym, a second office for Ilya, and a gorgeous one with the same balcony as the bedroom suite that he tells me is my office. It's mind-blowing, just like the kitchen downstairs, the living room, the dining room, and spare room. And the library and second office and...

I shrug. "It's okay."

"Okay?" His eyes narrow as a smile teases at the edge of his mouth. "This is what you described to me. Upstairs office, balcony. What more do you want?"

"Are we alone?"

"Do you see anyone else, Kira?"

"I mean is anyone going to come in to tell you we're safe?"

He gives an impatient hand wave. "My people don't do that."

"So?"

"We're alone."

I'm wearing one of the simple, loose sundresses I like to wear at home. Ilya isn't a fan. Then again, if he had his way, I'd always be wearing skin-tight outfits. Anything that teases my figure without me being completely naked. He likes to unwrap things. Like me.

Still, we've been together a month, and we haven't had sex. It's driving me insane. I was, however, recently told that I'm nearly completely healed, so...

"Alone?"

"Yeah, Kira. Alone."

"Good." I look about and then go back into the bedroom. There's a bed, a new one. "You chose a bed."

"Same as I had before." He points to the rest of the place, "but I'm waiting on you. If you like this place, we'll move in and get all the furniture together."

He sounds all disgusted again. Which he keeps doing every time he claims I've ruined him or domesticated him. I tell him it's the other way around, and then we end up kissing and cuddling and...

This time, I'm getting what I want.

I dressed for the occasion.

"I'd like to see if it's a good fit."

"There's a line, woman," he says, smiling, "and you, princess, are coming up on it. Fast."

In response, I kick off my shoes, grab him by the shirt, and tug him to me. Then I shove him on the bed and pull the dress down over my shoulders.

He helps me rip it away. I throw it to the floor.

"Now that's a look I can get behind," he says.

I jump on him. It's been too long.

"So hard," I note with a smile, reaching between his legs.

"For you? Always."

"And look what you do to me." I sink down on him, and he shudders. If he can't see how wet I am, he should be able to feel it.

I moan at the stretch, the fullness. He's perfect.

"You are a fucking gift," he growls.

I start to ride him, and he takes my hips, thrusting deep into me. It's wild. Hot. Fast.

After we cum, I fall onto him, and he mutters, "Fucking hell, I think that's the fastest I've ever cum."

"Me too," I smile.

He rolls us over so we can look each other in the eye.

With a big, devilish smile, he caresses my jaw.

"I fucking love you."

"What a coincidence," I smirk back. "I love *you*."

"Holy shit."

I stare at the newspaper in disbelief.

My piece has finally been published in the Chicago Daily.

At first, Mr. Calhoun told me I was too late. He changed his mind when he realized what I sent him was missing a vital piece.

After that, told me I could have my job back, as long as he took the head writer job, and me assistant on it.

So I'm completely shocked when the article has only my name on it.

I want to scream with joy, but I know that would only send everyone in the household running.

My brother moved into the floor below us, as he's working closely with Ilya. Every once in a while, we go out to dinner as a group.

Other times, we stay in. Ilya teaches me to cook. It often ends up with both of us naked and the food ruined, but it's always fun.

We fit together so well, even if I'm spending more and more time at the office. How could I not? My job has become what I dreamed of. Or it's starting to be. Mr. Calhoun still isn't paying me much, and I bitch about it to Ilya. Some of the articles I'm given leave a lot to be desired, but I know I'm lucky.

I'm a junior reporter with a huge article under my belt, one that's led to arrests, all kinds of political fallout, and I'm only just getting started.

I've been working on countless exposes. Sometimes, Mr. Calhoun will hold back on giving me new stories, but I still do my version and shop them around.

Eventually, they all get published, thanks to my own connections.

Still, it'd be nice if Mr. Calhoun actually let what happened slide, so I didn't have to fight him on everything.

Time passes, and the constant back and forth gets tiresome. There reaches a point where I hand in my notice. And he doesn't say a thing.

One night, Ilya calls me. It's early, but I'm home working on a freelance piece.

"Leave what you're doing and meet me. We're having dinner. Your outfit's in your closet."

I roll my eyes. "I just need to—"

"Leave it. You have thirty minutes. I'll send the address."

The outfit isn't sexy or revealing, but it is breathtaking. A very 'thirties' style suit, from the heels to the soft dark gray of the pants and jacket, to the dusty rose silk pussy bow shirt. Business with flare.

Curious now, I put it on.

I'm finishing my hair when there's a knock on the door. Since there's a dedicated doorman at the building's foyer—and outside our door on our floor—I rush over, not worried about who's there.

My brother whistles low. "I'm your car service."

"I'm capable of getting a cab."

"Have you met the man you're living with?"

I ignore him but still follow him to the car.

It's a quick drive.

When Mikhail pulls up outside the Chicago Star, I frown up at Ilya as he opens the door from the outside.

"I don't work here," I say, "Not anymore."

He takes my hand, kissing it. "Stunning."

"Likewise."

I pull this impossibly handsome man in for a kiss as my brother drives off.

How Ilya gets better looking daily is beyond me. But he does.

"Why are we here?" I widen my eyes. "Don't kill Mr. Calhoun, please. He's a pain, but—"

"No one's going to die." He tucks my hand in the crook of his arm.

We get through the front doors, and I'm fumbling for my credentials that I no longer have when the guards straighten up as Ilya nods at them.

They let us through.

"Ilya... what..." I pull him in. "What's going on?"

"You'll see."

The top floor is where all decisions are made by the editor-in-chief. When we arrive, I look around for him, because I'm not sure he'll want to see me.

Fortunately, his door's shut. But Ilya leads me to it and gestures like I should open it up.

"I don't want to talk to that man," I mumble under my breath. "What kind of—"

"We aren't here to see Calhoun," Ilya says. "This isn't his office. Not anymore."

It takes me a few moments to register the placard on the door.

And I'm fucking shocked.

Kira Zhirkov

Editor-in-Chief

I stare at it.

"I-Ilya..." I turn. "Where's Mr. Calhoun?"

"I fired him."

"You...?" I'm being stupid, but I'm having a hard time comprehending this. "You fired him? How could you even—"

"You're usually a lot smarter than this, Kira." Ilya opens the door and leads us in.

I gasp in awe. It's beautiful. It's still the same office, but now the walls and furnishings have a feminine touch with a very professional vibe. The walls are pale honey and white. The desk is made of glossy, dark golden wood, and there's a new computer on it. The chair matches the desk.

In place of the filing cabinets, which I never once saw Mr. Calhoun use, there's a small sofa, chairs, and an oval coffee table.

"This," he says with an expansive hand, "is all yours. You can do what you want, but I thought this fit you."

He takes a breath, an extra pause, and I'm struck. I think he's nervous.

"If it's wrong..." he takes another lungful of air. "We can start—"

"It's perfect. I just don't understand how."

"Oh." He grins. "Easy. I just bought the newspaper."

I stop in my tracks.

"That isn't easy, Ilya."

"No, it was actually harder than I thought, considering how stubborn journalists and media moguls can be with their freedom of press ideals… but I managed it."

"Of course you did," I say, unable to hide my smile.

He kisses me. "And you Kira are now in charge of the entire operation."

I shake my head. "I'm twenty-one. I can't run a paper."

"You're smart."

"It's not that. I'm…" I look at him. "Not experienced."

"You'll gain experience. I will get you the best assistant editor."

"Ilya," I say. "No one's going to do that, not someone with the right experience."

He frowns for a moment before a confident smile replaces it. "I'll pay them so much they won't be able to refuse."

"Like… a silent mentor for me?"

He nods.

I lean against the desk. "I don't want to become another Calhoun."

"Don't," he says, coming up to me. "Fucking run it your way. Share the glory as long as this person knows you're the ultimate boss. Get stories, let them get stories. Run the best paper, turn this into the best paper."

"But how could I be impartial? I'm in bed with the literal mob. You."

He coils an arm around me and lifts me to the desk, stepping between my legs. "Don't write about us."

I sigh. "It's not how it works. And if it's not me, someone else might."

"Then…" He kisses me, tiny kisses that pepper my face and neck. "I only tell you what won't harm me. And then you can't write about it."

"How about we agree to keep anything I learn or see off the

record." I take his face and kiss him. Then I frown. "But if someone else—"

"Princess. I know how to run a tight ship."

I sigh. "Ilya."

"How about this," he says, "you follow your passions and intuition, wherever they lead, and be committed to exposing the dangerous crime around the city."

"You mean your rivals? Because, Ilya, your rivals are mostly drug lords and violent factions. Seems a little... convenient."

"Convenient, but it happens."

"Not good enough." I shove him away a little. "You buy me a paper, and I agree to have off the record information. Also, I can report on your rivals, but I need more. That's still one-sided. I need to be a fair and honest reporter."

"Editor-in-chief."

"Ilya."

He goes still, thinking, then comes back to me. "How about this? I promise to never cross certain lines, because if I do, you're allowed to expose them too."

"Those lines are?"

"Fucked if I know. We'll work them out."

I get up and stare out the high-rise office windows. Up here, it feels like I float above the city, but I know I can't get a big head. I have to be fair when I work. "If we can hammer those lines out..." I nod to myself. "I agree."

Suddenly, I see Ilya's reflection move in the glass of the window. The skyline outside blurs as I focus on him.

My heart stops beating when he gets down on one knee.

I turn. "What-what are you doing?"

"Kira, you really are my princess, my fucking life." He opens a tiny black box, and the oval solitaire inside is so big and beautiful that I'm nearly blinded. "So make me the happiest man alive. Sure, we could live together without the ring and vows, but I want the world to know you're mine. More than that, I want to come home every day and see my life, my heart, my wife. I want to see you. I love you, Kira. So... will you marry me?"

Despite my shock, there's no hesitation in me.

"Yes." I grin. I run to him, and he's on his feet swinging me in his arms. "I want that, too. I love you, Ilya, I always have."

He kisses me deeply, possessively, with all the love there is.

And I'm finally where I belong.

I'm finally home.

Finally whole again.

This is my family. Together, we can do anything... even be happy.

EPILOGUE

KIRA

1 week later...

Oh, God. I fan my face.

Ilya moves so fast I can't really breathe. It's not that I don't want to have the engagement party and the wedding soon, it's just... couldn't he have given me time to make some friends first?

I fix my hair yet again and tug at the dress. Nothing's right.

My brother is with Ilya downstairs. They've both assured me it's only going to be a few people, but I'm still beyond nervous.

It's probably all men. Big, bad Bratva types, and a wife or two. I don't know.

And... this dress sucks.

I walk out of the upstairs bathroom to the bottle of whiskey I left on the counter and pour a shot, downing it. Then I pour another, hoping it'll give me the confidence to go help set up the party. Ilya said not to, but I can't spend the next hour by myself, driving myself insane.

I text my brother. ***I can't do this.***

Sure you can. Plus he'll kill us all.

I roll my eyes. ***Not the wedding, I mean tonight. I don't know anyone.***

Me. You know me.

Help!

Hold tight, he texts.

I get another drink and sip it, returning to the bathroom to try and do something with my hair and maybe run up to the third floor to get another outfit. It's why I'm down here, so I don't try on every single thing I own. Still...

Someone knocks at the door, and I rush to it and open it. "Mik—"

It's not my brother.

A tall, dangerous-looking, very handsome man stands there. "Ilya?"

"Kira," I say. "Ilya is taller. Less... girly."

"You're as bad as him," the man mutters, stepping past me, looking around. "No wonder you're marrying him."

There's a woman too. She's got her back to me as she's orchestrating a slender man to wheel in a clothes rack.

"Valentin, stop that," she says, then turns and smiles at me.

Oh my god.

It's her.

I'm gobsmacked. It's the fashionista, the one who was almost my big break into the mob all that time ago. I thought she'd be my lead into the big time. But she fell behind their iron curtain before I could get to her.

"Yelena?" I ask. "Is... is that... oh my god, it's you!"

"Hi Kira." She beams.

"Is this all the booze you have?" comes the dangerous man's voice. He looks familiar too. I remember him stalking close to Yelena back when I was trying to get a story out of her.

He disappears for a moment, then returns with the Japanese whiskey.

Yelena takes it. "Thank you for the help. That's all for now, though. Go down and play with the others."

"As you wish," he mutters, taking her and kissing her thoroughly. "Don't be too long."

Yelena watches him go with love in her eyes. "That's my husband, Valentin."

"You make him sound like a teddy bear."

"Sure... a teddy bear... If it had teeth and liked to cause death and destruction."

She looks happy and healthy, and I remember the last time I saw her in the nightclub, worried for her.

Guess I didn't need to be.

Because I can see the same thing that happened to her happened to me. We fell in love with dangerous men who will do anything to make us happy.

Valentin gave that vibe every time he looked or touched her.

We smile at each other.

"I'm so happy you found Ilya. He needed someone special," she says, "someone who can match him. And he told me you loved the suit."

"One of the most gorgeous things I have." I gasp. "You made it?"

"Yes, for you. He asked. And he looked so in love I couldn't say no." She pulls the rack close. "He suggested you might want something special tonight."

My smile slips a little. "Friends? I've been so wrapped up in my ambitions, in surviving that I never had time, and—"

"You've got something better than friends. A little family. I'll introduce you to the women. But Kira?" She holds up a glorious blue gown the color of my eyes, and presses it into me, nodding. Then she meets my eyes. "We're friends, but also family. So... you're not alone tonight."

"Thank you, it means so much to me." My eyes blur with tears made of happiness. "I love him so much. And thank you."

"For what?"

"Your friendship," I whisper. "I know we had our differences while I was researching that story, but—"

"We don't need to talk about the past," Yelena stops me. "All is forgiven."

I nod, feeling like an idiot. And feeling a little lost. Because I want to shine and make Ilya so proud of me that he can't see straight, but there's so much I don't know.

"At least I'll have someone out there I know," I smile, finding comfort in this little thread from my dark past.

"You have Ilya, your brother. And me." She hands me the dress and hugs me.

"Thank you," I say. "God, I could use a drink..." But when I look around, I notice the whiskey is gone. That's when it hits me. "Did your Valentin steal my whiskey?" I look at Yelena and laugh.

She nods. "Welcome to the family, Kira. Let's get you dressed and blow Ilya's mind. We can talk while we get you ready. We've got a lot to catch up on..."

EPILOGUE

ILYA

6 months later...

No one ever told me how satisfying married life could be. If they had, maybe I'd have tried it earlier.

Then again, I don't think earlier would have worked. No Kira. And Kira's what makes it all so fantastic.

The sex is off the charts. It doesn't matter if we get kinky all the way or go at it like fucking machines. It doesn't matter if it's a long, slow day in bed or a quick fuck somewhere new. It's amazing. She can get me off in minutes, and I can do the same with her. It's why I've taken an interest in her badass reporter ways.

She's meant to be in her office doing whatever the fuck an editor-in-chief does, but she constantly ignores that tradition to get her hands dirty in the field.

And that means I do too. Like a predator, I stalk her around the city. And when I catch her, I take her.

We get daring too.

But it's not just the sex. And it's not just the thrill of keeping my intrepid troublemaker safe. It's how she keeps trying to get stories from me. Nothing to put me behind bars or ruin my Bratva, but she wants the dirt that'll get her accolades, me in hot water, and the Bratva with a new round of enemies.

I have to stay on my toes. If I'm off my game with her, she'll turn the tables and catch me—a thrilling game of cat and mouse between crooked husband and ambitious wife. Not that things ever get too serious.

There are things I've ordered her to keep away from—things that could get her hurt, things I hear on my grapevine. Once in a while, I have to come up with a fun distraction. She doesn't mind. Neither do I.

"And how's your wife?" Mikhail asks as I sit down for the meeting I have with him and Semyon.

The two have become fast friends.

"Still prefers me to her dumb-ass brother."

"You do have an advantage. For now. She'll grow weary of you, though," he says.

I sigh and grin. "Doubtful. That feisty little reporter never has a boring day with me around."

"Let me guess," Mikhail says, "she's twisting you around her little finger to get the scoops?"

I glare at him. "She tries."

Thing is, I'm a man who helps her get them while keeping her safe. And at the same time, I also negotiate and renegotiate our terms to keep her from my shady shit.

This involves a lot of naked negotiation.

Something we're both happy with.

"You disgust me," mutters Mikhail, shuddering at the expression on my face.

I grin. "I didn't say anything."

But as we start to talk strategics of the job Mikhail just did for us, I can't help thinking how similar he is to Valentin and Andrei.

Did he do well? Fuck yes.

He saved a very important liaison and blew the lid on more corruption coming in from Russia.

Like I told my wife the other night, once you remove the seal from something, it'll never fit on again. Things will leak.

She's fucking smart. She knew what I meant. Kira seduced me, rode me, gave me her ass, and I refused to elaborate. Not because I know this will get her in deep, but because it involves Mikhail.

And the fact is that while Andrei and Valentin are fucking insane, Mikhail's insanity isn't out of love of the chaos or the fight—at least, not like it used to be. Something changed. Something's made him single-minded. Precise when he needs to be, chaotic when it calls for it. And all of it comes with a drive that says death wish to me.

He's easygoing, intense, all the best of the parts that make up and have always made up Mikhail. But this... it's different. Another level.

And Kira will stop at nothing if I tell her. So I don't. Not until I uncover what's behind it.

"This faction, a part of the Triad?" I ask.

Semyon looks up from the computer and shakes his head. "No, but we took them out all the same." He nods at Mikhail.

"We did. And the Triad helped."

"Mikhail, you did this with the help of the Triad?" I ask. "Fuck."

Mikhail shrugs. "It worked. Right, Semyon?"

I raise my brows as Semyon swings the computer to me. I look at the numbers he's got there, and I nod. But I say, "Owing the Triad a favor is like owing us. Never good, never worth it."

Mikhail's face says bring it the fuck on, but he doesn't say that. All he says is, "A mutual act which canceled out debts that might arise from certain other collaborations. As far as they're concerned, no one owes anyone anything. A mutual threat has been neutralized. That's it."

I shoot a look at Semyon. "Andrei?"

"On board," he says.

"Mikhail, you're quickly becoming part of the Chicago Bratva," I say quietly. "But if it comes to it—"

"I've fucking proved myself," he snarls, which is pure Mikhail. "I was born here, my sister's here—"

"You left her thinking you were dead for years." I meet and hold his gaze as Semyon serves witness.

It's got to stick in Mikhail's side, knowing it's me questioning him. And while I don't know if he'll believe it, I take no pleasure in this.

Mikhail narrows his eyes. "You think I don't regret that?"

"I don't know." I look him up and down. "Do you?"

Mikhail bounces a leg on the floor, clearly trying to hold back his anger. Hold himself in check.

"Of course I do," he mutters.

"You have contacts in Russia." There's a slight shift in his expression, one that only I can read. But maybe Semyon can too, as he goes completely still.

This is why Semyon's worth twice his weight in gold.

He's smart, intuitive, dark-souled, and loyal.

But this isn't about him. It's about Mikhail, who can read me pretty much as well as I can read him. Which is why I need to push all the buttons.

It's the only way I can see the truth.

The only way I can see if he really is loyal to us before I take the next step.

Once upon a time, if he'd asked to join my outfit, I'd have said a flat yes. Now? I'm inclined to lean that way, but I have to stop myself from that flat yes. Because we've spent so many years apart, and he spent so long in that seat of near ultimate power.

And power isn't for the weak or the corruptible.

I don't know if he's incorruptible.

Not anymore.

"What if things go wrong here?" I ask.

He looks at me, expression tight. "You don't think I can deal with bad fucking weather?"

"I'm not sure," I say, "if you can say no to the kind of power Russia can offer you again."

"I can't go back."

"That," I say, "is no answer. You want to really be in our fold, then you need to fucking convince me. Not Andrei, not anyone else. Me. The man who loves you like a fucking brother."

"The man," he says, "who wanted me dead and then turned around and married my fucking sister."

"In spite of you."

"So," he mutters, "I'm damned either way. You've got a grudge against me, and that's going to keep me down."

"Maybe," I say. I know Semyon's taking this in.

He picked up on that small vibration, but I also know he's not reaching for a gun or even thinking about it. As my second-in-command, he wouldn't have the rivalry he's got going with Mikhail if he thought he wasn't one of us. Right through to the bone. I know the rivalry's a fun thing, one I pretend not to notice. But this is different. If he thought there was a chance Mikhail would sell us out, he'd kill him. If he believed I thought that and gave the order, he'd carry it out.

I haven't done that, but if I did, he would.

"Mikhail, I've just made a decision on something. And it's big. But first, this grudge? If I do have one... What the fuck are you going to do about it? And don't say you can't go back." I pause. "I'm different. I was publicly banished, and there's no back from that. But you? Those who can back you or blame you are dead. You have all those contacts. You can use them."

He doesn't say anything for a long time. Then he sighs. "If I was going to fucking go back, I'd have never left. But you're wrong, Ilya. I can't go back because I won't. Not to work in that Bratva. Not to take up that kind of role. So, if I don't get inducted into the Chicago Bratva, I'll find something else. But not in Russia. And those contacts? They're helpful until they're not." He pauses. "So spit it out. What's this big decision?"

Semyon knows my decision was already made before I told Mikhail I'd made one, but we exchange a look. No one smiles. I let Mikhail squirm.

I stand. "I think, Semyon, we have an answer." I hold out my hand for the knife. "We always need more power and contacts from Russia, but you?"

I close my fingers around the knife's hilt.

"You, Mikhail, are to remain dead."

Semyon clears his throat. "A ghost is better." He pauses. "Boss."

"A ghost can get information better than the dead." I hand him the knife. "Welcome to the Bratva."

He frowns and takes the knife. "You… bastard."

I look at the knife. "It's American."

"It's plastic." He glares, even as he starts to smile.

"It cost… Semyon?"

"Five bucks."

"Assholes."

Semyon pats him on the back. "I'll take this to Andrei."

When he's gone, Mikhail punches my arm. "You scared me."

"I wanted your reactions because while you're in, we have very sensitive stuff coming up. And if I thought for a second…" I shake my head. "I'd recommend not using you until you were ready. You always have a home here, Mikhail."

I wrap him in a bear hug. "I've missed you."

"You're a lucky guy." He hugs back. "You got two for one."

"Kira's the better part of the deal."

There's a soft smile on her brother's face. "She is."

I want to tell him he can have what I have—money, power, love. Both he and Semyon want it. And they deserve it. But something happened to him in Russia. Something he hasn't talked about.

Something that turned him into a self-professed monster. It's the one thing he doesn't talk to me about. The one thing I don't ask.

Because a man's allowed secrets. As long as they don't fuck me or my Bratva over. His Bratva now too.

It's why I took a silly made-up ceremony down a serious path.

There are demons clinging to him.

"You know, I heard some rumblings," he says. "Last night. I wanted to hear and see what's been said in the trenches."

"What was it?"

He looks at me, rubs a hand over his head, and slings his bag over his shoulder. "I'm not sure."

"Russia?"

"No, this was closer to home. It wasn't much." Then he lets out a low breath. "Dinner?"

I hold open the door and stop. "That's not the story."

He hesitates. "No, it isn't, but... Things happened in Russia. Things I have to deal with. And it seems as though something I thought was put to bed is still kicking. Not from Russia, not that I could tell. But if it's to do with that. With her, then we should be ready for anything."

"I'm confused. You said it wasn't Russian or to do with Russia?"

"It's not, as in not Bratva. But it happened there. And, as soon as I find out more, I'll tell you. Until then..."

"Yes?" I ask.

"It's my cross. My burden."

"Kira?"

"Is safe." Then he claps me on the back. "Let's get the kid. Show her the knife."

I know Mikhail. He won't talk until he's good and ready.

As we head out to collect the love of my life, I can't help but think that Mikhail has the kind of dark secrets that fit in with a death wish, the kind that will bring trouble crashing down.

I just hope he knows that, if he needs me, I'll be there, fighting by his side until the very end.

Printed in Great Britain
by Amazon